The Sea

The Seasoning

Manon Steffan Ros

Honno Modern Fiction

First published in the English language by Honno Press in 2015
'Ailsa Craig', Heol y Cawl, Dinas Powys, South Glamorgan,
Wales, CF64 4AH

2 3 4 5 6 7 8 9 10

A catalogue record for this book is available from the
British Library.

Published with the financial support of the Welsh Books Council.
First published in the Welsh language by Y Lolfa, in 2012

ISBN 978-1-909983-25-0 paperback
ISBN 978-1-909983-26-7 ebook

Cover design: Graham Preston
Text design: Graham Preston
Printed by 4edge

For my grandparents
Una, Jean, Dafydd and John

The author would like to thank the following…

Everyone at Honno press for their support and enthusiasm. The editor, Caroline Oakley, for all her hard work. Everyone at Y Lolfa, especially the gentle genius, Alun Jones. Sioned Puw Rowlands at the Wales Literature Exchange, without whom this book would never have happened. Beth Wennell, my kind, funny, inspirational English teacher. My family, and especially my boys, Efan and Geraint, for their love and patience.

Peggy

2010

On my eightieth birthday, Jonathan gave me a notebook. Hard-backed with brown and pale yellow marbling on the cover, like chocolate in cream. I thumbed the bare, thick pages and touched the rough grain of the paper with the pads of my fingers. 'I want you to write something for me,' said Jonathan, his dark eyes locking on to mine. 'I want you to write your story, Mam.' 'No one wants to know. Don't be silly.' I broke away from his stare. My thin, creased fingers were almost as pale as the paper, and my wedding ring clung, dangerously loose, on to my bones.

'I want to know,' he answered softly, resting his big brown hand on mine. I felt his gaze on my face, but I didn't meet it. His kind face would convince me to do anything: he had always been able to.

'I can't believe how many people turned up.' I turned to the cafe door, trying to redirect the conversation. I had sat there all afternoon, accepting gifts, greeting guests, with Jonathan moving constantly between cafe and kitchen, bringing tea and coffee and cake. Francis sat by my side, talking and laughing his big deep chuckle, adding a bass note to the chatter of the party. A string of children came in on the way home from school, and Jonathan set silver bowls of jelly and ice cream on the tables for them. They had made a huge card for my birthday, which breathed dots of coloured glitter over my hands and clothes. It felt odd and awkward to have such small children at an old woman's party. Jonathan had arranged everything, had gathered the whole village to celebrate my big birthday: the old folk, like me, the young babies and their mothers, the farmers and the teenagers. I couldn't remember their names. Though I would never admit it, the party made me feel isolated. I only half-knew these people, and there was something perverse in celebrating a birthday when my own sons were themselves old, with ghosts of grey peppering their hair.

'I'm serious, Mam. I want you to write your story.'

'An autobiography?' I turned to him, facing those black eyes.

'If you like.'

'People like me don't write autobiographies.'

'No, they don't, and it's a great tragedy.'

Jonathan sighed and arose from his chair. The top of his head nearly grazed the ceiling. 'A book of your memories would be such a comfort to me when you've gone.' He collected a few dirty plates from the tables. Beside me, Francis snored softly, fast asleep on the sofa. A half-smile played on his face, and I wondered what occupied his dreams.

I turned my eyes to the window. It was a miserable day, and the grey-almost-brown clouds threatened snow. Jonathan's tender reference to my death had shaken me: a ridiculous thing to be bothered by on my eightieth birthday.

'I'm going for a walk,' I called, rising from the sofa.

'I'll come with you!' Jonathan called from the kitchen. 'Just let me finish tidying up.'

'No.'

'Should I wake Dad?'

I looked at Francis, asleep on the sofa.

'If he wakes, tell him to wait for me. I'd like to go on my own, if you don't mind.'

I reached behind the door for my coat and hat. Turning to say goodbye, my memory, for a short moment, took me back to another time, when there were no tables here, no tasteful sepia photographs on the wall. For a few seconds, I saw shelves against

2

the wall, full of tins and packets, and someone smiling at me from behind the shop counter, his apron as white as his hair was black. My stomach jolted with the clarity of the memory.

'All right.' Jonathan appeared, and the present flooded back into every corner of the cafe. I smiled at him. 'Take care as you go, Mam.'

'I'll see you in a bit.'

The wind immediately pierced my clothes and hair and skin, and the cold clung to my cheeks with its teeth. Almost five o'clock, and the darkness was coming. I walked down to Llan Bridge, painfully aware of the slow stubbornness of my steps. I had run down this lane, once upon a time, the kind sun kissing my ankles as I sped past the houses...

Light spilled out from the windows of the cottages, puddling the road with squares of yellow. I imagined the comfort of the chairs that rested by their fireplaces, and felt foolish for persisting on walking this way every day. It had been a rest, a sigh in the throes of a busy day. But now, it was a challenge to walk on the long, flat lane, a daily battle that made my joints ache and creak.

There were ghosts all around.

Two Chapel Square, and Rose Cottage where Annie lived with Jack and the children. That was home to a young family from Tywyn now, and they had painted the walls blue and cut down the cherry blossom tree in the back garden. The dark lane which led to Riverside, where I had lived with my mother when I was a little girl, and where I lived again with Francis. There was another memory clinging to Llan Bridge, white in the water, floating silently, a ghost in the river.

Further down the road, the houses petered out into fields and hedgerows. The sky was blackening. I'd only walk to Beech Grove and back. It wouldn't take long.

Long-dead conversations, the whisper of tender moments long gone, seemed to sigh on the wind. Laughter with Annie about silly things. Pushing the pram along this stretch of road, smiling at the baby and being rewarded with a wet, toothless smile. Watching the seasons. Years upon years of them, colouring the mountains with shades of green, yellow, rust and then a silent smothering of snow.

By the time I reached Beech Grove, a half mile from the village, the night had blackened the road, and the old house arose from the trees, still as if it was waiting. There was no light.

The taste returned to my tongue, a shock of flavour as if I had only just eaten it. It froze me in its intensity, and I churned the sweetness around my mouth.

Was I losing my mind?

I turned back, frightened by the strength of my memories. I had never seen a ghost, but suddenly the shadows in the hedgerows frightened me. I peered into the window of Beech Grove as I passed. Was that Mrs. Davies' shape in the window, tall and dark, waiting for me to come crying to her doorstep?

Don't be ridiculous, Peggy, I thought. It was only a memory. I could see my breath, smoky and stolen by the wind, quickened by my own imagination. A vivid memory, as real as now.

I struggled back through the darkness, the village streetlights orange and still in the near distance. The taste still lingered on my tongue, and other memories came hand-in-hand with it, forceful as a winter wind: each one attached to a brown, sweet sponge cake with a complex, thick smell. Old fingers offering a laden plate. A cup of hot milk, honey-scented steam wisping from it like a fog. I willed my mind to return to the present.

I thought of Jonathan, a man approaching old age now, and his eyes gazing into the darkness through the kitchen window as he washed dishes. I thought of Francis, and his smiling dreams. I thought of the young children who'd come to the party, the children of the children of the children of the people who were my friends.

But the past was a stronger force than this pale present.

4

Something new had awoken in me. Was it madness, the winds of old age bringing back all the yesterdays, close enough to touch, to smell, to taste?

He was there, I was sure: Mr Daniels, Ffrancon House, tending the green tomatoes in his greenhouse, washing his windows with ashes from the fireplace...

Llan Bridge, its ghosts as pale as bedsheets in the water...

Two Chapel Square, and the stains of age removed: the pastor's house, and Annie Vaughan watching her baby sleeping in the pram under the soft sunshine...

Sunshine? It was night!

I pushed at the cafe door, and the little bell tinkled. I stood for a few seconds, filling my lungs with warm air, filling my mind with the present. When did I get so old that I couldn't walk a flat road without tiring?

'Did you have a nice walk?' asked Jonathan from the kitchen. The small lamps which dotted the cafe had been lit, and the place looked as if it was slowly fading in the half-light. Francis slept on, exactly as I had left him.

'Yes,' I answered, peeling off my coat. I would have liked to explain to him, somehow, how the memories were awakening, sharpening in my mind. But Jonathan wouldn't understand. I wouldn't have understood at his age.

The notebook still rested on the table. I sat on the sofa beside my husband, and stared at it. I couldn't remember the last time I'd written. I opened the book, and the naked page stared back at me accusingly.

I had nothing to say.

'I don't know what I'll bake for tomorrow,' said Jonathan, pushing a damp cloth over the oilcloths on the tables and collecting the crumbs in the bowl of his palm. 'I have a lemon tart and scones, and I think I'll make—'

'A ginger loaf,' I answered. 'With treacle, and syrup.'

Jonathan stood upright and still, looking at me. 'Yes,' he answered slowly. 'Why not?'

'Do you have a recipe?'

'Somewhere...' He moved to the space behind the counter, where his collection of cookbooks stood proud and colourful. He drew a finger along the spines of the books. 'Here...'

'May I borrow a biro?' I asked. Jonathan turned, smiled that bright grin that belonged to no one but him, his recipe book clutched tightly under his arm.

Mai Davies
Neighbour
1937

Ginger Cake

4 oz caster sugar   5 oz butter
1 egg   10 oz plain flour
1½ tsp baking soda   2 tbsp ground ginger
1 tsp ground cinnamon   ½ tsp ground cloves
10 tbsp golden syrup   2 tbsp treacle
2 small balls stem ginger   9 fl. oz hot water

Preheat the oven to 180°C. Grease a 9 inch
square cake tin, and line with baking paper.
Cream the butter and sugar. Add the egg,
then the syrup, treacle and grated stem
ginger, and mix well.
Sieve the flour, baking soda and spices
into the mixture. Add the water and mix
well.
Bake for an hour or so, until a knife
blade comes out clean.

It wasn't easy getting hold of stem ginger in a place like Llanegryn. I did ask Mr Phyllip Shop for it, several times, and he would always glare at me over his glasses as he answered, as if I was a child.

'As I've said before, Mrs Davies, there's nobody here who has use for grand ingredients.'

'Well, I would use them. As I've said before.'

Mr Phyllip Shop would then shake his head, bald and shiny as a sweetie jar. Cheeky sod. I could remember him as a child. He used to walk as if he had a poker up his bum then, too.

I plunged my finger into the jar of stem ginger (I'd had to make it myself in the end) and started grating the ball of ginger into the flour, inhaling as much as I could of the spicy sweet perfume into my lungs. I licked my fingers, and felt the sweetness of the ginger-infused syrup reaching my blood.

Without washing my hands (who would know?), I reached for treacle and golden syrup from the pantry, before opening the shiny tins with a bread knife. A tablespoonful of treacle, a thick black river into the snowy flour, and then the syrup. They melted into each other like oil and gold. Water from the kettle on the Rayburn, and an egg. Only one, but a big one from Black Road Farm, the yolk a cheerful yellow.

Ginger cake in the oven and the dishes all washed, dried, and back where they belonged, I sat in the easy chair by the window. The birds glided over the village, and I did my best to ignore the ache in my joints and the chewing pain in my fingers. Everything was all right.

A ribbon of scent wove its way from the oven to my nose. Ginger and sugar. Everything was all right.

Ginger cake had always been Tommy's favourite.

I could almost feel him here, his ghost entwined in the smell of baking. I could almost hear the click of the back door opening, the thump of his work boots on the slate floor, the groan of the chair by the fire as he sat. A curve on his lips underneath the thick moustache, his eyes smiling. 'What's cooking?' A joke, of course. He recognised the smell, nothing else was like it. He'd cut a big fat square of the cake, surprisingly big for such a restrained man. I would feel the joy squeezing my heart. I loved him, and he loved my food.

Time to fetch the cake from the oven. It was beautiful: brown, moist, risen to a little hill in the centre. Wearing my stained oven gloves, I slid the cake tin to the window sill, and watched, for a while, the steam rising like grey ghosts and fogging the window.

I had to slow down to catch my breath after walking from the chair to the oven. Was it because I was fat? There were certainly more doughy folds around my stomach since Tommy died. The oven bore the brunt of my loss, keeping my hands busy and my mind occupied. Mountains of cakes, scones and loaves rose on every kitchen surface, wrinkling my hands as the dough dried around my fingernails. My hair, which had kept its exotic blackness, became white as clouds of flour rose in the kitchen. I filled my empty house with the scent of baking. And slowly, though I ate my fill of it all, the food died too. The bread and cakes became hard crusts, and the biscuits softened into mush. I left them in the pantry until they grew green, and then left them on the roof of the coal shed for the birds, pretending not to see the rats coming from the river to feast.

And yet, I baked every day, making more and more and more.

'You buy enough flour to feed a family of five,' said Mr Phyllip Shop as he measured it out, his eye tight on the red finger of the scales.

'I enjoy baking.' I silently berated myself for bothering to justify myself to an old toad like Mr Phyllip Shop.

'You need to eat something other than cakes, Mrs Davies.' His smile was cruel as his piggy eyes wandered to my midriff. 'You need vegetables and protein.'

I pressed my lips together, hoping the hatred and sharp words would not escape from my mouth.

'Not that it's my business...' He raised his eyebrows archly. 'I've warned you now, haven't I.'

Reaching for my purse, I couldn't stop myself. 'Oh, but I'm not baking for myself.'

Mr Phyllip Shop looked up at me.

'Some of the folk in this village think that bread and cake are too expensive. Your prices are very high...'

The grocer opened his mouth, looking for the words. I bit back a smile as a sheen of frustrated perspiration greased his bald head.

'Perhaps some of these terribly poor folk who think my goods are so very expensive should stop having children,' he said, as I left the shop. 'They're like a plague around this village...'

His voice had risen an eighth of an octave as his temper bubbled. I turned back, and smiled at him. That would annoy him more than anything.

'And how is little Francis?' I asked, remembering his young son's pretty, olive-skinned face. 'I never see him around the village.'

'Francis does not need to run around like a feral animal. He is perfectly happy in his own home.'

How odd that I would look back on that very moment as a rebirth, the dawn of my new life. This new woman would make a difference. People would treasure her, and remember her as generous and kind.

I began to give away my food.

The elderly were first. They knew me well enough. Some of them were just a few years older than me. I would get up early to bake, and by two o'clock my basket would be full of goods in small brown greaseproof packages. The pain in my joints grated as I walked with the heavy basket through the village. I knew who needed me: Mrs Ffrancon Mountain View, and Miss Delia End House, both of

10

them frail and both took a long while to open the door.

Then, I started giving to families too: Helen Cader Lane, who had nine children and lost most of her husband's pay to the bar in the Corbett Arms. She deserved a large donation for all the hungry mouths she had to feed. Two milk loaves, a bara brith, a small cake for each of the children and a bag of scones. Helen looked as if she couldn't understand what I was saying.

'Don't think me rude, Mrs Davies, but I'm not a charity. These children get everything they need...'

'I know that!' I had predicted this reaction, Helen was a proud woman. 'The thing is, Helen, I love baking, and since Tommy died, I have no one to eat it. So it all goes to waste. My own son has moved away...'

Helen sighed, and bit her lip. She was weighing her pride against her children's rumbling stomachs. Nothing is stronger than hunger.

'If you don't want them, please, don't take them,' I added quietly. 'I'll give them to someone else. I know that your little ones have plenty. They're such strong children... Full of energy! I'm only offering what will go to waste. You'd be doing me a favour...'

That was enough for Helen. She smiled, relieved, and accepted the packages. She knew, of course, that it *was* charity, and that I pitied her, but to pretend otherwise was important. As I left, after refusing a cup of tea, she touched my arm gently, and I turned back to the tired young woman.

'Thank you, Mrs Davies.'

I nodded and smiled, and felt warm all the way home, my gnawing arthritis forgotten.

In a few weeks, I was feeding the whole village. The children of Llanegryn learned that the old fat woman from Beech Grove was giving out food for free, and a knock on the door became a regular occurrence, with little eager faces when I opened it. I made a promise to myself that no one would be turned away empty-handed. Beech Grove grew lively, as it had been when Tommy was alive and Kenneth was a boy. I had a purpose again: I was mother to all the children of the village.

Every spring, the gypsies would come in colourful caravans, and hordes of pretty dark-eyed children would spill out onto the common. They were my favourites, and the mothers and grandmothers accepted my offerings without embarrassment and with a smile, and would make me a cup of tea with water boiled over an open fire. Their children encircled me, hanging onto my legs, making me feel wanted, as if I was part of something.

I loved the look of surprise that dawned on faces when they realised that I'd brought them food for nothing. And yet, I did receive something from them in return: A feeling that could not be measured in coins.

I opened my eyes suddenly, before letting them settle into the darkness for a while. The fire was almost out, the last few desperate flames licking up from the orange log. I had fallen asleep in front of the fire again, I realised, yawning. This was becoming a regular occurrence. I was exhausted after baking and delivering all day.

Slowly rising from the chair, my back ached. The arthritis. I moved from one piece of furniture to the next, leaning on them as I went. From the chair to the dresser, from the dresser to the corner cupboard, and then on to lean on the doorframe between the parlour and the kitchen...

Knock, knock, knock.

I froze, then stood up straight forgetting the pain in my back. The embers gave just enough light for me to be able to read the fingers on the clock. Half past eleven.

I felt my heart thumping.

The tramp: The one that came yesterday. It must be him. He was an odd character, not a single tooth in his mouth and stinking of manure. He had asked for food, and I'd soaked some bread in milk so that he wouldn't have to chew with his gums. Had he seized the opportunity to attack an old woman at night?

His toothless smile flashed into my memory, and sent a bolt of fear down my spine.

Knock, knock, knock.

Slowly, and as quietly as I could, I tiptoed over to the front door. A different sound, now: very, very different.

Gentle crying.

All my fears forgotten, I rushed for the door. I pulled the heavy oak and stared out into the blackness, narrowing my eyes so that I could focus on the small face that stood in the doorway.

'Peggy?'

She nodded, wiping her tears with the sleeve of her jumper.

'Come in, my dear!'

I moved to one side to let her in. Peggy Riverside! What was she – six, seven years old? What in God's name was a little girl doing out of bed at this hour, never mind walking the dark roads?

'Sit by the fire, my dear.'

I shut the door, before rushing to put another log on the embers.

'Will you take a hot drink?'

Before she had a chance to answer, I had rushed to the kitchen to warm some milk on the stove. Standing above the saucepan, I watched the little girl in the next room, sniffing and wiping her nose on her sleeve.

Peggy Riverside was a tall, thin, and rather plain child. Her hair was long, and hung like rats' tails around her shoulders, and her skin had a faint yellow tinge. Many of the poor children had this sallow complexion, their parents too poor to buy fresh vegetables and red meat. Her nose was long and narrow, her lips thin, but it was Peggy's eyes that drew attention. They would have been beautiful on any other face, big and grey like stone. I had taken a few baskets of food to Riverside, but not as often as I did to others.

Something about Jennie, Peggy's mother, made me uncomfortable – the lack of a smile, the lofty thanks, and the perpertual darkness Riverside cottage seemed to be in. She wasn't thankful.

She had her reasons, of course. Things hadn't been easy on Jennie Riverside, raising Peggy alone, without the comfort or salary of a man. But that wasn't the point. It wasn't too much to expect a little gratitude, was it?

I added a spoonful of gloopy golden honey to the milk, before pouring it carefully into a tin cup. Peggy was still and silent, sitting by the fire.

'Careful! It's hot!' I warned before she sipped some of the milk. 'What are you doing here so late, my dear?'

Peggy sniffed. 'I'm sorry, Mrs Davies.'

'You don't need to apologise. But you'd better tell me, in case your mother gets worried.'

A few fat tears escaped from her grey eyes.

'There you are,' I soothed, sitting beside her. 'Don't cry, now.'

'I think that there's something the matter with my mother.' Peggy pushed the tears from her eyes with the tips of her long fingers.

'Why do you say that?'

'She does such strange things sometimes, Mrs Davies.'

Peggy looked up at me, and stared into my eyes for a few long seconds. I felt a bolt of horror passing from her eyes to mine, and tried to hide my nervousness from the child.

I swallowed constantly, as if I could swallow my fear.

'Like what, my dear?'

'She never sleeps, you know.'

I stared at Peggy.

'She sits in her chair in the kitchen all night, staring at the wall.'

'She probably snoozes in the chair. It must be nice and warm there, by the stove.'

'She never says hello to me, or anything. She pretends I'm not there.'

Peggy coughed until there were more ugly fat tears rolling down her thin face.

'Oh, my dear Peggy...'

I enveloped her bony frame in my thick warm arms, and held her close to my breast, biting back my own tears as I felt her small body shaking with sobs.

'And today, she made a soup on the stove, with potato and carrot and turnip. But when I looked into the pot to get myself a bowlful... She'd put a rat in it. Whole. The fur and the eyes and everything.'

I wondered if Peggy could feel my heart drumming in my chest. I bit my lip as I tried to clean my brain of that horrific image, that vile rat soup, but it refused to leave. My mind's eye insisted on showing me the little claws, the shiny black eyes, the curling tail like a rope in the pot.

Jennie Riverside would have to go to Denbigh Asylum.

'Where is she now, Peggy?'

'Still in her chair by the stove. I got up from my bed and told her I was leaving because I was frightened, but it was as if she couldn't hear. She stared right through me.'

'Did you tell her where you were going?'

Peggy shook her head, much to my relief. A small, skinny woman like Jennie should be no match for a woman of my size, arthritis or no arthritis. But I had no idea how to deal with a mad woman.

'Your mother is ill, Peggy. She's going to need to take a holiday for a while.'

'What will happen to me?'

'Don't worry. We'll go and see the Reverend tomorrow, and he'll sort everything. You can stay here tonight.'

'Thank you, Mrs Davies.'

'You can take off your jumper and socks, and I'll get you a blanket.' I turned towards the stairs, before facing her again.

'When did you last eat, my dear?'

'Lunch time.'

I pressed my nails into the palm of my hand. It was nearly midnight. She must be famished.

After fetching a woollen blanket and tucking it around Peggy's frail frame, I cut her a square of dark, dense ginger cake. The smell momentarily took me to another time – Tom's workboots on the slate floor, the dustiness of his work coat. I shook my head to shake off the memory. Peggy would like the cake. Peggy would have liked the cake hours before, as she reached her little hand to open the saucepan lid, as she stirred the soup with her spoon, exposing the wet grey fur in her supper.

Discontent settled like a storm inside me as I placed the ginger cake on a plate. This is who needed my bread, my cakes, and I had avoided her because her mother was not sufficiently thankful. Was that at the root of my generosity? Did I chase that warm glow of appreciation?

'Here you are, cariad, something for you to eat before you sleep.' I handed her the plate, and after thanking me, Peggy started picking at the cake with the tips of her fingers.

'Oh, Mrs Davies, this is wonderful!' She broke off bigger pieces of the brown sponge and stuffed them into her small mouth. 'Oh, thank you Mrs Davies!'

A tear pushed its way out of the corner of my eye, and glistened down my cheek like dew. I don't know exactly what touched my heart. A mixture of things, perhaps: Tommy's ginger cake; the hungry mouth of a child and her eager fingers tearing the cake; the cruel neglect of Jennie Riverside. And something else, something that was planted deeply in my consciousness since before I could remember: the inherent joy of seeing somebody enjoying my food.

The next morning, after a breakfast of fried bread and bacon,

I pulled my coat on and led Peggy by the hand along the small road to the village. A knot of something vile hardened in my chest as we walked, a mixture of fear at seeing Jennie, concern for Peggy, but mainly my desperate yearning to keep the little girl, to nurture her and make her feel safe once again. I knew that Peggy's grandparents lived on a farm a few miles away and that they would now be her natural guardians, but that didn't change the longing that was pawing at my heart. I could make her happy. I could make meat form on those thin bones.

'Can't I stay with you?'

I couldn't look down at Peggy, but I could feel her grey eyes gazing up at me. 'We'd better see what the Reverend says, sweetheart.'

A silence stretched between us. The songbirds twittered in the hedgerows, and the school bell rang from the hilltop. Peggy's friends would be standing in a line on the schoolyard now, waiting to go into the classroom. Had they noticed that she was missing?

'I'd be a good girl for you, Mrs Davies, I promise.'

I stopped. Though my back ached after sitting in the chair all night, watching Peggy sleeping, I stooped down to the same level as the little girl. She looked better after having some meat and grease in her stomach. I had combed her hair, too, bringing some life to the fine, mousy hair, and teasing out the matted knots which hid at her nape.

'Sweetheart, I'd take you if I was allowed to. But I won't be the one who decides. Wherever you go, you'll be safe, and that's the important thing.' Peggy nodded as if she understood, watching my eyes. 'And if you're unhappy, you're always welcome at my house. I'll look after you any time.'

We walked together towards the village. It was a fine morning, and there were a few people in their gardens, pegging clothes on the line or pulling dandelions from their lawns. I waved, and wished everyone a good morning, but I didn't stop to talk, though

17

my neighbours were clearly curious as to why Peggy was walking with me so early in the morning.

Rose Cottage, the home of the Reverend Vaughan, stood opposite two chapels in the village square, the river whispering nearby. No-one was in the garden, only a knot of a rose bush under each window, small pink buds starting to form amidst the thorns. I knocked the door firmly. Mrs Vaughan came to the door, her face caked in make up and her dark curls perfectly in place. She could not hide her surprise at her morning visitors – a fat old woman and a skinny young girl.

'Good morning, Mrs Vaughan. Is the Reverend here, please?'

'He's in the chapel, Mrs Davies. Is everything all right? Peggy?'

Peggy nodded and smiled warmly. 'Mrs Davies is looking after me.'

Mrs Vaughan looked up at me questioningly, but I did not want to explain. 'We'll go over to the chapel, then. Thank you.'

The chapel was cold, though the sun was warm outside, the long windows casting their shadows over the wooden pews. The Reverend Jack Vaughan stood in the front, surrounded by towers of hymn books. He raised his eyebrows in surprise when he saw us. 'Mrs Davies!' He ran his fingers through his red hair to try and flatten the tuft that would not be tamed at the back. 'And Peggy! How are you both?'

'Good morning, Mr Vaughan.' I hurried over to him, pulling Peggy along.

'Is everything all right?'

'Yes, yes. But I need to speak with you about Peggy.'

Mr Vaughan stared at me, the same look in his eyes as the one his wife had given me a few minutes earlier. There was something odd about the way I was asking advice from a man who couldn't be any older than twenty-five. 'Of course. Sit for a while. Or would you prefer to go to the house?'

'No, that's fine, we'll stay here.' I settled my wide behind into one of the pews. I didn't want to go to Mrs Vaughan's spotless home. Being in the company of somebody so perfect would only make me feel my own shortcomings. And yet, I was happy enough in the company of the Reverend. They were such an odd couple! What kind of marriage tied two such extremes?

I told him everything. Peggy remained silent. I watched his face trying to disguise the disgust as I described the rat soup, and noticed his Adam's apple juddering when I told him that Jennie utterly ignored her little girl. When I came to the end of the story, Mr Vaughan nodded, wisely, and gave a little cough. 'Well Peggy, you did a very clever thing, going to someone kind like Mrs Davies. And she's right when she says that your mother's just sick.' He sank to his knees to speak to her, and she stared at him in complete seriousness. My heart jolted with appreciation that this young man knew how to speak to children. 'You mustn't be afraid. I'll send for Dr Thomas, and someone will fetch your grandparents. They'll want to care for you.'

'Grandparents?' Peggy half-whispered. The Reverend nodded.

'Your mother's parents. From Hare House.'

Peggy stared at him for a few moments. 'I don't know them.'

I bit my lip to stop myself from offering a place for her with me. Her place was with her family, but they were strangers... What use was a bond of blood when she knew me, trusted me, had asked to share my home? There had been an argument between Jennie and her parents some years ago. They were barely related now.

'They're kind people. They'll be careful of you.' Mr Vaughan stood up, and I did the same. 'Thank you for looking after her. You've been very caring.'

'It was my pleasure.' My voice was gruff, exposing my emotions. 'Shall I take her home with me for a while? While we wait for her family?'

Mr Vaughan shook his head and smiled kindly. 'You've done more than enough. My wife will look after her now.' I nodded, though I wasn't at all sure whether Annie Vaughan had the faintest idea how to care for a child, what with her painted lips and her wide-skirted frocks.

'Remember what I told you, Peggy.' I stroked her hair with my thick fingers. 'Come back to me if you're ever unhappy.'

She didn't answer. I bit my lip as I walked to the back of the chapel, feeling the tears rising. As I placed my hand on the doorknob, Peggy turned in her seat and yelled, 'Thank you, Mrs Davies! Thank you!' I turned back, my cheeks wet, and waved at the little girl sitting in the front pew.

Sion Pugh
Peggy's grandfather
1936

Barley Pudding

3oz pearl barley   2oz brown sugar
2 pints milk   1 oz butter

mix the ingredients and place in the
oven at a low temperature for two
hours. Add more milk if necessary,
and spices if you so wish, until the
barley is soft.

Goodness, she was small! A frail, thin slip of a girl, her summer dress hanging from her bony shoulders like curtains into an empty space. Almost small enough not to be there at all.

I hurried up the road. I was used to the isolation of my own home, and the windows of the small, squat houses seemed to stare at me coldly. The river ran alongside the road, chilly and whispering and, as I crossed the bridge and strode into Two Chapels' Square, I felt the significance of the moment. I knew I would remember this forever – the crunch of my feet on the stony road; the smell of new flowers in the hedges; the claustrophobic feel of being in the village again. My eyes fixed on a tiny figure which stood still by the gate of Rose Cottage. The Reverend Jack Vaughan stood by her side, tugging uncomfortably at his dog collar in the heat. He was a tall man, skin pale as milk and hair the colour of marmalade. He was barely a man at all, or so I thought at the time; he stood, walked, moved like an awkward schoolboy. My eyes were drawn back to the child, and she stared back at me, her eyes dark in that pale, sickly face.

'Mr Pugh,' The Reverend greeted me with a sad half-smile as I neared them. 'Thank you for coming so quickly.'

'No, thank *you* for looking after her....'

To my own ears, my voice sounded gutteral and gruff, like an old dog's bark, and it broke a little as the words faded. The Reverend's voice had a soft sing-song lilt, as if he were reciting a poem. No wonder he'd joined the ministry.

I stared at my granddaughter's face for the first time.

She was the image of Jennie. Plain, with thin lips and a weak chin, and the stone-grey eyes I had never seen in others. Old women's eyes, in young faces. I turned away from her for a moment. I didn't want to see her mother in the child, but Jennie seemed to possess the little girl. I steadied my mind, and turned back to her.

'Margaret, is it?' I asked the girl.

'They call me Peggy.'

'Oh.'

That was enough to stun me. The name of the grandchild I had harboured in my mind was not Peggy, it was Margaret, and her ghost had stood by my bed at night, teasing my conscience, keeping me awake. How did I not know that she was called Peggy? How could I have never known her name?

'I'm your grandfather.'

Peggy stared at me, starting at my beaten old boots until she reached the worn cap on my grey head, and then, imperceptibly slowly, she started nodding. 'I've packed a bag.'

She showed me her canvas bag: It looked almost empty. Even in the midst of this poignant scene, I had to suppress a smile at her sober seriousness.

'Good girl. We'd better go, then. Your nain will be waiting for you. She's been fussing all morning.'

'This is for you.' Mr Vaughan took an envelope from his breast pocket and offered it to me. 'With all the... All the *details*.'

I looked up and caught his eye for a few seconds. *The details.* Of course, I knew what he meant, but something in the simplicity of the words gave them a revolting flippancy. *The details.* It was so much crueller than that.

The Reverend lowered his gangly body to kneel on the ground, and held Peggy's limp fingers in his own freckled hand.

'Now listen, Peggy. I'll come to Hare House next week to see that you're settling. You need not worry about anything anymore.'

Peggy nodded, unsmiling. 'All right. Thank you very much.'

The child and I started on our journey, walking side by side towards Llan Bridge. I had not visited the village for years, and the place retained memories of childhood for me, vivid colours and sweet tastes. The road ran on a gentle slope before levelling out, long and flat as the village became fields. As an old man, the whole place held, for me, an almost eerie feeling of a toy town – a small, twisting river; a perfect, tiny stone bridge; brightly coloured flowers in perfectly kept gardens. I knew that behind Riverside, on the village common, things became wilder – the river wider, deeper, darker, the nettles allowed to grow and wave dangerously in the breeze. But the village itself was quiet and calm, and it made me nervous.

I was a stranger to awkwardness, and yet I felt tongue-tied whilst I walked with my granddaughter for the first time. Was I expected to hold her hand? Carry her on my shoulders? I felt the eyes of the Reverend watching us from the shadows of Rose Cottage.

We walked across Llan Bridge, the birdsong in the trees making the silence between us unspeakably loud. It was one of those rare perfect days, childhood-warm, with butterflies dancing their rainbows from flower to hedge to tree.

'I didn't know I had grandparents.'

I stared at Peggy as we walked, and she returned my stare. Was she joking?

'Your mother never told you about us?'

She shook her head. 'She doesn't talk a lot.'

I nodded, as if I understood, though I didn't. Jennie used to unsettle me with her incessant commentary when she was a child at Hare House.

'Is it a long way to your house?'

'No. Three miles, or thereabouts. Under Bird Rock.'

'Oh!' Peggy did not conceal her surprise. 'That's not far at all! Isn't it funny that we never met before?'

As we left the village behind us, I stole a sideways glance at her. She was grotesquely thin. Did she have worms? I had harboured my own invented image of her for years, but never like this. In my mind, Margaret was a small, round child, red-cheeked and with her father's dark, curly hair in swirls around her face. That imagined child was not at all related to this ghostly girl by my side, who gazed at the road with such seriousness.

'Peggy!'

24

I followed the voice, and saw Mai Davies behind her iron gate, clutching a brown paper package. I swallowed my shock at how her body had thickened in the years since I'd seen her. Years ago, Mai had been a pretty girl, shattering hearts when she settled on Tommy Davies as a husband. I almost did not recognise the corpulent figure leaning on the gate for support, sweat beading on her forehead, and yet something of the young, lithe girl I remembered remained in her – the heavy-lidded eyes, perhaps, or the way her mouth pouted ever so slightly.

'I cut it into slices for you to eat on your way home,' she said, offering the package to Peggy.

'Thank you, Mrs Davies,' said Peggy politely, taking the gift from the swollen hands, and holding it as tenderly as if it were a newborn. I thanked her, too. I had lost touch with her long ago - it had been so long since I'd visited Llanegryn. Aber and Bryncrug were my villages now. Mai and I were no longer the same two as the little children who'd sat next to one another on their first day of school, almost sixty years earlier.

Having said goodbye to Mrs Davies, Peggy and I walked silently along the road, passing the Lodge and the Soldiers' Hospital with the sound of a few weak voices laughing from one of the wards reaching us through the open window. A mile or so across the flat fields and the dark patch of forest around the grand Peniarth Estate, a crag rose high into the warm air, jutting improbably like a bird's proud breast. The road dug further and further into the valley, changing from this wide, flat expanse on which we now walked into a single-track road, darkened on both side by high hedgerows. One day, perhaps, I could walk with Peggy along the whole expanse of road, until it became a path leading up to Cader Idris mountain, fields and fields of slope dotted with old ruins.

Peggy looked up at me.

'Would you like a piece of whatever it is Mrs Davies has made?'

The seriousness in her face made me smile: I stroked my beard in an attempt to hide it from her.

'Is she a good cook, then?'

'All the Llan children go to her for cake. And she brings food to the village, too. Especially the poor people. She brought us a milk loaf, once, and she'd put nuts and rosemary in the bread.'

Peggy pulled the bag off her shoulders and set it on the road, before opening the string that was knotted at the top. She had no idea that she had, in a brief sentence, revealed to me that she and her mother were among the village poor. She had no way of knowing that her words had knotted a hard ball of guilt in my heart.

She held the paper package in her hand, using her thin fingers to unfold the sharp creases. I watched her face, lit up as if she was opening an oyster shell and finding a shining pearl. The grey eyes open wide, her lips parted in anticipation. When she recognised the contents of the package, her mouth widened in a triumphant smile, showing her crooked teeth. She turned that smile to me, holding her hand in front of her eyes to shield them from the sun.

'Look, Taid! Ginger cake!'

My own lips parted slightly, just as hers had done seconds before. I had never been called Taid before. I had not thought how that one syllable, the Welsh word for Grandfather, would suit me. But there I was, an old man on the quiet lane between Llan and home, rebaptised by this small child, and my new title vibrated like the sound of an unheard song within me.

Peggy offered me a thick slab of cake, and I accepted it eagerly. Peggy was right: Mai Davies was a wonderful cook. Little wonder she had grown so big.

Perhaps it was that 'Taid', which shattered the ice between us, or perhaps it was the thick sweetness of the cake, but from that moment, all awkwardness between Peggy and I disappeared. We chatted and laughed all the way to Hare House, our fingers still sticky with the remnants of ginger cake. Peggy was exactly as her mother had been at that age, an eternal circle of questions: who lived in that ruin in the olden days? Why did the important people on the Peniarth Estate hide their mansion with trees if it was so grand? How did it feel to be old? I was pleased to find that I had more patience to answer unanswerable questions now than I had done twenty years previously, when Jennie was a child. My granddaughter was a gentle, pleasant child, her eyes constantly searching the verges for songbirds and flies.

As we neared Bird Rock, I stopped for a moment and asked, 'Would you like to see Hare House?'

Peggy nodded, her eyes wide. I picked her up in my arms for the first time: she was no heavier than a lamb. I pointed over the hedge, beyond the grey rocks which dotted the fields. In the distance, the small, squat building could be seen nestling on the line of a hedgerow, a ribbon of smoke curling from the chimney.

I could feel Peggy's bones through her thin cotton dress. There was no cushion of fat to protect her scrawny body.

'Nain has made a fire, even though it's warm today,' she noted.

'She's waiting for you. She couldn't sit still this morning, trying to make everything perfect.'

'Why are there so many rocks here?'

I put her down on the verge, her shoes sighing softly as they hit the grass.

'They probably fell down, long ago. They may have been a part of Bird Rock once.'

'What if it happens again? What if Bird Rock falls down on you and Nain whilst you sleep?'

'Don't you go worrying about that, now. Everyone is safe at Hare House.'

So I was Taid, and now Elen was Nain: Grandmother, carer, protector. My wife was born to be a nain.

I remember it so well, her standing in the door frame, watching Peggy and I walking up the track towards the house, white apron

27

swaying in the breeze and the windows reflecting the white summer clouds. Peggy stared back at this tall, muscled stranger, who must have looked far too young and fit to be her grandmother. As we reached the farmyard, Elen started to run.

'Margaret! My Margaret!' she gasped as she wrapped her arms around the child. Peggy stood still, muted in the glare of affection. 'Are you all right? Are you all right, my love?'

'They call her Peggy,' I said softly, insecure in an important moment. Elen looked up at me, a wound in her eyes that had been hidden for a long while.

'You're like your mother. You're exactly like Jennie,' Elen mumbled, her eyes hungrily searching all the details of the child. 'Well now, come in to Hare House. It's all right! I have everything ready for you.'

And so it was. The stove in the corner roared, though the heat of the sun would have been enough on such a day. The house was unbearably hot. Wild flowers – buttercups, Welsh poppies and wild roses – were arranged in a pretty posy on the table. The scent of fresh bread laced the hot air, though it was a Thursday, and Thursdays had never been baking days in Hare House. Peggy looked around her, looking small and lost. Everything was new to her.

'Would you like Nain and me to show you the farmyard, and the back field?' I asked, to save her from the heat of her new home. Peggy nodded quickly, and escaped to the fresh air.

'Nain,' Elen repeated softly before we followed our granddaughter into the softness of the breeze.

'Yes.'

Peggy adored our smallholding, our small clutch of animals. I awarded her the job of egg collector, and her face immediately straightened with the seriousness of such a responsibility. She laughed at the pig and the goat, and by the time we had shown her the little we had, it felt like she had always been with us. In a way,

I suppose she had.

'I like Hare House,' she proclaimed over a cup of goat's milk in the kitchen, later. 'Although it is very hot here.'

Peggy went to bed that night without complaint or uneasiness, though she was surprised that her grandmother went along to help her wash herself and get undressed. It was clear she had been doing those things herself, until now. Her bony arms stretched around my neck before she climbed the stairs, and she kissed the grey bristles on my cheek.

'Your beard tickles my cheek,' she giggled. 'Goodnight, Taid.'

I sat in the flickering light of the fire, watching the sunset through the window. The town of Tywyn was five or six miles away over the flat bottom of the valley, and beyond that, a sliver of ocean, rust-coloured as the day bled its sunset over Cardigan Bay. It was strange to hear the sounds of a child within these walls again. Bare feet on the wooden floor, high pitched giggling and a sing-song lilt drifting wordlessly from upstairs. Like a language, long since spoken but not forgotten. Peggy. Our grandchild, who had been only a ghost on the marches of our minds until that morning...a shadow in the darkness of our imaginations, one we could not bear to speak of. And suddenly, she had transformed from a spirit girl to being a real child, meat and bone and voice and laugh, all within one day. A day that had started with the tall figure of a stranger approaching our home.

'Do you know him?' I had asked Elen as we watched him crossing the farmyard towards the house. She had shaken her head, her loaded spoon frozen halfway between her mouth and the porridge bowl.

'A note from Jack Vaughan, the Reverend,' said the young man, passing me a folded piece of paper.

I knew, then, that this would concern Jennie.

It had been six years since I had spoken to my daughter. Six years since we had spat cruel words at one another across this kitchen table. Words sharp as shattered things, words that wounded. I still thought about her, still felt like her father, and the weight of that feeling lay, a constant failure, on my shoulders. Elen and I could no longer visit Llan, and the name of our only child was a word that was unutterably sad, so we no longer spoke it. Sometimes, when I was alone, I curled my tongue around the vowels and consonants of her name, tasting the forbidden syllables once more. In the cowshed. In the sty. In the back field, standing in the midst of grazing sheep: 'Jennie', barely a whisper, just enough to remind myself that she had existed, that she remained, somewhere, alive.

I wondered if Elen ever did the same.

I knew my daughter well enough to know that it would not be long until I was summoned to the village to correct a wrong she had committed. The note was short: 'Come immediately. Jennie taken to Denbigh. Your granddaughter needs a home.' The unintelligible signature of the Reverend, and the blank spaces between the words more revealing than what was written.

And then there was Peggy, with us, suddenly, an incarnation of the memory of her mother, sleeping in her bed, with the same face, the same voice, the same babyish habit of curling the end of her plait around her fingers. She had already enchanted me with the possibility of a second chance, for righting old, unforgettable wrongs.

I couldn't believe she was back, and yet, she wasn't: she had never been here before.

After almost an hour, Elen descended the stairs to the kitchen, her steps slow and heavy. She sat in the chair beside me.

'She's a lovely girl,' I muttered into the twilight.

Elen started to cry.

She had never been an emotional sort of woman... Not since Jennie left, screaming a promise that we would never see her again. Elen had not cried at her parents' funerals, nor when the note was delivered that morning. But after putting her granddaughter to bed for the first time, she sat by my side and cried until her cheeks were slick with tears in the half-light.

'She's starved, Sion,' Elen whispered through her tears. 'Her nails haven't been cut, her body is unwashed. What did our little girl do to her little girl?'

I longed for her to shut up. I would have preferred not to know.

I recalled the feel of Peggy's protruding bones through her cotton dress that afternoon as we gazed across the field towards Hare House, her yellow-tinged skin reflecting the sun. I felt at fault, neglectful, as if my frayed, cracked care of Jennie had been thrown down cruelly onto a new generation.

'I don't know what to tell her, Sion,' said Elen breathlessly. 'I don't know whether I should talk about Jennie.'

'No, no, don't mention her.' I turned towards the window the face the approaching night.

The next morning, before anyone else woke up, I rose to milk the cows, so that Peggy could have the first cream with her breakfast. It was another fine day, and the dew shined my boots.

After I had done the milking, with a jug full to the brim waiting on the kitchen table, I listened for a few seconds, but the house was still asleep. I escaped to the wide flat rock in the back field. This was where I had sat as a child, pretending to be aboard a ship, the green pasture acting the part of choppy oceans, the sheep hungry crocodiles. The breeze breathed softly on my face as I sat, and reached into my pocket for the letter given to me by the Reverend Vaughan the previous afternoon. I would have given the world to be able to forget about it, but knew myself well enough to know that the white folds would prick at my conscience until the black words were read and understood.

The Reverend had done his best to fit the bare facts into plain, unadorned sentences, whilst being full of sympathy, and releasing Elen and I from any responsibility for the actions of our daughter. The story was a sharp, cruel thing, every word reaching razor-like claws further into my soft, tender skin, scratching at my conscience.

I came to understand why Mai Davies had been so kind, having found Peggy on her doorstep in the depths of night. I came to realise why Peggy was so thin, why her skin so pale. But there was nothing to explain why Jennie had done this. I was not told the details of my daughter's neglect towards her own child, only of the effects. No, the details were left to my imagination, in all its horrific glory.

I never told Elen that such a letter existed. She didn't need to know.

An hour later, Peggy sat at the table as Elen stirred the barley pudding, mixing the skin into the creamy thickness of it. She poured it into three large bowls, slowly, careful not to spill any.

Peggy turned to me, and smiled.

My breath caught in my throat. She was the image of her mother.

'Where have you been, Taid?'

'I milked the cows so that you could have the first cream, and then I had a walk around the back field, checking that all the sheep are all right.'

I pulled off my boots, and set them by the door. Elen laid the bowls heavily on the table.

'Was everything all right, Taid?'

'Yes. Mr Fox didn't come looking for his supper last night.'

I sat beside her at the table, stirring my breakfast with a spoon. 'If you like, you can come with me after breakfast. The pig needs to be fed.'

The way Peggy ate frightened me, as if she hadn't been fed in years. She forgot that she was being observed. Overloading her spoon with the thick, creamy pudding, she plunged for the next spoonful before she had swallowed the one in her mouth. Her forehead was creased in complete concentration on this task of consuming.

'This is lovely, Nain. Thank you.'

Elen looked at me. I had almost laughed as I watched the child until I saw my wife's eyes. Suddenly, I had to swallow back a choke of tears, understanding, in a second, the tragedy behind this feral hunger.

Half an hour later, whilst throwing handfuls of seeds to the hungry chickens, Peggy vomited her breakfast over the farmyard, her frail body quaking with the violence of it. She had rarely, if ever, had cream before that morning, and the weight of it had been unbearable for her small stomach. The chickens picked at the white, speckled sick, seeds forgotten. Elen had to water down the barley pudding after that, but within a year Peggy's stomach had expanded and toughened, and she could eat a whole bowl of barley pudding before she set off for school in the morning.

Gwynfor Daniel
Gardener
1939

Peggy's Second Breakfast

A thick slice of ham or bacon, roasted and cooled

Fresh tomato

Basil

Eat them together, in the morning sun.

I was certain that it was one of Helen Cader Lane's boys. Yes – they would be responsible. I was sure of it.

They were feral, those boys, and Helen had far too many children and far too little control. I pitied her, in a way, with a drunken husband who left her with a rainbow of bruises on her chalky skin. But the boys! I could not allow them to steal my tomatoes. I had spent time and care on them, had nursed them patiently as they grew fat. They were my tomatoes. *Mine.*

The first to disappear was a beauty – large, bulging, blushing deeper every day on the stem. I held back from picking it too early, reminding myself of that wonderful sharp tomato taste, freshly picked, still warm from the sun. I knew exactly what I would eat with it. A slab of cheese, a pinch of salt, and a slice of fresh bread from Phyllips' Shop, a thick wad of butter spread from crust to crust. I had been anticipating the tomato for days, visiting the greenhouse in the back garden several times a day to marvel at the vivid colour, the glossy skin.

The day came, and I had prepared everything before lunchtime: the bread and butter, the cheese and the salt cellar were waiting expectantly on the kitchen table. I grabbed the gardening scissors from their nail by the back door, my tongue restless in my mouth as I imagined the feast to come.

It had gone.

'Buggers! Bloody buggers!' I swore loudly, shooting a pearl of saliva across the greenhouse. There were no more tomatoes, and I would have to be satisfied with a simple lunch. It may have only been a small fruit, but it would have been the highlight of my day.

It may seem an over-reaction on my part, to break my heart over a stolen tomato. But so much more than that was tied to that little fruit. Months of labour – composting, watering, tending the plant softly, like skin. And then there was the praying! *Oh Lord, thank you for all you give, for my home and my health, and please make the tomatoes grow nice and fat and don't send any greenfly...*

I had purchased the seeds from a glossy colour advertisement in a magazine, had pushed them gently into the earth, nursing them like children, touching the smooth green leaves with craggy old hands.

'You must find them!' I complained to PC Williams as he did his rounds astride his bicycle.

'I'll do my very best, but...'

'It may be tomatoes they're stealing now, but those boys of Helen's will move on to bigger things... I've seen that very same pattern a hundred times before...'

'Mr Daniels,' the policeman replied, gravely, 'I am taking this seriously. I'll have a word with their mother. But without proof, there isn't much I can do about it...'

I swore under my breath. What did a young lad like him know about anything?

It became clear that PC Williams did, indeed, have a word with Helen, and that she, in turn, relayed the message to her sons. In the twilight of that evening, the sound of something solid and wet thudding against the parlour window broke the silence. I rushed out onto the road, and saw the eldest boy, Keith, at the far end of the street, double over and flashing his bare behind at me, pale and waxy like a couple of unripe apples. He pulled up his trousers, and shouted with venom, 'I wouldn't eat your horrible tomatoes if you gave me fifty pounds, you old sod! I've seen the cow shit you put on the soil!'

The next morning, I stood outside the house, a bucket of ashes resting on the road by my side. The mud on the window had dried, and after scratching it away with a leaf, I rubbed the ashes into the glass, using scrunched newspaper to do the job.

The village awoke as I worked.

The bread van passing, its scent of loaves like a perfume in its wake. Mai Davies on her way to the shop, walking slowly, painfully. Peggy, on her daily trek from Hare House to school, her plait hanging limply down her back.

'Good morning,' I called, as I always did when I saw the child, remembering the shine of the black car which had carried her mother to Denbigh Mental a few years previously.

'What are you doing?' she asked, surprised to see me out and about so early.

'Cleaning the dirt from the windows. One of the Cader Lane boys.'

She sighed knowingly. 'They're always in trouble at school. Do you not have any soap, Mr Daniels?'

'Well, yes, I do, but this is the best way to make windows shine, Peggy.'

'Really?'

I nodded. 'This is how my mother did it.'

I spotted the suspicion in her eyes, but she didn't say a word.

As the spring matured and the plants in the garden bloomed, the thief became bolder. More tomatoes, a cucumber, lettuce, rhubarb. They would be there at night and gone by morning, and every hope and expectation that I would enjoy them for lunch faded as my vegetables began to disappear. Those boys must have come in the night, silent, sly thieves, knowing that I was always early to bed.

And then, one morning, I learned the truth.

Eight o'clock, and I stood in the little kitchen at the back of the house. My stomach ulcer had kept me awake at night, gnawing at my insides as if it was chewing its way out of me. I arose early to fetch a glass of milk. That always seemed to calm the acid in my belly.

As I sipped, I happened to catch sight of her. She sat on the damp grass in the garden, her body curled up, knees to chest, matchstick legs stretching from the dark cotton of her school skirt.

Peggy? But she would never...

The tomato in her hand was the same size as her fist, and in her other hand she clutched a glinting penknife. I watched as she expertly quartered the tomato. The blade must have been sharp. Then, she reached into her pocket for a square of baking paper, before opening it carefully, exposing the wedges of pink ham within. With swift fingers, Peggy plucked a few leaves from my basil plant, and pushed the three ingredients into her little mouth at once. The juice and seeds of my tomato ran a teardrop down her chin.

It looked wonderful.

I opened the window slowly, but Peggy heard the sigh of the window frame and looked up, her grey eyes wide.

'It's all right,' I said, before she had a chance to escape. 'Does it taste good?'

She nodded, muted by the food in her mouth.

'Why do you take food from my greenhouse? Do they not give you breakfast at Hare House?'

Peggy swallowed, keen to correct me. 'Yes! A huge breakfast! But...'

I looked at her, raised my brow in a question.

'By the time I get here, I want more.'

I stared at her thin arms, her bony legs.

'Perhaps you should eat a bigger breakfast,' I suggested, thoughtfully.

'I eat as much as I can! And I'm not hungry, not exactly. But you know, Mr Daniels, I never feel full either.'

She escaped, then, and disappeared though the gate to school.

Nothing was ever taken from my greenhouse after that, and Peggy and I never conversed again: just a perfunctory 'good morning' and 'good evening', polite and shy. I got to keep my tomatoes, my cucumbers and lettuce, but somehow, they never tasted as good after that, and the memories of a painfully hungry child always seemed to surface as I put them on my tongue.

Davey Hoyle
Gypsy
1944

Trout

2 trout fillets   a lemon

2 tomatoes   salt

Drizzle a little olive oil on the trout.
Slice the lemon and tomato thinly,
then place them on top of the trout in a
small package of foil. Add plenty of
salt. Close the little food package and
roast in a moderate oven for half an
hour.

'What are you doing here?'

I looked up and saw her standing there, her arms folded across her chest. She was leaning against a crooked oak tree, silhouetted against the sun.

'What does it look like I'm doing?' I turned my eyes back to the fishing rod. 'Leave me alone.'

'My grandfather owns here,' she answered defiantly.

'Does he own the fish in the river?'

Her forehead creased as she considered it, before deciding to ignore my question altogether.

'You need a licence to fish.'

'I've left it at home.'

'In the caravan?'

'Yes! In the caravan!'

'Okay, okay. Don't bite my head off.'

I had come for the quiet, the coolness, the solitude, away from the village and the shrill voices that came echoing over the common. My sixteenth summer, and the world and all that was in it danced on my nerves.

She moved towards me, cracking the dry twigs with her bare feet. She wore a green dress, a kind of mossy damp-looking green that made her skin look pale, and a navy blue cardigan over it. I watched as she settled her thin body on a smooth flat stone under the shadows of the copse, and she turned her own face towards me.

'What are you doing here?' I asked.

'One of the sheep has wandered. Gone to find some shade, I reckon, but I thought I'd look for her all the same.'

'Well, she isn't here.'

'No, she isn't.' Peggy lay back over the smooth stone and stretched her arms and legs, groaning lightly. 'Do you know, this is one of my favourite places.'

'Oh.'

Peggy turned onto her side, and rested her face in the palm of her hand, staring at me.

'Why are you so angry?'

I laughed. Peggy was a stupid girl: too jolly by half. I had seen her with her friends in the village a few times, waving like a loon at everyone, smiling all the time. It made her look simple-minded, like there was something wrong with her: a slowness of thought, as if she was seeing everything for the first time.

'Everyone's angry with me. I'm just returning the favour.'

'Don't talk rubbish. Everyone's always very kind to you.'

I sighed deeply. What did she know? This long slouching farm girl, with her rat's tail plait hanging down her back. She was shielded from everything by her grandparents. I had seen them, and was jealous of the gentle way they looked at her, the fondness in their crows' feet as they smiled. Peggy was a fourteen-year-old child. She knew nothing of suffering. I had travelled the country, had seen the blown-out holes where bombs had raged; the mothers crying into telegrams on their doorsteps; heard the waspish rasp of enemy planes clogging the air. I had sat in a crowded, smoky cinema as a clipped voice read the newsreel over flickering images: 'Hundreds of thousands of Romany gypsies thought dead in concentration camp as Hitler seeks total annihilation.'

'Why do you think people hate you?'

'Why do *you* think?' I shot back. 'Now, bugger off to find your sheep, you stupid girl.'

I waited for Peggy to cry, yell, argue, or to get up, at least, but she didn't move. I could feel her grey eyes boring into me.

'Because you're a gypsy?'

I swore under my breath, loudly enough for her to hear. 'You wouldn't understand. Go home, Peggy, before your grandparents start worrying.'

'Oh, they won't worry. They know I'm a wanderer.' Peggy curled the end of her plait around her finger thoughtfully. 'Nobody hates gypsies here, you know. Everyone gets dead excited when you turn up on the common.'

Llanegryn common was one of the prettiest places we came to, shielded by a curtain of oaks and hazels. We always put the caravans next to the little river, and slept well to the sound of the water, like a breath through the greenery. Peggy was right, in a way. Hordes of children would come as we arrived, gleeful with excitement and keen to explore the caravans, to gawp admiringly at the bright colours on the walls. A few older people, even, would come down to the common to say hello. One old lady even brought baskets of bread and cakes for us, smiling as we ate them greedily.

But there were others. People who didn't want us there. It felt to me as if there were more of those kind every year.

'Something's caught on the line!' I exclaimed, shocked that I'd had a catch. I had never before caught a fish in this part of the river. Fishing had been a ruse: I'd come here to hide, to stew in my furious teenage hormones.

'Bring it in, then!' Peggy rose to her feet. 'Does it feel like a big fish?'

'Yes!'

I pulled on the line quickly, the sweat of enthusiasm dampening my forehead.

A trout, a thrashing slash of silver at the end of the line. A big, thick slab of a fish. I took the slippery body in my hands, and the fish battled against my fingers, its head and tail dancing madly, its black eyes staring and the furious mouth gaping.

Peggy knelt beside me.

'I've never caught a fish before,' she said breathily, staring entranced at the trout.

I glared at her. '*I* was the one that caught it, stupid!'

She laughed lightly. 'You know what I mean! We don't eat fish at home, just meat.'

44

'No one eats meat on rations.' I struggled with the fish as she watched.

'We're lucky. With the farm. My grandparents don't let me go without.'

Peggy reached out a long, thin hand to touch the fish, but thought better of it before her fingers touched the damp scales. 'What will you do with it now, Davey?'

'Kill it, and eat it.'

'What? Here?' She looked up at me in shock.

'If I take it back to Mam, I'll have to share it.' I thought of my boisterous little brothers and sisters, running around the common, tummies growling. No. This was my feast.

'How do you kill it?' asked Peggy, and looked up into my eyes.

Suddenly, I saw something in her – an unusual beauty, oddly awkward, something on the cusp of ugliness. I was aware, only then, that we were within touching distance.

'Will you help me, Peggy?'

'With what?'

'To kill it, and take out its guts. Then we'll cook it, and eat it.'

Peggy's thin lips parted as she looked from my eyes to the wild eyes of the trout.

'Teach me how to do it. Teach me how to kill it.'

I nodded, and smiled a brief but excited smile. 'Go and find a piece of wood.'

Peggy rose to her feet, and searched under the trees for a minute. She found something and picked it up to show me.

'I said a piece of wood, not a twig, stupid!'

She threw the twig away, and lifted a heavy-looking log. I nodded gravely.

'I'm going to put the fish on this rock, and it needs a heavy blow to the head. But, Peggy, you have to be quick, before it leaps away.'

'Okay.'

Peggy's lips spread into a tight line of concentration, as she lifted the log above her head, as if she was about to split wood with an axe. I held the fish down on the rock, pressing against its thrashing body.

'One... Two... Three!'

I let the trout go, and it started flailing madly, lifting itself inches into the air.

With all the strength she had in her thin arms, Peggy bashed the fish in its eye.

'Again!' I yelled, seeing the fish twitching, without rhythm now, as if it was having a fit.

Peggy hit it again.

'Its tail is still moving!' I lied, my voice loud and the words spilling quickly. 'Again, Peggy!'

This time, I didn't look at the fish; I turned my eyes to Peggy. Her grey eyes fixed tightly on her prey, the pupils pin-sharp. As she lifted the log above her head, I could see the darkness of the hair under her arms through the thin cotton of her dress. As she bashed the fish, her mouth released a gutteral throaty groan, and she looked like a woman, somehow, her pale flesh quivering as she swung her weapon.

'Well done, Peggy,' I smiled. 'You did well.'

She smiled back at me, her teeth gleaming. She had none of the squeamishness that other girls' showed at the process of killing, and that pleased me.

I reached for my pocket knife, and gave it to her. The metal was damp underneath my fingers.

'I've never lent this to anyone before, so be careful with it.'

She took the knife between her long thin fingers as if I'd given her a golden necklace, and stared at it with child-like wonder. 'What shall I do with it?'

'Turn the trout on its back, and find its bum.' Peggy glanced at me with suspicion. 'We have to take out the guts first, or we'll be eating all sorts of stuff.'

Peggy took the fish into her hands, and turned it on its back. The dead trout's blind eyes stared at her.

'Now, the blade has to face the head. You have to slit it from its bum to its throat.'

She slipped the knife into the fish without flinching.

'Don't cut too deep, or his guts will spill into the meat and poison it. There you are! Now, stop before you reach the gills.'

Peggy pulled the knife from the fish, and with her graceful fingers, opened the slit she'd just cut, showing the rose-coloured innards of the trout.'Perfect, Peggy, perfect. Now, pull all the guts out. It's connected by the throat, too, so you'll have to cut there.'

She obeyed, cupping the intestines in the palm of her hand and examining it before throwing it into the river. I leaned over, and took the fish from her. I opened the slit and looked inside.

'Did I do it well?' she asked.

'As if you'd done it a hundred times before.'

I smiled at her, and felt a quiver of something in my stomach.

'Now, go and wash it, and I'll make a little fire with these dry twigs.'

It took less than five minutes for me to start the fire. It had been a dry summer, and I had been taught how to make fires when I was a child. Peggy knelt by the water, and leaned over the dark river. She didn't know that I was looking at her, and I pretended to be stoking the fire while I watched her caressing the dirt off the fish, running her fingers through the empty space where its guts used to be, rubbing her thumb under the gills and the tail. Her plait hung over her left shoulder, the end curling like a question mark above her breast. She rose, and turned, but I was too quick for her. She never saw me watching her.

The flames licked the breeze by the river.

'How will you cook it?' she asked, and I smiled slyly as I reached for a square of folded foil from my pocket. 'You brought that with you?'

'I take it when I go fishing – just in case.' I opened the foil into a large silvery square.

I folded the foil like a shroud around the trout, Peggy's shadow darkening my shoulder as she watched. After tossing the foil package carefully onto the flames, Peggy and I eyed each other awkwardly.

'You're all right when you're not angry.' She wasn't joking. Her eyed fixed on mine.

'And you're all right when you're not laughing and chattering like a six-year-old.'

She was silent for a moment, and then nodded.

The flavour of that fish was the most vivid, wonderful taste I'd ever experienced. Peggy and I sat on the river bank, our fingers picking the skin and bones from the white meat, and ate as if we hadn't eaten for days. The trout tasted of the river, of a warm breeze, of summer.

I tried afterwards, many, many times, to recreate that taste, but never succeeded.

Peggy lay back in the moss after we had finished eating and closed her eyes, the remains of the fish and the glistening foil between us.

'Thank you for teaching me how to kill a fish,' she said lazily.

'You're a fast learner,' I answered, looking down at her. The branches above us threw long shapes across her cheek. 'Sorry I was so angry.'

Peggy opened her eyes and watched me. 'It's okay,' she answered, and, in a second, I leaned over her and pressed my mouth to her thin lips.

I felt her mouth opening a little. She tasted like the trout that she had killed, and my hand rested on her bony shoulder as we kissed.

I don't know how long we spent kissing and touching each other that afternoon on the river bank. My memory insists it was many

48

hours. When my fingers wandered to the hem of her dress, she entwined her fingers in mine, an old trick to keep hungry teenage fingers from reaching too far. She let me touch the soft flesh on the nape of her neck, and I stroked the damp skin with my rough fingers.

'You're sweating,' I said quietly, as we lay side by side.

'Am I?'

'Yes. Your skin's damp and smooth, like a fish.'

She laughed softly, her mouth open and her plait loose on the moss. I could see none of the annoying young girl who wandered into the copse earlier. She was different, her laugh knowing, womanly. She turned onto her side, resting her head on her palm, and watched my face as if she expected me to say something important.

'Some boys chased me as I was walking here. They threw stones.'

I surprised myself by telling her, as if I hadn't known what I was going to say before I opened my mouth. I barely knew her. A few hours earlier, I'd hated her.

'Why?'

'They shouted "gypo" and "thief" and "go home". I don't know what "go home" is supposed to mean for someone like me.'

Peggy nodded.

'It happens everywhere. Now, more than ever. People don't want to see us.'

Peggy lay back, sighing as she turned her eyes to the branches above.

'What's it like? Going from place to place, as you do?'

I swallowed hard. I hadn't spoken about this before. Who would listen? One of the boys from the other caravans? They'd call me a traitor. And I barely spoke to anyone else, not properly.

'I come to beautiful places, like here, and stay in the best spots – amongst the trees, in a field, by a river or a lake. And, Peggy, I start loving a place, and start finding the pathways and the prettiest places, and that is *exactly* when we move on.'

'Why don't you stay, then, when they go? You're old enough to find work, pay your own lodging...'

'I can't.'

'Why?'

'I can't explain to you, Peggy... Family and that... I just *can't*.'

She turned her eyes back to me, grey as clouds in her pale face.

'They call us so many names, Peggy... We were in a village last spring, and they sent a battalion of their men to send us away. They shouted and swore at us all, even the children. They said we were crooks and thieves.'

Peggy laughed. I stared at her.

'They hate me. Never mind what kind of person I am, or what I do with my life. I'll always be a "gyppo".'

Her smile fading, Peggy turned away from me again. She pulled her cardigan tighter around her body, as if she was hugging herself. 'I'm getting cold.'

'You'd better go home. Your grandparents will be worried.' I didn't know whether I'd said something to upset her, but suddenly, the atmosphere changed under the trees, and the woman I'd kissed faded into a girl again.

'Yes.'

Peggy arose, brushing the moss from her hair and clothes with the back of her hand. I sat up and watched her.

'Thank you for helping with the fish,' I said, although I was actually thanking her for something more, something I couldn't describe.

Peggy turned to me, the dark branches of the trees framing her head. 'Thank you for teaching me.'

She walked away, her bare feet choosing their steps carefully through the dry twigs.

'You'd better get used to what you are,' she called, without turning back. 'You can't get rid of what's in your blood.'

I paused and swallowed. 'How is it that you understand?'
Peggy stopped for a second, before turning to face me.
'Mam,' she said, and then disappeared through the trees.

Jennie Williams
Peggy's Mother
1948

Oatcakes

8 oz oatmeal	8oz plain flour
1½ tbsp yeast	½ tsp salt
1 pint milk	½ pint water
½ tsp sugar	

Mix the milk and water. Mix the flour, oatmeal and salt in a bowl. Blend the yeast and sugar in a splash of lukewarm water. Mix all the ingredients thoroughly, and leave in a warm place, covering the bowl with a tea towel.

Warm the griddle and oil it lightly, then spread a little of the mixture on it, creating a thin pancake. When small holes appear in it, it is time to turn the pancake.

Place ham, cheese or something sweet to melt on it as the other side cooks. Roll into a tube before eating.

She was waiting for me when I returned. Standing by the gate in the garden, her hair in a long plait down her back, her plain face painted with an eager-to-please smile. I had hoped she might have lost her similarity to me, but no. She was the image of who I had been at seventeen, that fragile, tender age that rested awkwardly between childhood and womanhood.

I walked up Church Road towards her. Smoke curled into question marks from the chimney, and the windows shone as they had never done before. She had been preparing for my homecoming.

'How are you, Mam,' she said as I neared, though it was not a question, just something to say. Anything to fill the quietness that had stretched for years between us. I stood a few yards from her, staring. My own two eyes stared back at me from within that same blank, uninspiring face. 'Welcome back to Riverside,' she said.

She wrapped her arms around me – strong arms, surprising given her slenderness. She squeezed me lovingly, rested her cheek on my shoulder.

I did not know how to take it. She was too close.

She pulled away, took the bag from my hand. 'Come into the house, Mam. I made tea for us, with fish from the river. And your bed has been aired, ready for you.'

I followed my daughter into the house. Shadows still darkened that dank old place, though Peggy had tried to lighten it by making a fire, hanging light coloured curtains and a huge new mirror on the back wall to reflect the sun.

Everything else was the same. The same table, the same dresser, the same pots and pans hanging from the ceiling. The same little face, waiting eagerly for my attention.

'More than ten years,' I said quietly, feeling as though that time had melted into nothing. I would have preferred a different house, somewhere new, but Riverside had been kept for me for all those years. I had not asked who had paid the rent on an empty house for me, but supposed it was my parents' penance money. I wished they had let the dark cottage go.

'Yes, Mam.' Her voice was quiet. 'But you're better now.'

As I peeled off my coat and removed my hat, as I sat by the table, as Peggy made a pot of tea, she did nothing but chatter. Perhaps it was her nervousness, but she had an unfortunate tendency to comment on whatever she was doing, and expected no reaction from me. I should have been appreciative, but I was not.

'I bought this milk from the shop, but I can tell it won't last very long. You always said Mr Phyllip Shop was a sly old fox, and you were right! He still charges more than the shops in Tywyn, but that's it, that's what he's always been like. And the vegetables he sells... You wouldn't give them to a horse. Would you like more hot water in your tea? Oh, you're all right. I wanted to speak with you about that, Mam, about maybe getting a goat and a few chickens, for milk and eggs...? There's three goats and a billy at Hare House, and they have milk with every single meal, and they've started churning butter...'

Her voice faded into nothingness, then, and she stood for a while, the bread knife stilled in the middle of cutting a slice, her mind three miles away with her grandparents.

'Did they look after you?'

She turned her eyes to mine. 'Yes. Oh yes.' Her voice was quiet and tender. 'Very well.'

I committed the longing in her face to memory, so that I could use it again to torture myself. I was seething with jealously already.

After slicing half the loaf and spreading the slices thickly with globules of blackberry jam, Peggy sat in the chair opposite me, and poured herself some tea.

'Did you make the bread?'

She shook her head, a rosy hue blushing her cheeks. 'I've tried so many times, but somehow, my loaves don't turn out as they should... The jam is home-made.'

Blackberry jam. My mother used to make it when I was a child.

'About Mr Phyllip shop,' Peggy started again, choosing her words carefully now. 'I was speaking to Francis, his son, this morning. Do you remember Francis, Mam? He was in my class at school...'

I had known the boy since he was an infant, and he had been annoyingly gentle and effete, spending his hours birdwatching instead of chasing girls.

'Francis was saying that they need someone to help in the shop. Mr Phyllip has ulcers on his legs, and he can hardly stand... Well. Francis asked if I would be interested in working there.' She searched my face for a reaction. 'Would that be all right with you, Mam? We need the money, and I'd like to work in a shop...'

'Do as you like.' I tried to smile at her, but my face insisted on contorting into a grimace.

'Thank you, Mam. I'll tell him tomorrow.'

Peggy turned to the bread, and ate it with such hunger that my eyes could not turn away. Mouthful after mouthful, each one thick with butter and jam. She had no dignity, just a small, eager mouth, tearing at the food like a baby bird snatches at scraps from the mouth of its mother.

I picked up a piece of bread, chewed it slowly. The bread was light, the crust thin.

'Nain and Taid mentioned they might visit over the weekend,' said Peggy after devouring her first piece of bread. 'With eggs and butter, and barley pudding.' She gazed at her hands. 'Nain never forgot how you love barley pudding.'

I moved from my chair at the table, and settled in *my* chair, the one in the corner, the one I always used to sleep in, the one I sat in when Peggy was a child, my mind enveloped in the darkness.

'I haven't liked barley pudding for years,' I answered. 'And the doctors at the hospital told me I wasn't to see my parents again. They made me ill in the first place, before you were born. They are not to come here. I forbid it.'

I could see the desperation on Peggy's face from the corner of my eye. 'Mam...' She tried to think of something to say, but the words didn't come, and she was silenced by her own eagerness to please me. After a while, she started clearing the plates and cups, washing them thoroughly, her back to me. I sat back in the familiar embrace of the chair, in blissful silence.

It was unfair, but her ugliness scratched on my nerves more than anything.

When Peggy arrived from Hare House, she was thin but muscled, skinny but strong. After six weeks of shop work and nothing at home but a silent mother, her muscles melted away, and the shine left her eyes. After two months, her skin became grey, and after six, her hair hung greasy and limp, and her face took on a yellowish sickly tinge as she lost all the joy from life. I saw all my own faults reflected in her, and I hated her for that.

Peggy grew to hate me, too. She had no idea how to convey it, either, and so we lived in silence, and in darkness, too, as the oil for the lamps became a luxury for us. Her unhappiness, her melancholy was my family. It pleased me.

I was at my worst on Wednesday evenings, the night before Peggy's day off from the shop. That was the day of her weekly pilgrimage to Hare House to see her grandparents, calling on Mai Davies on the way to chat and laugh. She always arose at the crack of dawn on a Thursday, making breakfast for us both although I never ate mine. I would watch her though the window as she walked down the lane towards Hare House, her walk lighter than usual, her spine straight, not slumped. When she returned in the evening, the weight had returned to her shoulders, and she didn't greet me as she came in.

I was certain that they were all talking about me.

My mother and father and daughter, sitting in my childhood home, forming a dirty patchwork of ugly words about me. I entertained myself by imagining their avid mouths curling around knife-sharp adjectives: 'selfish'; 'cruel'; 'cold'. I searched my memories for painful words spoken long ago, my father's words, yelled across the kitchen table of Hare House, the wet black glint of my mother's eyes as I ran away, shouting that I would never be back.

No one came after me.

I longed for the Asylum, the nurses with their blank, detached faces. I remembered the white rooms, unadorned, soothing me into stillness amidst other people's madness. More than anything, I craved the drugs which melted the solid mass of emotions and memories. I craved the horrific electric shock therapy, the months of delicious emptiness it gave my mind. I was too tired to face Llanegryn and Peggy, too tired to make the effort to be kind. It was easier to be cruel.

My tongue became my sharpest knife, and I began to voice my disjointed, terrible thoughts. Oh, the relief of it! Tripping the cruel syllables from my poisoned maw; allowing the wounds of my mind to bleed though my mouth.

She never answered back. I believed she had succumbed to the same black hopelessness as I had at that age. One Wednesday evening, I became particularly vicious, with the conversation I imagined she would have with her grandparents the following day scratching on my mind. I sat in my chair all day, trying to ignore the birdsong which drifted like hymns from the garden. She would tell them that I had complained about the state of the windows, though she had washed them a few days before. She would tell them about my refusal to eat, the ugly angles of my bones protruding from my pale skin. Perhaps she would cry, wiping her cheeks on the cotton of her sleeves, weeping her heartbreak into the pattern of her dress.

Peggy walked in after a day in the shop. She looked exhausted, her stony eyes like grey shadows.

She said nothing as she arrived home, and I remained silent. She didn't even look at me as she fetched a mixing bowl, eggs, flour and the blackened griddle from the dresser.

'Pancakes again?' I spat with all the venom of a silent day.

'They're cheap. Francis Shop gave me some milk, and he wouldn't take any money.'

'It'll be sour by tomorrow.'

I watched as she poured clouds of flour and oatmeal into the mixing bowl, water and yeast, milk, and stirring it all, her thin fingers grasping the fork, knuckles white.

'I don't want you to go to Hare House tomorrow.'

She paused her frantic whisking, but didn't look up. 'Why?'

'It's not good for me. I feel uncomfortable that you spend time with those people.'

She turned her head to me, then, and stared into the pools of my eyes for a while, before turning back to the pancakes. She added more water to the bowl, started whisking again.

'I'm going.'

I looked at her, surprised at the sliver of strength in her that I hadn't seen before. She hated me, I realised, and somehow that fact sent a vibration of satisfaction through my body.

'The doctors told me I was not to allow myself to become anxious. Do you want me to go back to Denbigh?'

Peggy rested the mixing bowl on the kitchen table, fetched a tea towel to cover it.

'It is! That's exactly what you want, you cruel little bitch. You wish your own mother back in the Asylum so that you can swan your way back to Hare House and be fussed over like a child.'

A wave of rage shook me, and I leapt to my feet and grabbed the mixing bowl off the table, threw it against the wall. It smashed, sending shards of white ceramic lightning across the kitchen, thick batter weeping fat tears down the wall.

'Do you think I want to eat this shit? The hospital food was a thousand times better!'

Peggy calmly reached into the cupboard for another bowl, fetched the same ingredients again – flour and oatmeal, milk and water- and prepared the batter, again, as if nothing had happened.

That night, I slept more soundly than I had since I had left the hospital. I could not remember the last time I had dreamt, and suddenly, there I was! A little girl, again, in the field at the back of Hare House, with Bird Rock jutting out above me and the sheep's bleating and the screaming of a red kite singing a cosy symphony. I felt the grass tick my bare ankles, the smell of wild flowers rising invisibly to envelop me.

My parents in the dairy, Mam churning the butter and Dad washing the milk bottles.

'Come and try this!' grinned my father, dipping a cup into the pail. I swallowed it all at once. It was cream, foaming thickly on the morning milk.

I awoke in my chair by the stove. Everything was black. The birdsong was silenced, the only sound was the whisper of the river, murmuring words I could not decipher.

The mixing bowl I had shattered had disappeared, every drop of the pancake batter cleaned away. Peggy must have worked as I slept.

I arose, leaning on the stove as I got up. I had not eaten since yesterday morning, and then I had only chewed on a piece of dry bread. It was blissful, that light-headedness of hunger; it felt as if I was in a dream.

I stumbled through the kitchen into the parlour, grasping onto the shadows of furniture. The stairs sighed under my weight as I climbed them, slowly.

Peggy was asleep under a thin blanket. The window was open

slightly, the curtains swaying like a dancer's skirt in the night breeze.

I stood in the doorway for a while, watching her. She slept in the same position as she had done as a child – on her side, her knees pulled up to her breast, like a ball.

I don't know from where it came, that sudden shock of longing, regret, realisation. The dream, perhaps, with its vivid images, tastes, and scents of long ago exploding like a bomb of ceramic shards in my mind.

I sat on Peggy's bed, touched her cold cheek.

She and I were so very similar.

Peggy opened her eyes, and saw me. The black in her eyes was wide and deep.

'I'm sorry, Peggy,' I whispered. She nodded, silent and unsmiling. 'I don't know why...'

'Don't think about it.' Her voice was deep and gravelly with sleep.

'If I could cut out the sick part of my mind, I would do it. But it's growing like a cancer, and I'm afraid that it's poisoned every part of me now. Every day is a battle with my own instincts... My mind *wants* to be cruel, *wants* to harm. It's always been there, Peggy, and all the doctors in Denbigh couldn't blunt the sharpness of it.'

I started to cry, hearing my own voice, child-like and pathetic.

'Don't think about it,' Peggy repeated.

'I want to go home,' I cried.

'But you are home, Mam.'

'To the hospital. I want to go home, to the hospital.'

Peggy arose from her bed and helped me down the stairs, her hand on my back until I was safely back in my chair. I grabbed her, held her close to me. I couldn't remember if I had ever embraced my daughter before.

I pitied her.

'Go to sleep now, Mam,' Peggy pulled away from me. 'You'll be all right.'

She had felt bony in my arms, uncomfortable to hold. Too thin, all sharp angles, no softness.

Peggy didn't go to Hare House the next day.

Perhaps I should have felt a sense of achievement in my victory over her freedom, but I didn't. The sharpness of my tongue was blunted, and the tiredness of last night's tears felt thick behind my eyes.

'I'm going to the shop,' she said as she knelt in front of my chair in the morning, as if she was speaking to a child. 'I'll be ten minutes.'

She left, and when she returned, the dew of the common shining her shoes, the basket on her arm was half-full.

She made tea for me, and left it steaming in a cup on the stove, and opened the windows and door with vigour, allowing a summer breeze into the kitchen.

I watched as she cooked quietly, her eyes concentrating utterly on her ingredients. I must have fallen asleep a few times throughout the morning, because things seemed to appear suddenly, out of nowhere. A posy of wild flowers in a cup on the table, fresh scones cooling on the window sill. Around midday, she offered me a sandwich, but I had no appetite. She didn't say anything, but sighed hopelessly, quietly, before preparing her own lunch.

I didn't know I was asleep until she awakened me with cold fingers on my cheek. The oil lamp had been lit, and the summer's day had faded into a velvety navy blue, the cheese-coloured moon staring at us, open-mouthed, through the window.

'Look at what I made for you.' Peggy smiled sadly, placing a warm bowl into my hands.

Barley pudding.

Exactly as my mother used to make, all thick cream and

fat pearls of barley. She had put a spoonful of jam in it, too, a glistening bloody nugget in its centre. She must have prepared it in the morning. It must have been cooking slowly in the stove throughout the day.

Peggy lifted the spoon from the bowl, formed a hill of barley pudding, a ribbon of jam throughout it. My daughter blew the steam from the food, and offered it to me. I opened my mouth like a baby bird.

It was painfully lovely. It was everything that had been precious to me, everything I had lost. The creamy pudding that my daughter had made for me was sharper in its softness than any shattered dish.

Peggy scooped up another spoonful, blew on it again. I opened my mouth eagerly.

'It's salty,' I said.

'Because it has your tears on it, Mam,' she answered, wiping my face with her sleeve.

Why was I cruel?

Why had I refused to acknowledge Peggy when she was just a child returning from school? Why had I pretended that she did not exist? Why had I harboured venomous hate toward my parents throughout the years? Why was I breaking Peggy's heart all over again? Why did I want her to feel worthless, and sharpen my words before aiming them at the tenderest corners of her heart?

Something was lost in my mind, perhaps, or there was something there that ought not to be. A knot of flesh, a tumour, nestled within my brain, poisoning all the goodness within me. I could not control it. Neither could anyone else. I was born to die.

Barley pudding was a thin thread that connected both versions of me, something small that belonged to both the happy child and the cruel, terrible madwoman. I had not considered the comfort of

63

my mother's food before I was spoon-fed it once more by my own daughter thirty years later.

Unhappiness is emptiness, the constant gnawing of something lost. I did not realise that until Peggy fed me the barley pudding, spoonful after spoonful, and I returned to a feeling I had not experienced since I was a child.

I was full.

Francis Phyllip
The boy from the Shop
1948

Raspberry Ice Cream

½ pint double cream
½ pint Greek yoghurt
8 oz icing sugar
tin of raspberries in syrup

Whisk the cream and yoghurt until stiff. Sieve the icing sugar and stir in. Add the raspberries and syrup, and whisk for a further five minutes. Place in a plastic tub, and freeze overnight. Remove from freezer half an hour before consuming.

That sweet vibration, deep in the tummy, that comes when a new love awakens. It feels like hunger, a craving to be satisfied. Of course, it fades with time, transforms into a comfortable satisfaction, the full feeling one gets after a large meal. But those first weeks, the meeting of coy eyes across the room, the accidental touching causing lightning... Nothing compares to it.

I was in bed, and it was morning. The whistling of the songbirds had awoken me, pouring like air through the open window. I couldn't muster any frustration towards them. My bed was warm, and I lay, quiet and still, and thought of Peggy. The previous day played like a film in my mind.

Gathering courage, to start with, as I walked across the common at lunch time, the bees droning drunkenly around me, nervousness amassed in the pit of my stomach, almost strong enough to induce sickness. Collecting the flowers, wild poppies, their petals soft as a baby's cheek. And then, I stood by the gate to the common, the posy in my hand, staring at the brow of her home on the corner, my heart pounding and my hands hot. I tidied my hair with my fingers, forced myself to open the gate and walk towards her house. I *had* to do something about her. Her presence in the shop, the gentleness of her laugh, her sweet scent... She filled my senses, tripped up my mind.

Peggy must have heard the garden gate creaking, because she appeared as I shuffled up the path. She opened her mouth to greet me, but then she noticed the flowers in my hand, and they were enough to silence her.

I offered her the posy. 'For you, Peggy.'

Her grey eyes arose to meet mine, and she took the flowers. A smile crept across her face, spreading from her soft mouth to her eyes, the colour of the sea in winter.

'They're so pretty, Francis.'

I failed to swallow the sigh of relief, and it escaped from my lungs loudly. She looked happy.

'Well...' I stood before her, feeling a lick of sweat accumulating at the base of my spine. I had not thought any further than this. I should have had wise words or poetry to offer her now. '...I'll see you in the shop tomorrow.'

She nodded enthusiastically. 'Of course!'

I turned and walked away, painfully aware that her eyes were on me. I turned back to smile at her as I shut the gate behind me.

'Thank you, Francis. Wild flowers are my favourite.'

'And mine.'

As I lay in bed, the clock ticking its way towards the alarm, I recalled the coy smile on her face as she thanked me. She knew, now, that I liked her. That I liked her *in that way*. She didn't laugh, or tease, or become cold. She had seemed happy to receive my admiration.

The footsteps came crunching over the birdsong, the small stones on the path from the common to the shop being walked swiftly, hurriedly. It wasn't half past six yet. Who on earth...?

Knock, knock. Soft rapping on the back door. I leapt from my bed before my father woke, and rushed to the window. It was Peggy, standing on the doorstep, as if she'd magicked from my imagination to my home. She gazed up at my window, hoping I was awake. I pushed the window wide open.

'Peggy... Are you all right?' I half-whispered down to her. Her plait was messy, uncombed, and her cardigan was buttoned up all wrong.

'Please, Francis, I need your help.'

She lay in the water, facing the pattern of small stones on the riverbed. She wore a long white nightgown, her flesh swelled with water and the flow billowing her hair and gown as if she were an angel, flying.

I had never seen a dead body before.

Peggy stood on the arch of the bridge, gazing down at the Reverend Jack Vaughan and I, as we waded into the river. She wasn't crying, just staring, grey eyes wide and empty. As I lifted Jennie's lifeless body from the cold flow of the river, I almost stumbled as I saw those same grey eyes gazing at me from the pale face of the corpse.

With wet fingers, the Reverend closed her eyes for the last time.

I had expected her to be heavy, especially with sodden clothing, but she was as light as a child in my arms. Her bones felt like sticks through her skin.

Peggy watched as I carried her mother from the water, across the stony riverbank, onto the road, but she didn't move, didn't say a word.

'Bring her into the vestry,' said the reverend, quietly. 'People are starting to wake up.'

I snatched a glance at the windows of the nearby houses, and saw a few faces gazing from their bedrooms, their eyes tight on the dead body in my arms.

Those hungry eyes staring at the unfolding tragedy was the most terrible sight I ever saw: worse, even, than a lifeless form in the river on a summer morning.

I crossed Two Chapels Square to the vestry, ignoring Annie Vaughan, the reverend's wife, who stood in the doorway of their home, an infant at her feet and a newborn in her arms. What would I say to her on a morning like this?

The vestry had not been prepared, of course, and I had to place Jennie Riverside on the floor, her wet nightgown soaking the floorboards. She was gruesome, her skin a waxy yellow and her face hardened and ugly.

'Poor Peggy,' said Mr Vaughan, and I rose to my feet to face him. He looked shaken.

Peggy.

Her face and grey eyes smiling as I handed her a posy of wild flowers. Was that only yesterday?

'Did she say what had happened?' asked Mr Vaughan.

'She came knocking at the back door this morning. She said there had been an accident.'

Her hand on my arm, asking me to help her, as I stood on the doorstep pulling on my boots. Her stillness was eerie under the circumstances, and yet I could not swallow the quake of excitement at her touch.

'She said that Jennie had been missing when she got up. Peggy had gone looking for her, and found her like that, in the water, in her nightgown.'

She had tugged at her messy plait, and there had been a dreamy, odd timbre to her voice.

'She must have gone for a walk in the middle of the night. She must have fallen into the water,' Peggy had told me, though we both knew that no one could fall from Llan Bridge.

I had run straight to Mr Vaughan's house, had asked for help fetching the body from the water. I had no idea what to do in that situation. Where did people take corpses?

'I'm sorry I woke you so early, Mr Vaughan. And your wife and children.'

The redheaded reverend placed a pale hand on my shoulder, and shook his head. 'Don't mention it again. I'm glad you felt you could come to me.'

We stood for a while, staring at the dead body on the floor.

'Someone ought to tell Jennie's parents in Hare House,' I said, finally. 'Half the village will know by now. I'll go... After I've changed into dry clothes.'

'No, no.' The Reverend shook his head, as if he was sorting things in his head. 'You go and look after Peggy. I'll go to Hare House.'

I nodded, weakly.

'And Francis?' I looked up at him. 'You will make sure she's all right, won't you?'

The funeral was long and uncomfortable, the sky dark and the thick air threatening a storm. I tried my very best not to stare at her, but my eyes always found their way back to Peggy as she sat between her grandparents. I looked at her in the cemetery, over her mother's coffin, and imagined kissing her thin lips. The guilt, instantaneous. Even at her mother's funeral, the hot stormy breeze made me think of Peggy's breath on my skin.

After the funeral, I went to see her. The house was quiet, the birds muted by the promise of a storm. I walked down the path, knocked the door softly. Perhaps she was crying. Perhaps she was sleeping. Perhaps she wasn't there at all.

The door was opened quickly, and I was suddenly facing the thin, pretty face of Elen Pugh.

'Francis! Are you all right?'

'Oh! Um… I'm sorry,' I answered. I had no idea what to say. I had not expected Peggy's grandmother to be there, though I knew they were close. Now, of course, it was obvious – it made perfect sense. Her grandmother would never leave her, not on a day like today.

What could I say to a woman who had just buried her daughter?

'I came to make sure Peggy was all right.' The explanation stumbled off my tongue awkwardly. 'I didn't like to think of her on her own.'

A shadow of a smile crossed Elen's thin face, and she opened the door wide. 'Come in.'

'Oh no, I don't want to disturb…'

'Don't be silly.'

The kitchen was quiet, and Peggy and her grandfather sat by the kitchen table. Peggy smiled warmly at me, and even in this most uncomfortable of situations, I felt a shiver of joy touching the most primitive part of me.

'Francis.'

Sion Pugh arose from his chair to shake my hand. I had only met Peggy's grandparents a week ago, after Jennie had died, but it seemed to me that they had both aged a decade in that time, as if years had passed in days. I looked into his eyes, and looked away immediately, recognising the glaze of tears.

'It's so hot, I thought you wouldn't want to be cooking in this heat. I bought some ice cream. Don't eat it if you don't want to, I won't take offence.'

I set the pot on the table.

'Ice cream!' exclaimed Peggy, lifting the lid and peering in at the pink cream.

'Did you make it, Francis?' Elen asked.

'Yes. I convinced my father to buy a deep freeze to put in the back of the shop. It was expensive, but if I can make ice cream to sell, it will pay for itself.'

'I've never had ice cream before.' Elen fetched four bowls and spoons from the dresser.

'Oh, I won't have any,' I protested weakly. 'I have some at home.'

'Sit with us, Francis, for a while,' Sion insisted, and though I felt like an outsider, I could not bring myself to refuse.

I sat in the chair next to Peggy. She smiled sweetly.

There was silence as we ate.

The ice cream was wonderful... Fat dots of raspberry lost amidst a pillow of frozen cream, the pink juice like the little whirlpools in the river.

I watched Peggy from the corner of my eye, and adored the way she ate. After inspecting her food for a while, she decided which part she wanted to eat first. She loaded her spoon with the pink cream. Then, she opened her mouth wide, and sighed as the taste reached her, obviously adoring it. Seeing her pleasure excited me, made me want to touch her. I looked at the three who sat with me at the table: Peggy, Sion and Elen, the three tasting and appreciating this small gift I brought them. Today, every other sense was dulled by the weight of the occasion: only taste remained.

I wanted to cry.

'What will you do now?' I asked later, after Sion and Elen had returned to Hare House, after I had promised solemnly that I would keep an eye on their granddaughter.

'What do you mean?'

'Will you live in Hare House? Your grandparents certainly want you there...'

We walked across the common, searching for an evening breeze after a humid day. It was the first time we'd walked together, and I noticed anew the elegance of her movements. The ball of hair had loosened on the nape of her neck, and a few strands hung loosely around her forehead. The midges danced around us.

'I haven't decided yet,' she answered, thoughtfully. 'I enjoy working in the shop.'

'We're lucky to have you.'

She smiled, shook her head slightly. 'You father would disagree.'

Damn him. I had hoped that Peggy hadn't noticed his snobbish glares in her direction from the throne of his wheelchair in the back room. She had never reacted to his sniping. He would never have employed her had I not insisted, for once, and threatened to move away to Dolgellau or Machynlleth to look for work. 'I'm sorry, Peggy. I'm ashamed of him.'

She laughed softly. 'Don't worry about it, Francis. It doesn't worry me.'

'It worries me. I don't know why people still come to the shop, the way he looks down his nose at them.'

'They come to see you,' she answered simply.

I looked at her, but her mind was far away.

I started to speak, but Peggy lifted her finger to her thin lips. I became silent.

'No sound at all,' she said. 'Nothing, except the river. No birds, no bees.'

Her eyes rose to meet mine, and something leapt inside me.

'The wild things know that the storm isn't far.' Her voice was

72

soft as a drop of rain.

I stared at her face. This girl should be ugly, I thought. Everything was imperfect, plain, odd. Why did I want to kiss her?

She turned away, and resumed walking.

I let her walk a few yards in front of me, watching her enjoying the common. It was becoming wild, the grass too long under our feet – one of the farmers would soon bring a few sheep to graze it to size. The common ran in a green strip alongside the wildest stretch of the river, and trees hung heavily over the water, heads hanging down as though in prayer. It was where the children played, where lovers walked, where the elderly wandered to enjoy a part of the village that had remained unchanged for years. Best of all, the common was hidden from sight. The peering eyes of the village did not penetrate the surrounding woodland. We were utterly alone there.

Peggy's fingers reached for the low hanging branches, her eyes wandering from colour to colour, bloom to bloom. She still wore the funereal black dress, but I could see a small stain where she had spilt some ice cream, and it had dried like a scab on the blackness of her body.

The first clap of thunder was powerful enough to shake the earth under our feet, and then a flash of light, as if heaven had opened the door a crack to let some light out. Peggy and I became still.

The rain came in a heavy wave, without warning, soaking us in seconds. Peggy turned to me slowly. Her face shone with rain.

'Storm,' she said, fixing me with those thundercloud eyes.

'Yes,' I agreed, unable to take my eyes off her.

I ached to hold her.

She began to run, a strong, child-like victorious run, towards her home. I chased her, watching her through the screen of rain. The black dress clung to her long, thin legs, and the wetness slicked her brown hair black.

She swept up the path, the thunder booming like a fanfare

around her. Down the lane, through the gate of Riverside, and into the house, her feet leaving disks of prints on the doorstep.

I stood by the gate, watching the door. I didn't know if I should follow her.

Staring through the rain, my shirt and trousers were heavy with water, my hair dripped rivers down my back. Every part of my body was wet, and yet, I stood there by her home, silent and still in the rain.

Peggy came back to the doorway, and stared at me.

And then, she, too, was in the storm again, her arms around my body, her lips pressing against mine. There was an odd perfection about everything... The kiss, the rain, the forks of electricity in the sky, the taste of raspberries on her mouth.

I remember nothing of walking home that evening.

My father swore as he saw me arriving home soaked head to toe, and he barked a greeting: he was going to telephone the asylum to come and fetch me. I didn't answer. Standing by the airing cupboard, completely naked, I rubbed a towel over my hair, the crevices on my body.

'Don't even think about hanging around that Peggy Riverside,' he spat from his wheelchair in the corner of the kitchen. That is where he always parked himself. It had a good view through to the shop, and through the window out onto the trees which masked the common. 'She's cut from the same cloth as her mother. Women like that aren't good enough for a businessman like you.'

I wrapped the towel like a skirt around my waist, and strode down the stairs. My father recoiled in horror as he saw me.

'Put on some clothes, you bloody fool! What if someone sees you through the window?'

'Say one more bad word about Peggy, and I'll take you straight to an old folks' home. Don't think I won't do it, because I swear to you, I will.'

My father stared at me, open-mouthed and wide-eyed. I had

74

been silent for too long.

'And if anyone does see me without my clothes, they can look all they want, because I belong to Peggy for the rest of my life, and one day, she'll be my wife. You'll see.'

My father opened and closed his mouth like a fish in the river, and I left him there, stunned and horrified.

Annie Vaughan
The Reverend's Wife
1951

Pork and Apple in a Cider Sauce

8oz pork	2 cooking apples
~~mooking~~ cider	pork stock
1 onion	half a doz. mushrooms
2 cloves or garlic	a few sage leaves
2 tsp cornflour	

Fry the pork, onion, mushrooms and
garlic for twenty minutes. Add the
stock and cider, and cook for an
hour. Chop the apples into wedges,
and add to the pan. Simmer for a
further 45 minutes. Add the sage.
Mix the cornflour with a little water,
and add to the saucepan. Cook for a
further five minutes.

One tin of condensed mushroom soup. Two packets of red jelly for Ruthie's fifth birthday on Saturday. A jar of Camp coffee, and a loaf of bread.

'Have you had any more of that black treacle in? I fancy making a ginger cake.'

'Goodness. I haven't tasted ginger cake in years.'

Peggy turned to face the shelves on the back wall, and stretched for a shiny red tin of treacle, before placing it in my basket on the counter.

'There's not much space for you behind that counter.' I smiled.

She touched her swollen stomach lovingly, and nodded. 'I knocked some tins of tomato soup off the shelves yesterday, and I couldn't bend to pick them up afterwards. Francis stood in the door, laughing as I was struggling to grab them.'

She had a shine in her grey eyes, a new glaze that had never been there before. I recognised it. Excitement. The once-in-a-lifetime sheen of being on the cusp of something new. A birth! I had been the same when I was expecting my first child, John, seven years previously. My imagination carried me to the nursery, everything clean and tidy, waiting, waiting. Cream coloured paint. New blankets, sheets ironed into crisp squares, and a shiny new cot under the window.

And yet, there was something else about Peggy... A depth in her eyes that I couldn't pinpoint. When she thought that no one was looking, when she let the smile slide from her face, there was a darkness, shadows. Perhaps it was my imagination, inventing things from the memory of her as a helpless child.

'How is Mr Phyllip?' I asked, though he never changed.

'The same. He can't walk without help, and he refuses to come into the shop.' Peggy lowered her voice. 'He isn't happy with the ice cream business. He refuses to acknowledge that we're making money from it.'

'I wouldn't worry about him, Peggy. He's always been like that.'

She smiled, appreciatively, pleased to have found an ally in me.

'And what about you, Susan?' Peggy turned to the baby in the pram. 'Are you sleeping like a good girl for your mother?'

'Teething,' I answered, rolling my eyes. 'She was awake from half past two until four, bawling her eyes out. I'm surprised you didn't hear her.'

Peggy shook her head hopelessly.

'Put these on the slate, will you Peggy? I'll send Jack in to settle the bill before the end of the week.'

'See you soon. Bye-bye, Susan!'

I turned the pram and struggled out of the shop. It was a hefty, awkward thing, and I had insisted upon it when I was pregnant with John. Now, with Susan approaching her first birthday, it had carried four children and was battered, the navy blue cover fraying. It looked nothing like the shiny picture I had seen in a magazine years ago. I had been like Peggy Shop. Older, perhaps, and more desperate, maybe. I had nothing else to do, whilst Peggy had the shop, at least, to keep her occupied. Before the children, I had been waiting for my life to begin, and then, when they came, I urged time to slow down so that I could enjoy them. But yes, I recognised Peggy's enthusiasm, her hope, her excitement. She wanted to see the baby *now*, to meet him or her this minute, to begin this new adventure immediately.

I pushed the pram down the road towards the square. Susan sat with her fingers in her mouth, removing them only to point to the songbirds.

Perhaps I should return to the shop, I thought as my high heels click-clacked on the road. Perhaps I should go back to Peggy, tell her, honestly, how things were going to be.

This is going to hurt, you know. More than anything. You will think that you're about to die. No, you'll want to die. But there will be no escape, no matter how much you call on those you love to do something, to help you, there will be nothing they can do. It's a pain you'll have to endure, and there is no escape. And if there is the smallest crack in the relationship between man and wife, there is nothing like a baby to underline every single fault.

The guilt came, then, and I reached over the pram to tickle Susan's fat cheek. My daughter smiled at me, and I pushed the four horrific births from my mind. They were here now, my babies. That was the most important thing.

I reached Two Chapels Square, and lifted Susan onto my hip. With the baby on one arm and the shopping basket on the other, I had to push open the front door of Rose Cottage with my behind.

The kitchen was a chaos of breakfast dishes, and Ruthie had smeared marmalade fingers over an already dirty wall. John had abandoned his crusts, though I had threatened terrible things if he did, and Audrey had left half the porridge she had begged for drying like wallpaper paste in the bowl.

I sighed as I set Susan on the floor. She immediately crawled to the dried food that had fallen to the floor, and slipped a blackened disc of banana into her mouth. I should have stopped her, but I didn't. I couldn't face the din of her protestations, and I had too much to do.

As I washed the dishes, Peggy still on my mind, a memory thudded back into my mind. A slip of a girl on my doorstep with a fat old woman beside her, asking for Jack. Had that girl really grown up to be Peggy? She had come into the house alone to wait for her grandfather. She had felt whole generations younger than I, but now, she had become someone who was my age. How many years were between us? Twelve? More?

I had felt so lonely then.

Llanegryn had felt like a punishment after my childhood in Machynlleth, which was a constant bustle of shops, gossip and girls like me, smart girls who wore make-up and styled their hair each morning.

'Will you have something to eat?' I had asked young Peggy,

feeling awkward in the company of this limp-limbed, stormy-eyed child.

'No, thank you,' she had answered. 'Mrs Davies Beech Grove made me a huge breakfast.' She'd paused for a while, before adding, 'But I wouldn't mind something small, if it's not too much trouble, please, if it's all right.'

As she sat by the table chewing on a ham sandwich, I had carried on with the housework: brushing the floor, dusting, scrubbing the stove.

I felt her watching me.

'Are you all right, Peggy?' I asked after a while. 'Would you like a drink?'

She shook her head. 'You're so clean, Mrs Vaughan.'

I stared at her, pleased beyond reason by the praise of a six-year-old child. I was only nineteen myself, and was bored right down to the marrow of my bones by this life of washing and cleaning and cooking. It was important for Jack and I to be tidy, to look as a reverend and his wife should look. But it felt like a game, as if I was a girl playing at being a wife in the large rooms of my new home.

'Thank you Peggy,' I'd answered, blushing, as she stared at me without a smile.

She was an odd child.

Who had changed the most, I wondered as I washed the breakfast dishes of four untidy children, Peggy or I? She had become a woman, a wife, respectable. The scars left by her mother had faded away. She would be a mother herself in a week or two. I had given birth to four children in a few short years, and tried to keep my hair and make-up tidy whilst losing the battle with housework every single day.

'Mamamam...'

Susan's voice burbled me from my daydream, and I turned to look at her. A dark damp patch on her dress indicated that her nappy had leaked again.

Peggy had a boy. Huw Sion Phyllip, seven pounds and three ounces and a happy and gentle soul from the day he was born. Peggy was back behind the counter of the shop within a fortnight, and Francis was usually with her, instead of being hidden in the stock room as he had before the birth of his son. He doted on the infant, chatting with him as if he understood. Peggy rolled her eyes at him, but with a smile that betrayed her.

She had always been one for long walks. To escape from her mother, originally, but her wayfaring had continued after she moved to Hare House, and after that, too, on her breaks from the shop. After a few weeks of rest following Huw's birth, she began to walk again, striding purposefully with both hands on the pram handle. One morning as she crossed the bridge, I called out to her. She turned her eyes towards me, and raised her hand in a wave.

'Would you mind if Susan and I came along?'

A shadow of a question crossed Peggy's forehead, and then she nodded. She was probably wondering why I would want to be in the company of a young girl like her. She knew nothing of the loneliness of being a reverend's wife, the respectable distance the other mothers kept from me at the school gate. She didn't know, either, how I felt like I hardly recognised myself to be that same girl who came from Machynlleth, all lipstick and neatness. I didn't know who I had become.

'How old is he now?' I nodded at the little baby in the pram. He was gazing up at the clouds, blue eyes reflecting the sky.

'Three months,' answered Peggy. She reached a bony hand to stroke Susan's cheek. 'Did her teeth break through?'

'A few of them, yes. The back ones haven't appeared yet, so the worst is yet to come.'

There were only a few days to go until the school closed for the Summer. Sweet, warm days, baking the earth. I was looking forward to having my children's company in all their chaotic, messy glory, but a part of me dreaded the bustle, the anarchy. I would miss the afternoon hour when the eldest three were safe at school, and Susan was asleep in her cot: That golden hour when I could ignore the dirt and mess and sit in the rocking chair in the bedroom, trying to clear my mind of everything. Sometimes I would stare through the window, and other times I would shut my eyes. The world would stop turning until Susan awoke, and then, everything would return – the dirty floors, the pile of laundry.

'You enjoy walking, Peggy,' I said, as we passed the village sign and walked along the long straight road, it's horizon jagged with mountains. 'Do you go far?'

'Further than I should! I ought to be in the shop, but the summer is so mild, and I enjoy it.'

'I should walk more,' I confessed, with a sharp, painful truth on the tip of my tongue. I swallowed it back.

'You can join me, if you like,' said Peggy, with a bashful quietness to her voice. 'I go every day before lunch. Except on Thursdays, when Huw and I walk to Hare House to see my grandparents.'

'You don't walk all that way with the pram!'

'It's a flat road, and it doesn't take that long.' Peggy tilted her head towards me, as if she was about to impart a secret. 'Huw began to cry on the way the last time, wanting to be fed. So I sat on the dry stone wall to feed him.' She touched her breast softly. 'When I looked up, there was a row of old soldiers in the window of the military hospital, staring at my breast!'

I giggled. She was sweet, and mischievous, and she was unabashed by my status as a reverend's wife.

The chatter between us was easy and light as we walked, our children watching the canopy of trees. I noticed her eyes being drawn to Beech Grove, Mai Davies' home, as we passed.

'I haven't seen Mrs Davies in a while,' I ventured.

Peggy shook her head. 'She isn't well. Doesn't leave the house any more... Can hardly walk... I take her some groceries twice a week, and stay and have tea and cake with her. And d'you know what? She still gives me a box of cakes and bread, and asks me to hand them out to the people in the village who need them.'

I stared at her. 'I didn't know that.' I was stunned that anything might happen in this village without my knowing about it.

'Francis takes them with the rest of the deliveries from the shop. People aren't embarrassed, then.'

'That's so kind of her. Especially as she's not well.'

'It's not easy for her, but she insists on doing it…'

Peggy abandoned the sentence, steered the conversation away. Perhaps thinking of Mai Davies reminded her of that cold night, and how dark this road must have seemed to a six-year-old girl.

'I go up there, sometimes.' Peggy pointed to a narrow lane which led to the hills as we came to a curve in the road. 'But it's steep with the pram. Do you know what I'd like? Tying the baby close to my body, like the women do in Africa. Did you see the photographs in the paper? Like a long scarf, and the children are safe and cosy close to their mothers.'

'The Black Road,' I said, looking at the winding lane. 'I never walked further than a few miles along it!'

'My grandparents say that a tribe of wild people lived there in the olden days, and that they used to attack people who walked along it to Dolgellau. Do you think that there are a few of them still up there?'

I stared at her, wondering if she was joking. 'Of course not! That was probably in ancient times… Things like that just don't happen anymore. What would they eat?'

'Who would notice if a sheep or a bird went missing? It's so bleak up there…'

'You've got some funny ideas, Peggy,' I answered. She liked my honesty, and began to giggle.

We reached the old ruin before we had to turn back. She would have to go back to serve a hot lunch to Francis and Mr Phyllip, and Jack would be wondering where I was. Before we turned the prams back towards the village, Peggy pointed towards the little stone house nestled at the foot of Bird Rock.

'Hare House,' she said. 'Nain will be making lunch now. A stew, probably, and Taid will be milking the goat.'

Was this the reason Peggy walked so far each day? I watched the tenderness on her face. Did she have a longing for the home where she had been so happy?

As we walked back, we chatted about small, unimportant things: what was for supper, the children's sleeping patterns and what to plant in the garden next spring. I could not connect this confident, witty woman to the wispy child, bent over with hopelessness, years before.

'Would you like me to call for you tomorrow?' asked Peggy as we neared Two Chapels Square and Rose Cottage. She stared at me with a glowing glaze in her eyes.

I nodded, enthusiastically. 'Great! See you tomorrow, Peg.'

'Bye!'

The house was silent, with only the rhythmic click of the clock keeping time as I struggled to bring the pram in. In the kitchen, the dirty dishes waited for me, the smell of breakfast's burnt toast clung to the curtains.

I sat by the table and sighed. Susan stared at me, perplexed.

I had not realised until that morning how lonely I had been. Missing that easy chatter that could only ever happen between two women. Comparing lives, without competition, light laughter about silly things.

Amiable company, and sweetness... Things I hadn't experienced since I'd left my school friends in Machynlleth. There were other mothers in the village, of course, and everyone was kind – some even called for a cup of tea every once in a while. But I was the reverend's wife, and God put a distance between me and everyone else, as if being attached to a man of the cloth meant I couldn't partake in life in the same way as other women.

'Are you home?' Jack's voice came from the study, and he wandered into the kitchen to see me sitting by the table, wearing my coat and no comforting food smells this lunch time.

'Yes. I've been for a walk.'

To Jack's surprise, I reached across the table and kissed him on the lips, leaving the stain of my lipstick on his pale mouth.

'Well! Who's walking like a big girl!' Peggy exclaimed as Susan toddled uncertainly on into the shop. Susan looked up, and smiled when she saw Peggy grinning at her from across the counter.

'Geggy,' she said.

'Come to your Auntie Geggy!'

She strode around the counter to the shop floor, her apron tight around her slim waist. Lifted Susan into her muscly arms, stuck out her tongue at my youngest daughter.

'I'll put the kettle on,' she said to me with a smile. 'Come on through.'

I followed her to the back of the shop, passing through the storeroom with its wonderful rainbow of scents: biscuits, salt and the still hunk of ham which hung from the ceiling. Francis stood in there, whisking a bowl of cream to make another batch of ice cream.

'Good morning, Annie,' he said cheerfully.

'Hello, Francis. What flavour are you working on now?'

'Cherry. Not easy, but it'll be worth the hard work if it comes together. How is everyone?'

'Fine, thank you.'

'Would you mind taking a pot of ice cream home for them to taste? I have some apple flavour, and Peggy and I don't agree about it. I think it's wonderful, and Peg can't stand it...'

'Please, Francis, let me pay for it this time...'

'Not a penny. You'd be doing me a favour.'

86

'You're ever so kind. The children will love it. And Jack, too... He was smitten with the chocolate biscuit flavour...'

Francis chuckled, and turned back to his work. He was a wonderful, gentle man. Goodness knows where he got his smile, because I had never seen one gracing the face of his father. Peggy had told me that she had never seen him lose his temper. She didn't know if he had one. He would start and end each day with a smile. Some would say he was too kind. Whenever anyone was caught stealing from the shop, he refused to notify the local police, but would react, instead, with a furrowed brow and mutter that he was disappointed. He reminded me of Jack in many ways: Friendly, gentle and kind. But there was something in Francis that I had never witnessed before.

He adored his wife.

His eyes would follow her round the shop; he brought her tea as she worked; notice her clothes, commented kindly on the way she wore her hair. He smiled at her, even when she wasn't looking, as if he couldn't believe his luck at landing such a woman. He was a handsome, kind and rich man, and he was smitten with his plain, bony wife.

I smiled at him before walking through to the kitchen – the best room in the house, blessed with sunshine throughout the year. Peggy was not a proud woman. The clutter of family life abounded – papers, books, crockery and letters. I felt the need to clean manically before having visitors, but she didn't seem to care about things like that. I never saw her wearing make-up, and she didn't enjoy getting her hair done at the salon in Tywyn. But there was something about her, all the same, something deeper than beauty.

'You go and play over there, sweetheart.' I set Susan on the floor in the midst of a mess of toys. 'Huw will wake up in a bit, and he'll come and play with you.'

In no time at all, there was a cup of tea steaming in front of me on the table (no saucer), and a packet of biscuits that were new to the shop: 'with brazil nuts in them! They cost a bomb!' Susan gurgled happily as she pushed Huw's wooden red tractor along the floor.

'Are you all right?' Peggy asked after she had settled in the chair beside me, her grey eyes searching mine.

She had no idea.

I wasn't one to cry, even in front of my best friend, so I did nothing but cover my face with my hands, and swallowed, swallowed, swallowed, hoping the tears would keep at bay. They didn't. I felt them escape, hot and salty, through my fingers, down my wrists.

'Oh, Annie. Don't cry.'

Peggy moved her chair closer to mine, placed her hand softly on my back. I kept my hands on my face, thinking of the smears of make-up that would now be blackening my cheeks.

'You're crying all over the biscuits, and you really don't want to spoil them, Annie. They're *lovely.*'

I could hear the smile in her voice, and I started laughing through my tears. I pulled my fingers away from my eyes, and dried them with the handkerchief I kept up my sleeve.

'Everything all right, Annie?' Peggy asked softly after she'd devoured two biscuits and swallowed half her tea. For the hundredth time since we had become friends, I considered the difference between us. Had she been the one weeping, had she dripped tears onto my kitchen table, I would have panicked. I would have rushed to her, pleaded to know what was wrong. But she was not of that nature. There was a calm stillness which permeated the atmosphere she carried about her.

How could I explain to her what was wrong? That the constant bickering between John and Audrey, my eldest children, was shredding my nerves. That I was worried that there was something the matter with Ruthie because she didn't recognise her letters or numbers. That Susan still awoke several times a night, and that I hadn't had a night's uninterrupted sleep since she was born. That I still wasn't sure, wasn't completely certain, that Jack and I were meant to be together. He was so untidy, so quiet, so different to me. I barely knew him on the day of our wedding, and though I conceded that he was a good husband, faithful, uncomplaining, something was missing. A flame, a passion. These things, these everyday, usual things, felt heavier than they should.

Things ought to be better than this.

'I'm so tired, Peggy,' I said, weakly, and that, somehow, explained everything.

'Well, go home then! Why didn't you say? Go to bed, leave Susie here. She'll be perfectly happy with us. She can help me in the shop this afternoon, she'll love that! Won't you, Susie?'

Susan looked up at Peggy, and smiled widely.

'I couldn't...'

'Of course you could! And the older children can come for tea after school, too. Everything will seem better after you've slept, you'll see...'

'Peg...'

'Stop making excuses! It'll be good for the children, and for you.'

I could have come up with a thousand reasons why I shouldn't leave the children with Peggy. She had Huw, the shop, her father-in-law sniping at her. And what would people say about me, leaving my children in the care of someone else?

But then I thought of my bed. The white sheets, soft as a whisper, the solace of a pillow. Heaven.

I rose before I changed my mind, and planted a kiss on Susan's downy hair. I smiled appreciatively at Peggy, who looked pleased that her plan was working.

'I'll do the same when you have eight children, and...'

Peggy chuckled. 'Just go, Annie!'

As I left, her voice said quietly, 'Thank you for telling me.'

I turned back, perplexed. 'What?'

She avoided my eyes, choosing to stare out of the window at the swaying treetops. 'Telling me that it's difficult. And for crying, as you did. It's important, you know. It's a sign that you'll be fine.'

People don't realise, before having children, but waking in a completely natural way, simply because you've had enough sleep, is a privilege. It is utterly wonderful, slow and dreamy, as if the world is softened.

I looked at the clock, and swore in a way a reverend's wife should never do.

'What is it?' Jack croaked, halfway between sleep and wakefulness.

'The children! Where are they?' I calculated quickly. It was ten past nine, and from the light that escaped through the curtains, I could see that it was not night.

I had slept soundly for eighteen hours.

'They begged to stay at the shop last night. Something about a tea party in their beds.'

I sat up. 'All four of them? Susie, too?'

'Don't worry, Annie,' Jack smiled lazily. His red hair stood at untidy angles from his scalp. 'I went there to wish them good night, and all four were happy and settled. And little Huw! Peggy promised to send them off to school as usual this morning, and said she'd keep Susie as long as you wanted.'

I sighed, and lay back.

'What would I do without her, Jack?'

He nodded, smiled thoughtfully. 'She was so happy, Annie. A houseful of children, Francis and Peggy in the middle of them all. I bet you they'll have a load of little ones, like us.'

'I can babysit for her, then,' I said, though I didn't really know whether I could be so selfless.

'She left some food for us. Pork and apples in cider... I had some last night. It's lovely.'

'Cider?'

Jack smiled at me.

'I can't believe that she's the same girl that came here all those years ago with Mai Davies. When her mother went...'

Jack shook his head. 'And yet, there's still something of that girl in her. Last night, with the children... She was one of them, somehow...'

That morning was one of the sweetest, tenderest moments that ever happened between my husband and I. It was simple and gentle, and we satisfied one another in a way we had never done before. We stayed in bed until after eleven, laughing and chatting and making love, and then we wandered down to the kitchen to warm up the food Peggy had made, which was creamy and delicious and tasted like freedom. Jack had even attempted to clean.

Nothing had changed, not really. The place would be in chaos again for the next day, and I would still be pondering over love as it was in the films, so different to this friendly co-habiting that was our marriage. But I could cope with everything again. I was satisfied, even happy. By the time I went to the shop to fetch Susie, I was ready to receive my children once again, ready to love and treasure them, exactly as they deserved.

Isaac Phyllip
Peggy's Father-in-law
1953

Turkey in Cornflakes

8oz turkey strips   8oz cornflakes

salt   Cumin

coriander   an egg

Grind the cornflakes into fine crumbs,
and mix with the spices and salt. Soak
the meat in the beaten egg, and then
coat in the cornflakes. Fry in oil for five
minutes on each side, until it browns.

'Shall I open a window? It's stuffy in here.'

Peggy didn't look at me as she came into the room. She crossed the room towards the window, her footsteps soft on the oak floorboards.

'Don't touch it,' I answered, gruffly. 'I'm cold.'

'I'll fetch you another blanket.'

'I don't want one.'

Peggy reached for the tin bowl of water on the dresser, and sat in the small chair by my bed. I watched her testing the temperature of the water with her long, bony fingers. The previous day, I had complained that it had been freezing. I shivered with disgust at the thought of those witchy fingers touching my flesh.

Peggy folded back the blanket, denuding my feet and legs. They were candle-pale and skinny. I couldn't stand the fact that she could see them.

She removed the dressing from my wound, and examined it. 'It looks better today, Mr Phyllip. Less bloody.'

'It doesn't feel better,' I answered, tightly. I could feel my heartbeat in the ulcer as the air reached the open wound.

'I'm going to wash it now, Mr Phyllip,' said Peggy, wringing out the cloth in the water. She held it over the wound, and a few drops fell onto the open flesh of my leg.

It was almost enough to make me faint. A white, furious pain, biting its jaws up my leg. Peggy ignored my groans, continued cleaning the ulcer. Sometimes, I believed that she persisted in stretching out the task, enjoying a thrilling, evil pleasure from my pain.

'There we are,' she said, quietly. I felt as if a beast had gnawed a lump of flesh from my leg. 'I'll just put the ointment on. It's almost done, Mr Phyllip.'

I do not know why her persistent kindness grated on my nerves as it did. I could say anything to her. She always refused to take the bait, refused to answer back. I longed to hear her spit a cruel, bitter word in my direction. There must be some poison within her, if I could only scratch it to the surface.

I groaned again as she applied the ointment to my wound. It felt cold for a few seconds, before the heat of the ulcer warmed it.

'That's it,' Peggy said softly as she placed a fresh dressing to my pain, then folded the blanket back, covering me once more. 'We're finished.'

Until tomorrow. The only human touch I experienced, and it was a sharp, fierce pain. I would have preferred not to treat the ulcer at all. I would have preferred to be allowed to rot in my own sallow company, letting the poison devour my body until I became one large bloody wound, silent and seething.

'Lunch will be in an hour or so. Would you like me to help you down the stairs? You can eat with us, by the kitchen table.'

I shook my head definitely. Peggy offered the same every day, but I never accepted. Eating at the same table as them would make me feel as though I should be thankful of their company, and the very thought was repulsive to me.

After she had gone, I lay in bed, listening to the sounds of the shop beneath my bedroom. Francis laughing, Huw yelping, Peggy trying to soothe him. The shop was no place for a three-year-old child: it was unprofessional. Why did she not keep him in the kitchen? That is what I had done with Francis when he was an infant. He had been perfectly content on his own, playing with his toys – I would check on him every now and again.

I could still feel her fingers on my legs. Perhaps she was worsening the ulcer. Her bony fingers, killing me gently.

On temperate mornings like that one, I would sometimes fall into a half-sleep. My eyes open and my body still, and a tsunami of memories filling the emptiness around me. She led them, always, appearing by my bed, a smile on her raspberry-coloured lips.

Mary.

Sometimes, her ghost was so real, so lifelike that my very breath would freeze in my lungs, convinced that she was resurrected.

'Isaac! It was a mistake. I'm not dead. How could I be? It could never be... May I lie with you, Isaac?'

I would reach out my hand to touch her, but she was never really there in my cold bedroom with its heavy, dark furniture. I was imprisoned in the bed where she had died.

Francis' newborn screams, filling the sound space where Mary had been groaning for hours. The doctor's footsteps, heavy on the wooden stairs. Quiet words over the shop floor. 'She could not be saved. I'm sorry. But you have a son.' He handed me a tiny wriggling figure in blankets. Mary's blood stained the baby's pink head. 'He's a strong boy, Mr Phyllip. Congratulations.'

The infant struggled in my arms. He was nothing like Mary. I didn't know what to do with him. I had never held a baby before.

The doctor suggested that I employ someone to nurse and care for Francis. I didn't want anyone to take Mary's place – calling the shop home, cooking in her kitchen. One of the young mothers of the village came in to nurse the baby, and that, in itself, disgusted me. Mary's little baby at another woman's breast. She would sit in the corner of the kitchen, her own baby in the pram by the door. She spoke sweetly to Francis as he suckled her, smiling and stroking his cheek before turning back to check that the baby in the perambulator was still asleep. 'There you are, Peggy.'

After being fed, Francis would gaze at Jennie Riverside, his eyes glazed with tiredness, and I would hate her, then, and her quiet little baby in the pram. How had an ugly, worthless woman like her been allowed to live, when Mary had died? Where was the justice in that? And how could Francis look at that woman with such peace and adoration in his eyes? His placidness in the absence of his mother was a betrayal.

When Francis reached six months old, I told Jennie Riverside that she was no longer needed, and I started feeding my son proper milk from a bottle. He gulped it greedily, but he never looked at me in that peaceful, sleepy way he had gazed at Jennie.

As he grew, Francis became like his mother. Dark, with large round eyes, a gentle grace to his movements. It made me love him, and despise him for reminding me what was forever lost. I would have given the world to have her back. I would have given Francis to have her back.

When she was only a young child, Peggy would come to the shop to fetch the week's groceries in a basket that was almost half her size. I knew, by that time, that Jennie was unstable. The village whispered about her. Although I suspected that things were difficult for the little girl, it still wasn't enough to stop me hating her.

'Here you are,' said Peggy, and I awoke from my past to see her, a woman now, carrying a dinner tray into my bedroom. 'Turkey for you.'

Long strips of meat in a golden crust, a bloody red sauce, new potatoes and peas.

'What is this?'

'As I said. It's turkey. I saw the recipe in a magazine.'

'Vile foreign food.'

I bit into the meat, the crust crumbling slightly under my teeth. It was wonderful and unfamiliar, and I hated her for bringing new tastes to my tongue. Only the bland was comforting.

'I can't eat it.'

Peggy stood still for a few seconds. 'If you would only try the—'

'I will not.'

I picked up the plate, and poured its contents over the white blanket on my bed. Peggy stared at the mess she would have to clear up with an almost deathly stillness. I felt the sauce seeping through the bedclothes, onto my bare legs.

'Go away! Leave me alone!'

Peggy raised her eyes from the blanket to my face, and she looked like a demon, brimming with hate and vitriol. I felt a lightning strike of joy at the poisonous gaze- At last! She was angry!

'All right. I'll leave you alone. I won't bring you any food or drink, I won't clean your ulcers, I won't empty the bedpan in the morning. You can rot here on your own. You're a cruel monster of a man.'

Adrenaline buzzed through my body, overjoyed that I had managed to rile her after years of trying. I felt more alive than I had done in years.

'Francis will tend on me. He's family.' I curled up my lips in a goading smile. 'He'll care for me.'

'Will he?'

'Don't think for one second that he'd take your side over mine. He's listened to me putting you down, complaining about you, being foul to you for years, and have you ever heard him speak up in your defence? Not once. *Not once.*'

I saw something flicker in her eyes, then, a shade of weakness.

'The shop is my home...' She began, and my temper flashed, hot as a wound.

'No! No, it is not! You will never be the mistress of this house. Never!'

'I am the mistress of the house. And you're nothing but an angry old man, slowly dying in his bedroom, a burden on his family.'

I smiled at her again, heart drumming.

'Goodness,' I said slowly, sharpening my tongue. 'You remind me of your mother.'

She swallowed, and left the room.

I lay back in my bed, quaking with the thrill of it. I knew that her mother would be her weak spot, but I hadn't foreseen that the fire in her eyes could be so easily extinguished.

I felt refreshed. For the first time in weeks, I felt well enough to get up, go downstairs. Yes, that's what I'd do – I'd go down to the kitchen and make a song and dance of preparing my own lunch.

It took ten minutes for me to dress myself in a shirt and a pair of trousers, but I was pleasantly surprised by how strong I felt. I'd show them. I wasn't dead yet.

Peggy was sitting on the stairs, midway down, with her back to me. She had not heard my footsteps, had not heard the bedroom door sighing open.

She was eating. No, not eating, devouring – pushing chocolate into her mouth so quickly that it threatened to choke her. Packet after packet, she ripped the paper off, her breath short and laboured through the volume of food. The wrappers glinted like treasure in the half-light.

I had been right. She was sick, just like her mother had been.

'I warned Francis about you,' I said, quietly, and Peggy became still. She did not turn to me, but I could imagine her face, stained with tears and chocolate.

Kenneth Davies
Mai Davies' Son
1958

Beef Casserole with Mustard Dough Balls

8oz cubed beef	2 carrots
An onion	A turnip
beef stock	salt
4oz plain flour	1oz butter
2 tbsp wholegrain mustard	

Fry the beef and vegetables for half an hour in a lidded pan. Add the stock, and simmer on a low heat all day. Rub the butter into the flour until it looks like breadcrumbs, then add the mustard. Form small balls of the mixture. Place the balls in the casserole, and cook for a further 45 minutes.

I had not been back to Llanegryn for a year. Nothing had changed in the meantime, and, as I drove through the village, it felt that nothing had changed since I was a child.

'It's so lovely here,' said Helen in the car. 'We should keep your mother's house.' She gazed at the small houses which huddled beside the road, at Phyllip's Shop, at the small path which led to the common.

'What for?'

'We could holiday here. We could even think about moving.'

I shook my head sternly. 'No. Absolutely not.'

Helen looked sideways at me, sighed quietly. 'You should at least consider it.'

'Never.'

She would not understand.

The car rolled to a halt outside the village, in the shadow of the house. The gate shone as if it had been polished a few hours before, the path swept.

Helen placed her hand over mine.

'Are you ready?'

I nodded slowly. I felt numb.

The birds whistled, disrespectfully loudly, from the trees and bushes behind Beech Grove, the same as they had done when I was a boy. The only sign that things were not as they should be was the bare clothes line which hung like a horizon across the garden. Mother would always have found something to hang on the line, especially in a sweet breeze like the one that blew that day. A hard seed of something came to the pit of my stomach as I stared at the space where a nightie or a teatowel should have hung.

My nerved seized when the front door opened as I walked up the path. Instinct made my hands fly to my chest, and a blackbird rose from the rosebush in the garden.

'Mr Davies,' said the Reverend. 'I'm sorry for scaring you.'

I shook my head, and took a deep breath. I had never met this one before. He had taken the place of Mr Edmunds, a cruel, grey-skinned old man who had terrorised us all when I was a child. Mother had mentioned this one in her letters a few times, but he was nothing like I had imagined him. There was something unkempt about him, his red hair uncombed and his summer-sky blue eyes tired.

'I didn't expect anyone to be here, that's all,' I answered, in Welsh, surprised at how awkward my tongue felt around the fat vowels and pointed consonants of my first, precious language. I offered my hand. 'Kenneth Davies.'

'Jack Vaughan.' His grip was firm and solid. 'May I say, Mr Davies, how sorry I am regarding your loss. Your mother was a special woman.'

I gave him a small, appreciative smile, and reverted to English. 'This is Helen, my wife. This is the Reverend Vaughan.'

'How do you do?' Helen smiled, coyly. 'We weren't expecting anyone to be here.'

'I didn't want your home to be empty when you arrived,' he answered, the Welsh accent thick on his tongue. 'I've made a fire, and Annie, my wife, has baked a cake.'

'Goodness! How kind!' Helen exclaimed. She was unused to the tokens of Welsh village life.

Everything was the same in the house, and everything was different. The grandfather clock ticked mournfully in the corner, the plates on the dresser shone like glazed eyes. Mother was gone, and everything seemed unfamiliar.

A shiver played on my spine as her voice echoed from my memory. 'Don't wander too far, Ken, your tea will be ready in a minute!'

'I'll leave you in peace,' said Mr Vaughan. 'But I shall come back tomorrow, if that suits you, to discuss the order of service..? I have a few suggestions for hymns that I know your mother enjoyed...'

'Thank you, Mr Vaughan. You were very kind to come here.'

'Not at all. I thought very highly of your mother.'

The reverend said a warm goodbye to Helen, and left. I rushed out after him.

'Mr Vaughan...?'

He turned to me. I could see wisps of silver lining his ginger hair.

'Where is she?'

He became flustered, opening and shutting his mouth a few times as if caught out. 'I'm sorry?'

'My mother. Where is her body?'

'Oh!' He nodded in relief. 'In the vestry. The funeral director has prepared her, and the coffin has been placed in the vestry.'

'I hope you don't mind my asking,' I said slowly. 'But what gave you such a start just now, when I asked you?'

'You asked where your mother was,' he answered with a bewildered smile. 'I didn't know whether you were hoping for a literal or a spiritual answer.'

When Mr Vaughan had gone, Helen prepared a pot of tea. The first ever she had been allowed to make in that house. I walked around the kitchen, almost afraid to touch anything, though I owned it all now. The detritus of my childhood studded the shelves, old colours on old crockery that I had not used for half a century.

'Good God. Kenneth!' I followed Helen's voice into the dark, dank pantry.

There was flour and sugar, honey and treacle, cocoa and syrup, bottles and packets lining the walls.

'She was hoarding food,' Helen sighed, dolefully, creases of sympathy in her brow. 'How sad!'

With that, Mother's hands came into my mind, thick fingers with dried dough under the nails, and I began to cry.

"Ef sy'n rhoi bwyd i bawb, oherwydd mae ei gariad hyd byth. Psalm

136. He gives food to every creature; His love endures forever.'

There was a pause as Mr Vaughan looked around at the mourners, his sea-blue eyes full of sympathy. 'Each and every one of you understands how that passage relates to Mrs Davies. She often spoke of Kenneth, her son, and clearly thought a great deal of his wife, Helen. But Mai Davies had more than one child. Yes – in fact, she had hundreds of children. She was mother to all of Llan's children.'

I turned my eyes to the window. It was a grey day, the rain drizzling lightly and the low-lying clouds hid the mountain peaks. I had been so sure that few people would turn out on such a dreary day.

I had not realised how much the villagers had loved my mother.

Walking from Beech Grove to Llan that morning, Helen and I enshrouded in black under an umbrella, we saw people leaving their homes, parading slowly towards Two Chapel Square. As we crossed Llan bridge, a sadness squeezed my throat as I saw that the square was a sea of black, as if Williams Wynne of Peniarth himself had died.

The crowd parted silently to let us pass through into the chapel. Every seat was taken, apart from ours in the front pew. There were over a hundred mourners. A few were familiar from my childhood, but most were complete strangers to me. Every one of them had come to pay their respects to my mother.

After the service, I followed the coffin through the crowd, and allowed myself to look at the people. The Reverend's wife was neat and fashionable in her suit and make-up, her children struggling not to fidget around her. Helen Cader Lane, who had been at school with me, looked twenty years older than she ought to – life had dealt her a cruel hand. Someone else... A young woman, plain, with a swarthy, handsome husband standing silently in her shadow.

Our eyes met, and a shiver reached the marrow of my bones.

Later, in the vestry, the young woman approached me.

'Mr Davies? I'm Peggy. I thought the world of your mother, and I'm very sorry for your loss.'

I looked at her. She was young enough to be my child, and yet, there was something ancient about her.

'Peggy... Mother spoke of you often. And now, at long last, we meet.'

She smiled sadly.

I could not tell her, but I knew her story. I had her life catalogued in my study at home, within the folds of my mother's letters. This was the girl that had suffered at the hands of her own mother. This was the girl that had appeared like a helpless animal on the doorstep of Beech Grove one night, long ago. This was the girl who found her mother facing the riverbed in the cold river one morning. And she was the only one who had visited my mother during her final months.

Peggy had been my mother's only true friend- a woman who wanted her company for the sake of it, and not for the cakes and loaves it brought.

'I've never seen such a big funeral. Not once.' Peggy looked around her. 'Everyone says the same. I can't think of a single villager who stayed at home today. People who have moved away have come back specially.'

'Everyone has been so kind,' I answered, awkwardly, unsure of what to say.

'It's only a small thing, isn't it?' Peggy fixed her grey eyes on mine. 'Coming to someone's funeral. It's a shame your mother can't see how important she was, how loved. Take care, Mr Davies.'

'Peg! Come here!' The young man behind the counter yelled. He smiled at me as we waited for her. I returned the gesture, thinking how much the shop had changed since I was a boy.

'There was a counter all the way around this shop, once, and everything was kept behind it,' I told the man. 'And Phyllip Shop used to keep an eye on everyone, expecting them to steal... Are you related?' I asked, though I couldn't see any shadow of resemblance between this dark, handsome man and the dry-faced old toad that used to work here.

'My father,' he answered, brightly.

The fact that old Mr Phyllip Shop had ever been married came as a shock to me, especially as I could recall the strange hygienic practices, the white gloves with which he handled everything, his complete lack of joy. I could not imagine such a man ever touching a woman, never mind creating a child with one.

'My parents were only married a year or so. My mother died at my birth,' the man explained, interpreting my silence.

'I'm sorry.'

That poor man. Fancy being raised by a man like Old Phyllip Shop...

'Is your father..?'

'He died last year,' he answered, still smiling. I could not blame him for his lack of sorrow.

He offered his hand over the counter.

'I'm Francis. Peggy's husband.'

'Of course. I'm sure my mother mentioned you in her letters...'

'Hello,' said Peggy from the door behind the counter. Her apron was tied tight around her waist. 'How are you, Mr Davies?'

'Call me Kenneth, please,' I pleaded. 'Take these, Peggy. Mother's old books.'

Peggy eyed the bag, as if she was unsure of it. 'Come into the kitchen, Kenneth. I'll make us some tea.'

Francis' eyes followed his wife, and he smiled at us as we disappeared into the darkness of the stockroom and came into the light again in the kitchen.

'Please, take a seat. I'll put the kettle on.'

The kitchen was lovely, an old fashioned one like my mother's, with pictures and objects on every surface. I almost sat on a pair of tin soldiers.

'You have a son?' I asked, putting the soldiers to stand on the kitchen table. Peggy turned, and laughed.

'Huw. He's seven. Quite a handful.' She poured hot water from the kettle into a teapot.

'Will you have any more?' I asked, and realised immediately how rude I sounded. 'I'm sorry, I shouldn't have...'

Peggy sat by the table, and smiled as she poured the tea. 'We were fortunate to have Huw, but we haven't been as lucky since. Not yet, in any case.'

I nodded. She would never know how much I sympathised.

We sat in silence for a while. Being quiet with her did not feel awkward; I felt as though I had always known her.

'May I see the books, Kenneth?'

I reached into the bag for the six volumes, and placed them, like a tower, in the centre of the table. 'You may as well have them. I'm not a reader, and Mother would have liked you to have something to remember her by.'

They were novels, old fashioned hardbacks. Peggy thumbed the thick, dusty leaves, tracing my mother's handwritten name with a soft fingertip: *'Mai Davies.'* She lifted one of the books to her face, inhaled the dust deep into her lungs. She savoured the scent in a way which made me swallow my saliva, bite my lip.

The last volume was larger than the others, and unkempt. The red cover was awash with dried stains. Peggy opened this one as if it were a treasure, using only the very tips of her fingers.

'Oh Kenneth!' she exclaimed, and her voice felt like a breeze.

'It won't be much use to Helen. The recipes are all written in Welsh. And it's not very easy to follow. Lots of the pages have been scribbled on or added to.'

'Mrs Davies' recipe book.' Peggy touched the pages as if they were made of gold, and she pored over the recipes slowly, as if she could taste each one. 'Oh! She made me this one when... A long time ago... ' She pointed to a ginger cake recipe.

'That was my father's favourite,' I answered, trying to banish the memory of rough fingers pushing the cake into a tired mouth a lifetime ago.

'And this one!' She touched the words on the page. 'She made this for me when Huw was born. She came to the shop with a huge dish of it.'

Beef casserole with dough balls, in Mother's handwriting, her fingerprint like a ghost on the corner of the page. Peggy became still, and stared at me.

'Thank you, Kenneth.'

'You're so much like your mother,' I answered, and regretted it immediately. I should not have mentioned Jennie, not with all the complexities that came with her.

'You knew her?' asked Peggy, with a slight sharpness.

'Not very well. We were at school together. She was a little older. You look like her.'

Peggy nodded, and stared into her cup. 'I see that every time I catch a glimpse of myself in the looking glass.'

'She was kind, at school. I remember that.'

'Really?' Peggy asked me, shocked. 'Are you telling me that to make me feel better?'

I laughed softly. 'Not at all. She was popular, always giggling. Silly, sometimes.'

Peggy shook her head. 'I didn't know that.'

I finished my tea, and rose to leave. As I said goodbye, Peggy faced me, fixed me with those eyes once more. 'I wouldn't be alive if it wasn't for your mother. I'm quite sure of that. There was no one else that I could depend on.' She turned her eyes to the recipe book, and seemed not to notice when I left.

The following evening, Helen and I sat by the fireside, looking through Mother's papers. The wind was moaning through the trees, and the house was dark and gloomy.

The statements had arrived from the bank that morning, showing a hole in her savings, as if a small mouse had burrowed its way into her money and gnawed its way out. I suspected an error, but upon mentioning it to the Reverend, all had become clear. My inheritance had been eaten by the people of Llanegryn.

'It's no wonder the world and his wife were at the bloody funeral!' I raged. 'She's been feeding them all for the last fifteen years!'

'She was just being kind. And look what a difference it made to people's lives!' placated Helen, who seemed to understand it all better than I did.

'But it's so much money, Helen...'

'What would you have done with it? We have our home, don't we, we're comfortable. And she left the house to you...We could sell it and make some money, if that's what you want.'

She was so reasonable, so sensible and wise that I wanted to yell at her.

'I've left my cigarettes in the car, I'll be back in a minute.'

I almost tripped over the casserole dish on the doorstep. It was heavy and cream-coloured. I knelt, the wind whipping leaves into my face. I lifted the lid slowly.

Beef casserole, with fat dough balls drowning in thick gravy.

Peggy had repaid my mother's favour.

I sat on the doorstep, and wept into the wind. Helen put her arm around me, and I realised, suddenly, why Mother had cooked for all those people, why she had spent time and money on others. Because some tastes, like some touches, are all about saying *It's all right. I'm here.*

Dr Thomas
General Practitioner
1966

Oat and Seed Flapjacks

3½ oz butter   1¾ oz brown sugar

2oz honey   5oz oats

2oz seeds and nuts – pumpkin or
sunflower seeds are best, and almonds
or cashew nuts

Preheat the oven to 200°C. Line and
grease a baking tin.
Melt the butter and sugar in a pan,
then add the rest of the ingredients.
Press into the baking tin, and bake for
ten minutes.
Leave to cool in the fridge for about
an hour before cutting into squares.

'My mother's illness... Is it something than can be inherited?'

Peggy couldn't look me in the eye. She stared at the wall behind me, as if she feared I would be able to see too much by looking into her black pupils. Her gaze lingered over the italic lettering on my medical certificates, which had hung limply on the wall for decades. She chewed her fingernails, and glancing down at her other hand, I could see dried blood where she had bitten down to the flesh.

'Why do you ask, Mrs Phyllip?'

'I need to know whether it's possible,' she answered, without answering at all. There was an edge to her voice, an almost manic pleading that the most primal part of me longed to soothe. Peggy touched her face, as if to reassure herself that she was really there, a real person, meat and skin on bone.

'You're uneasy, Mrs Phyllip. Do you suspect you may be suffering from the condition which affected your mother? Do you feel unhappy, or out of control?'

Peggy sighed, and stared down at her hands. I waited for her to answer, as it seemed she was just about to, but the silence stretched as she scanned her bony fingers.

They were the same, Peggy and her mother; similar enough to churn my stomach.

The same lank dark hair, slate-grey eyes, and plain, narrow features. The only difference was something I could not explain. Peggy was beautiful, strikingly beautiful, whereas her mother had been hard-faced and repulsive.

'There is a definite tendency for mental illness to run in families.'

Peggy nodded, without looking up. She grasped her other hand, as if her own touch gave her comfort.

'But if you feel that symptoms are developing, there are a great many things that can be done in order to stop it getting anywhere near as serious as it was for your mother.'

'I don't want to go to Denbigh.'

Her voice was small and whispery, like a child's, and as I looked at her sitting there in her thin cotton dress, lanky legs stretching down to her plain brown shoes, I could scarcely believe that this was a grown woman, a wife and a mother. She looked the same as she had done when she was a girl, neglected and sallow skinned from lack of nourishment.

'Would you like me to get you some medicine, Mrs Phyllip?'

She sighed, and looked at me for the first time, locking her eyes on mine.

A memory smashed into my mind. I saw those same grey eyes staring at me through a car window. Jennie Riverside, on her way to Denbigh Institution.

Why had I remembered that moment, and forgotten so many others? Half a minute. Holding my patient's elbow gently as she slid into the car. Slamming the door between us. The finality of the thud echoing over the whisper of the river. Jennie's thin hands folded neatly in her lap in the back seat of the car. A lurid ladybird crawling lazily over the sheen of my work shoes.

'It's the silence. The same silence as we had at home, when I was a girl.'

I nodded, trying to hide the throb of despair that threatened to choke me.

'I don't know why. I think about her all the time. Where she went during those years when I was at the farm with my grandparents...'

'She was in Denbigh Institution, receiving treatment.'

'But when she came back, she was cruel, and cold, and... I don't know. Disconnected. Worse than before. The things I've heard about Denbigh Asylum... They keep me awake when I should be sleeping.' Peggy shook her head gently. 'I was the one who told that she wasn't right. I was the one who sent her to Denbigh. Not you. Not really.'

I opened my mouth to offer some comforting cliché, but was struck dumb by a small tear which escaped from her eye and left

113

a trail on her cheekbone. Words were all I could give, and they would never be enough to fill the silence that her mother had forced upon her when she was a child.

'I promised myself that I'd never let her do this to me. I have everything I want, and she's still here, haunting me... A black fog in my home...'

'Have you discussed this with Mr. Phyllip?'

'No, not properly. Just that Francis said I wasn't myself, and insisted that I should come to see you.'

'Go home, Mrs Phyllip. Talk to your husband – and Huw. He's old enough to understand. And, if I may, I shall come over to the shop tomorrow, after closing time, to discuss it with the three of you.'

Peggy nodded, moving her gaze away from me, as if normality had now ensued. I felt a torrid longing for the stare of those stormy grey eyes on my face, before realising with a jolt how disgusting it was to hunger for Peggy's sad, desperate gaze.

On Thursday evening, after my wife, Mair, had washed the dishes and I had enjoyed my smoke in the study, I started towards Llanegryn. There was an unsettled quiver in my stomach, and I knew that I had been sharp and impossible to please since Peggy visited my surgery the previous day. Mair kept a concerned distance. I could not explain why I was like this, not even to myself. Peggy was a woman in her thirties, and I had been her doctor since she was a child. I was almost sixty – easily old enough to be her father, and yet, those long pale fingers had a hold on me. I despised myself for it.

Summer's warm breath had given way to a cool breeze, and I shivered under my thin sweater. The car roared through Tywyn, past a crowd of youngsters who stood in line outside the cinema, and along the flat road to Bryncrug. Through the village and over

114

Pontfathew bridge, and along the curve of the river before turning down into the lane which led to Llanegryn. In the distance, Bird Rock jutted its grey brow into the last of the day's sun.

Phyllip's Stores were closed, and the 'Camp Coffee – CLOSED' sign hung lopsided on the door. Four lads sped past on their bicycles as I parked the car, and faces appeared in windows at the sound of a motor. A doctor visiting Francis and Peggy after closing time. The rumours would keep the village in whispers for a while.

It was Huw that came to the door, and he greeted me warmly before inviting me in. He had changed beyond recognition since I saw him last, had reached that brief pause between boyhood and manhood. Tall and lithe, he had his father's dark hair and his mother's thin lips, but he wasn't startlingly like either. His looks were his own.

The shop was dark, but the sweet and salty smells coloured everything.

Peggy and Francis sat by the kitchen table, and Francis rose to shake my hand. His handsomeness was almost otherworldly, as if his face had escaped from a sleek moving picture and had settled on the shopkeeper of this small Welsh village.

'Thank you for coming, Doctor. We appreciate it. Don't we, Peggy?'

Peggy stood up, and turned to the stove and kettle. She was avoiding my eyes. 'Will you take some tea?'

'No, thank you. I had a cup before I left.'

Peggy sighed, as if her plan to delay the inevitable discussion had been thwarted. She sat down heavily, defeated, and Francis invited Huw and I to do the same.

'I'm very keen to give Mrs Phyllip the best possible treatment, and that is why I came here this evening. In cases like these, I think it's vital that the entire family understands what is happening. It is an illness like any other, and though there is a stigma, it is nothing to be ashamed of.'

Peggy stared through the window at the trees in the common.

'Are you talking about tablets?' asked Francis, his forehead lined with concern.

'Well, yes.' I pointed to my medical bag. 'I have some medicine. But I do have another idea, if Mrs Phyllip agrees to it.'

Peggy didn't look at me.

'You mentioned yesterday that you find it difficult to cope with the fact that your mother spent so many years at the institution in Denbigh. It's true that she was there for a long time, and I am aware of the rumours which circulate about the institution – though I do think they're unfair. It is a place where people go to receive treatment and to get better, not the hell you've been led to believe it is, Mrs Phyllip.'

'Have you ever been there?' The venom in Peggy's voice shocked me.

I shook my head. 'That's a fair point. But I would like to go, and I would like you to come with me. A visit to Denbigh may be exactly what you need. Seeing the reality may well soothe your mind. If you see the good work they do there...'

There was a silent stillness in the kitchen for a while.

'They let visitors into asylums?'

'Not usually. One of the doctors is a friend from university, and I telephoned him yesterday after seeing Mrs Phyllip. He is happy for us to visit, should Mrs Phyllip agree to it.'

Peggy shook her head, eyes darting from face to face like a cornered animal.

'It's a trap. A way to get me to go there quietly. I don't want to...'

'If that were the case, I'd be insisting that you come. It's only a suggestion. Don't come if you don't want to. In all honesty, I'm keen on visiting myself...'

'Was my mother's mother – my nain – very ill?' asked Huw slowly. He glanced at his parents, nervous that he'd asked a forbidden question.

'Yes,' answered Francis weakly, his face pale. 'Very ill.'

'Was she, doctor?' asked Peggy quietly, staring at the table.

'Yes,' I answered, hoarsely. I could not forget Jennie Riverside. The first extreme case of mental illness I'd seen as a young doctor. 'I never saw anyone as bad as she was. When she was sent away... Well... She was barely functioning.'

'How bad did it get?' Peggy asked, her voice almost a whisper. She covered her eyes with her hands, as if protecting herself.

My gaze settled on Huw, who suddenly looked more like a boy than a man.

'Mrs Phyllip... You *must* remember...' I started.

'I can't trust the memories of a child,' she answered. 'I don't know what's real and what I've invented. Please tell me how it was. I need to know.'

I turned my eyes to Francis, who nodded his blessing. He looked over at his son, no doubt afraid that the truth would scare him.

'She stayed in the house for weeks – months, maybe – and sent you to the shop. This shop, as it happens. To buy food. When she was taken to the hospital, she suffered from the effects of lack of sunlight: weak eyesight, sallow skin, brittle bones.'

Peggy nodded.

'A few weeks before she was taken to Denbigh, she was seen wandering the village in the early hours. And you, Peggy, were severely neglected… Little food, little water, a lack of hygiene, your clothes dirty and small and full of holes, your nails growing into your flesh. But worst of all was the lack of attention. Your mother had not spoken to you in years.'

Peggy's eyes were red.

'I remember.'

'Do you remember seeing me, all those years ago?'

She shook her head, puzzled.

'I was sent for by your grandfather. It was less than a week after you had arrived at the farm, and he was concerned by how thin you were. I checked you over, and asked whether you were all right.'

'What did I say?'

'You answered that you were happy that the silence had gone.'

Peggy nodded again.

'Your grandmother said that you ate as if you were tasting everything for the first time. Everything was new and vivid, every sense intensified. Mrs Pugh, your grandmother, had made tea for me, and I sat beside you as we ate – scones, cream and blackberry jam to begin, then an apple, then some pancakes. You ate as if you were afraid that the food would be taken away.'

I could see that child in the darkest pits of my memory:- thin, pale fingers curling around cake, a moustache of milk staining her top lip. She'd had a feral quality, almost animal, that, despite years of respectability, Peggy had never quite been able to get rid of.

'I understand that,' said Huw, nervous again of saying the wrong thing.

'What do you mean?' quizzed Francis gently. 'Your mother still cooks our meals, still goes out for walks...'

'I didn't mean that. I was talking about the silence.'

We all stared at him expectantly.

'It starts so slowly, you don't even notice it. And then, one day, you find the whole house is completely silent.' He stared at his mother dolefully. 'You don't sing anymore.'

Peggy stared at him, her grey eyes dark and wide.

'You know, like you used to. The old Welsh songs that you used to sing to yourself. The songs your grandmother used to sing. You're so quiet now.'

Across the table, I caught Francis' eye, and felt a sadness swelling within me as I realised how tragic this was for him. A silence, threatening his family like a poisoned fog, creeping invisibly into the corners of his home. And his wife, whom he loved, with the fine threads of her mind becoming undone.

'We'll go to Denbigh,' said Peggy, her eyes fixed on her son, tears wetting her eyelashes though her voice was strong and determined.

On a grey day, the air thick and close as smoke, the car wandered through the Dysynni valley and along the winding roads past Dolgellau and Bala. The sun was lost behind the threat of grey brown clouds, and the car windows were open. I glanced at myself in the mirror. I looked old, my forehead a map of lines, sweat greasing every sign of my age. I noticed, for the first time, how wayward and untidy my eyebrows had become, like wild hedgerows.

By my side, her slim frame barely occupying half the seat, Peggy leaned towards the window, as if she was trying to escape from me. Her attention was outside the car, on the land that we were passing, and though the heat was unbearable, there was not a lick of sweat on her.

I had forced myself to accept that I was besotted with my fragile patient, whilst swelling with disgust at my own foul hunger for her. The immorality of my thoughts did nothing to cool my imagination, which wandered into her bed, over her flesh, into her mouth, under her clothes. I became infatuated in a way I hadn't been since I was a teenager. I slept at night wishing she was beside me, and awoke disappointed to find my wife by my side.

I glanced at her in the car. She wore a thin cotton dress, patterned with green ivy. Her wrists, and the pale hairs on her arms, were enough to make me have to swallow hard, as if hoping the boiling lust would be swallowed too.

'Was this the way my mother would have come?' Peggy asked suddenly, having been quiet for a long time.

I nodded. 'I can't be certain, but this is the quickest way.'

Peggy turned her whole body to face me. 'Did she know where she was going?'

'Yes. I told her before she got into the car.'

'How did she react?'

'She didn't. She was completely silent.'

But I remembered Jennie's wild eyes, and that they were more similar to Peggy's than I liked to think.

A silence stretched over a few minutes, before Peggy said, 'You would have thought that she'd ask after me. Arrange for someone to care for me. Put up a bit of a fight to stay with me. I was only a child.'

'It was an illness, Mrs Phyllip. She had no control over the things she said and did.'

'So everyone keeps insisting,' Peggy answered quietly, before turning away again.

Memory is such a flawed, fragile thing. I can remember every detail of that journey to Denbigh. Every piece of clothing that covered Peggy's bony frame, every word she uttered. The almost-silent cadence of her breathing. I can remember the white rowing boats on Bala Lake, the leather-skinned men trimming the branches of an oak tree on the outskirts of Denbigh. But of the hospital itself, only wispy ghosts of memories remain, ghosts that visit me, still, in my darkest hours.

Peggy strode from the car towards the gothic towers of the hospital and they rose like storm clouds behind her. She paused and turned back, waiting for me, her skin pale and eyes dark.

She walked through wards of women her own age, each one stupefied by drugs, lying in their beds with an air of ethereal, dangerous calm.

'My mother would have been this age when she came here,' she said quietly, gazing from face to face as if she was looking for someone.

Screams from somewhere deep within the building, and Peggy turning to see, her face more alive, somehow, than I had seen it before.

The great hall, and patients dancing to a slow, steady song. They swayed to a rhythm that we could not hear, their limbs long and limp. Peggy watched them through a circular glass window in the door, the light pouring though and turning her cheekbones yellow.

A patient in a wheelchair was pushed hurriedly past us, the smell of piss and shit poisoning the sterile air around him. He had a swollen black eye, and a cut on his lips which had been tidily stitched. He wept like a child. A strong man, injured and broken.

'I'm ready to leave,' said Peggy, and then she strode down the corridors towards the doors, opening them with all the energy she could muster, letting the muggy grey light of day illuminate her entire body.

'You were kind to make a picnic,' said Peggy, biting into the sandwich. 'I didn't think of eating.'

'It was Mair's doing. It's a little late to call it lunch, but never mind.'

I watched as Peggy tore a piece of bread between her thumb and forefinger, before eating it quickly, hungrily.

'Lovely bread.'

'Mair is a wonderful baker.'

'Well, I respect anyone who can bake bread. I have tried and tried, and I always fail.'

Silence fell as we ate.

'I like it here.'

I nodded. It had been her idea to stop at Bala Lake. It was the first thing she had said since we had left the asylum. There was a smattering of people by the water, trying to find a cool breeze.

It was beautiful, but Denbigh asylum made it ugly, and made my food taste grey. I had never seen anywhere like it.

'I'm sorry, Peggy.'

She looked up from her sandwich. 'Sorry?'

'For taking you there. I thought it was a good place. I thought it could help you.'

Peggy chewed on a crust, and stared out onto the lake. 'It has helped me, in an odd way. Please don't apologise.'

'How do you mean?'

'When my mother came back from Denbigh, she was poisoned... She said things she knew would hurt me, put all her energy into despising me. And I thought that if the institution had cured her, then that cruel, soulless woman was the real her – her true character, not simply an illness.'

'And what has changed?'

'She couldn't have been cured in a place like that, could she? She would have been drugged and sleeping for long periods of time, and then simply left with others as ill as she was. So she wasn't herself when she came home. If anything, she would have been worse.'

'That makes you feel better?'

Peggy nodded. 'It was her illness that was cruel, not her. I can take the blame away from her, now.'

I reached into the bag that Mair had carefully stored in the car boot that morning, and pulled out a foil package. 'Mair made these, too. Take one.'

Peggy took one of the sweet golden squares, and handled it tenderly as if it was a treasure. A syrupy cube, full of seeds and oats, with a few fat almonds nestling between them. She bit into it hungrily, like an animal, and chewed slowly.

'These are amazing.' She groaned, contentedly. 'Please thank your wife on my behalf.'

'Of course,' I said, biting into mine. My favourite sweet, and Mair knew it. I spied on Peggy from the corner of my eye, besotted with the childlike way she ate, modesty and manners forgotten. When she had finished, she brushed her ivy covered dress with the back of her hand, before stretching her long legs and leaning back on the bench.

'Someone once told me that my mother was funny when she was younger. Full of life. Can you imagine? I never saw her that way. But I like to think that it was the real her.'

I couldn't respond to the feeble excuses she made for her mother. Peggy was still protective of her, after all the years. I turned my face to the lake, hoping for a breeze, but not finding a breath of relief for my sweltering skin.

The storm broke as the car wound its way through the mountains which led the way home, and the rain punched the windows violently. I felt the road vibrating under the tyres, such was the strength of the thunder, and lightning flashed angry forks towards Cadair Idris.

'Filthy weather,' I yelled over the storm.

'Never mind. Everything will be greener tomorrow.'

We arrived at Llanegryn, and I stopped the car outside the shop. Veins of rain patterned the windscreen. Peggy thanked me profusely, and reached for the door.

'Peggy?'

She turned her stormy grey eyes to me.

'I'm sorry.'

'What for?'

'I sent your mother to that terrible place.'

Peggy shook her head. 'You had no choice. And you didn't know.'

I waited for her to leave, but she was still for a moment, our silence punctuated by rain.

'Dr Thomas?'

I gazed at her, and wondered if she knew how much I wanted to touch her.

'Will you ever send anyone else to that place?'

Her eyes were her mother's, and it made my heart hurt. I promised Peggy that I wouldn't. She moved quickly, then, out into the rain, slamming the door between us. The rain stuck her cotton dress to her body, and by the time she reached the shop door, the ivy pattern seemed to grow thickly over her thin, bony flesh.

Menna Arthur
Pwllheli
1967

Lavender Biscuits

10 oz plain flour   4 oz caster sugar

10 oz butter, softened

3 tbsp lavender flowers, finely chopped

Cream the butter and sugar together.
Add the lavender and flour, and stir.
Leave the dough in the refrigerator
for an hour, then roll it out and cut
into shapes.
Bake in an oven at 170°C for around
eighteen minutes, or until the edges
have started to colour.

I watched her for days before we spoke. Something in her caught on the thread of my mind, and I became undone.

She passed my bench at ten past ten every morning, after I had washed my breakfast dish and struggled on my stick to the promenade. I did not know why I put myself through this daily struggle. Every step made my eighty-year-old bones groan and ache. No one waited there for me. I barely spoke to anyone.

I could not decide upon her age. She dressed like a middle-aged woman, but her skin looked younger. Her stride was tall and straight, her face turned towards the sea as if she was searching for something lost on the horizon.

She came to a sudden halt on her fifth morning, and sat at the far end of my bench without acknowledging me. Her sudden stillness was odd in someone who walked as though they had a specific destination. I watched her long face, the thin lips and narrow nose. Her hair was tied back in a bun on the nape of her neck, her dark, shapely brows like crescents over her eyes. She crossed her hands on her lap as she sat, and breathed with the waves.

'Are you on holiday?' I asked in Welsh, expecting an English answer to say that she didn't understand. Most of the tourists were English.

She didn't turn to look at me, but her answer came in soft, comforting Welsh. *Mewn ffordd*, she said. 'In a way.'

A warmth grew within me as I heard my mother tongue spoken from a stranger's mouth. Her voice suited her gait: deep and smooth as velvet. All the scratches and scars of my own voice seemed amplified. I had been young, once, in a different world, in a different life.

'Your accent...'

'Meirionnydd,' she answered, still watching the horizon. 'I've been unwell.'

'Convalescence,' I nodded knowingly. 'I was sent to Llandudno after having the measles when I was fifteen.'

The woman turned to face me for the first time, locking her eyes onto mine – grey, like the sea in winter. Her gaze swept over me, making me feel as self-conscious as a girl.

I felt ashamed of the woman she saw. A bent old hag, attempting to distract from her age with jewels – emerald on the right hand, ruby on the left, pearls in my ears, a diamond strung around my neck. Lace on my black clothes, and a shell-shaped clip holding my hair in place, put there carefully by quaking hands. I usually prided myself on these decorations, but sitting by this elegant woman, adorned only by a thin gold band on her wedding finger, I felt like a child caught playing in her mother's jewellery box.

She turned back to the sea without uttering a word.

'You look nice and strong, anyway,' I said, to fill the silence, though I thought she was too thin.

For some reason, this made her laugh. 'You're right.'

'The sea air makes a difference. It's as if that breeze can blow all the bad things away,' I added.

'I hope so.'

We sat for a long time, watching the waves. Her presence was a comfort. I had sat alone for so long.

'I sit here each morning,' I said after a while. 'Over a decade on my own.'

'How peaceful,' sighed the woman, and I turned to her, perplexed.

'Lonely,' I said, the first time I'd said that cruel word out loud in years.

She turned to me with a sad smile. 'Peace for someone who lives amongst people, lonely for someone who lives alone.'

She had a lovely smile, as if her face had been crafted to show joy – straight, white teeth and high, round cheekbones.

'Do you have children?' I ventured.

'One. Though he's no longer a child. Sixteen, and itching to leave home.'

127

'You've been a good mother to him, then.'

She looked at me, awaiting an explanation.

'Prepared him for leaving you. Made him independent of you,' I added.

The woman stared at me, as if she was seeing me for the first time. I held her stare, though it was not easy to gaze into those stormy eyes without breaking away. It was important that she understood what I was saying. She turned away, finally.

'I wasn't always the best for him,' she said, quietly.

'They have to know that parents are just people. Riddled with faults. No one is uncomplicated.'

'I was ill before, too... I think he may have been lonely, then.'

She smoothed some invisible creases in her skirt, and then stood up, faced the sea as straight-backed as a soldier.

'Will you come for supper tonight?' I regretted the question as soon as I asked. It sounded like a lonely old woman, craving attention.

To my surprise, she nodded.

'I'm in number seven. Six o'clock?'

The woman nodded again, and walked away.

'Your name?' I croaked after her.

'Margaret,' she answered without looking back, without stopping, without asking the same of me.

Things were awkward that evening. Two women, separated by generations, unsure as to why they were together at all. Though Margaret had changed her clothes, there was nothing grand about her – a long black dress, hair twisted into a ball at the nape of her neck, the bones of her face beautiful but too thin. She accepted a glass of sherry, and looked at the photographs on the sideboard as the food warmed in the oven. I admired her long fingers on the stem of her glass.

'Your sons?' she asked as she looked at the pictures of my boys, both smiling under the caps of their uniforms. I nodded, and the sapphire earrings tinkled as I moved. She ran the tip of her finger along Ed's cheek, leaving the faintest of stains on the glass.

'They're handsome. Do you see them often?'

I shook my head. She retracted her hand from the photograph, nodded with understanding.

As I served the food, I felt the blush of a young girl heating my cheeks underneath my rouge. Serving peasant food, to a woman like this...

'It looks lovely,' said Margaret as I sat opposite her. I had lit the candles, and their reflection danced in the grey pools of her eyes.

I smiled at her. 'My mother used to make it. We didn't have much money, but we lived by the sea, so there was always fish.'

'She'd be happy to know that you're still making it.'

'I'm not so sure. I think she would have hoped that I might have developed a more sophisticated palate by now. And it never tastes the same as it did when she made it.'

Margaret stared at her plate, and I could tell that she could see more than food.

The meal was good, and Margaret had a voracious appetite, which stunned me in someone that was so thin.

'This is perfect. It tastes like the sea.'

I smiled, and ate my fish slowly, carefully. Lately, my senses had started to fade, and the small pleasures that had been left to me were beginning to leave me. I wondered whether this was an indication that I was about to die. Taste was the first sense to abandon me, and the most difficult to part with. Vivid colours and the sound of laughter would live forever in my imagination, but there was something less solid about the memory of taste, the same as that foggy memory of dreams.

Margaret ate every mouthful, though it had become fashionable to leave a morsel. There was something to be admired in her feral

129

enjoyment, her lack of self-consciousness over her joy in taste.

For dessert, I served lavender biscuits, cut into pretty heart shapes. A light, sophisticated end to the meal. Margaret lifted a biscuit to her thin lips, and bit into the heart shape with her dainty teeth.

'Wonderful,' she said, turning that taste around her mouth. 'It reminds me of home.'

'How is that?'

'My grandmother used to grow lavender. She'd put some underneath my pillow so that I could enjoy that sweet, sleepy smell.' She swallowed hard, as if she was trying to get rid of whatever was in her head.

She did not touch her wine, and declined coffee, drinking only water.

'My husband and son are coming to fetch me tomorrow,' she said, staring at the crumbs on her empty plate.

'Do you feel better after your convalescence?' I asked.

Margaret sighed, stroking a long finger along the long leg of the silver fork on the table. 'Perhaps.'

'Did you have an operation?'

She shook her head, and in the dim light, I never saw anyone who looked so young and so old. A child's face, lined with middle age. She almost frightened me.

'I wasn't really ill. I need a week each year to myself, to remind myself of what's important. Francis calls it my holiday, and he moans that he can't leave the shop to come with me.' She intertwined her fingers. 'I don't show him my weaknesses, you know. They'll never know how delicate I am. No one knows.'

The candles threw long shadows across her pale face.

'They're only memories, but sometimes it feels as if they're trying to suffocate me, as if they have their own souls. As if I'd done something wrong. I can't tell Francis or Huw. That would be unfair.'

I remembered an old man who lived in our village when I was a child, talking to himself, screaming. I was never as scared of anything as I had been of him. He howled at the moon on clear nights, and I had lain in my bed, shivering under the sheets as I listened to him.

'I'm looking for something, I think. Looking for something, though I'm not sure what it is...'

That man had thin fingers, too, exactly like Margaret. Reaching for people who weren't there.

'I feel tired. I'd like to go to bed,' I said shakily.

Margaret looked up at me, shock in her dark eyes.

'You're frightened of me!' she exclaimed.

'Of course not.' My quaking voice said otherwise.

Margaret stood, almost knocking her chair over in her rush to escape.

'Thank you for the meal,' she said quickly, in a formal, tight voice, and disappeared.

'I'm sorry,' I called from my chair, and my voice sounded pathetic, like a lamb bleating. 'I didn't mean to...'

Margaret appeared in the door frame, her coat tied tightly around her slim waist. She stared at me wordlessly.

'I'm sorry,' I said again.

'Why are you afraid?' she pleaded, her voice thick with bruises. 'I never did anything to you.'

'I'm afraid of everything,' I confessed, to myself and to her. 'I'm old enough to know that it's wise to be that way.'

Margaret left. I could hear her quick stride on the path, slowly fading into silence. I remained by the table, the dirty dishes heavy upon it, and felt the shame and relief that she had gone heating my blood.

Francis Phyllip
Peggy's Husband
1969

Oat Biscuits

3oz self raising flour   3oz oats

3oz sugar   6oz butter

1 tsp cinnamon

Mix everything with your hands.
Shape into balls, and press onto
greaseproof paper before baking for
around ten minutes at 150°C.

Sometimes, after going to bed, I would pretend to read so that I could watch Peggy preparing for sleep. I found comfort in her patterns, in the familiar shadows of her body.

I had tried, a few times, to set my book face-down on the blankets, to openly watch her. Though she always smiled, then, something was different about her movements, a stiffness in her limbs that I found displeasing. She would always assume that my watching her was a game that would lead to making love, and though I enjoyed it, that was not why I watched.

Was it voyeurism? Was it perverted, watching my wife when she thought my mind was in my book?

Sunday nights were best, after she had had a bath. She would pad softly into the bedroom, a towel wrapped around her, her dark hair dripping tears onto her bony shoulders. She would rub the towel over every part of herself, under her arms, behind her neck, between her legs. Her naked body had improved as the years had passed, collecting mementoes as she neared her forties. The slack skin and silvery lines on her stomach were a testament to the fact that she had grown Huw inside her. The lines around her eyes were the scars of smiling, and the silvery strands that lined her black hair matched her eyes.

With her mind elsewhere, she would slowly put on her nightclothes – a vest to hide her dark nipples, a white nightgown to drown her. I would turn my eyes away, then – Peggy in a nightgown scratched at old memories of a sunny morning by the river.

I did not know whether the heat of my love for Peggy was normal, or healthy. My father had told me several times that is was unnatural for me to gaze at her as I did, and until he died, he insisted on reminding me of who she was, where she had come from, who her mother had been.

'It's in her blood,' he had spat once, when Peggy was out walking with Huw. 'And you'll see it in her one day. The girl is like her mother.'

The fear that he may have been right was enough to awaken me, sometimes, in the middle of the night. I would turn to Peggy, asleep by my side, and I would see Jennie.

Things had improved after she had been to Denbigh Hospital with Dr Thomas, though she never said a word about what she had seen there. Her laugh returned to the shop, her unselfconscious singing, and we returned to who we wanted to be.

And then, again, the silence came upon us like a wave.

'Please, Peggy,' I pleaded one evening, in the twilight of the shop after closing time. I had bitten my tongue for weeks, but her behaviour had become painfully strange. I found an empty box of biscuits and half a dozen Mars Bar wrappers shoved behind the wardrobe one morning. On that same day, Peggy had refused lunch and dinner. 'Go and see Dr Thomas.'

'He won't give me another chance. He'll send me to the asylum, like he did to my mother.'

'I wouldn't allow that! He must have some tablets or something...'

'Do you think I'm losing my mind?' asked Peggy suddenly, her eyes dark in that long, pale face. I shook my head slowly, trying not to show that I was becoming scared for her.

'No. But I think you have a sadness.'

Peggy sighed, and looked away. 'I need something... Something is missing...'

'We'll find it,' I comforted, making a promise I could not keep. 'Whatever it is...'

'I would have been all right if we'd had more children,' she babbled. 'I could have broken the pattern. I would not be like my mother, then. I'd have had more to love...'

Love me more, then! I thought, without uttering a word. *Love me enough to be who you once were.*

'I need to do something,' she went on, becoming agitated. 'To pay penance for all the bad things...'

'There are no bad things! You're a good woman!

'I need to go away.'

I froze.

'Go away?'

'Away from her shadow... My mother's shadow. Away to somewhere new, to think about... May I, Francis?'

'Leave?'

'Alone.'

I felt my father's spirit, then, cackling at me, smug that he had been right all along.

'A week – Pwllheli again, perhaps. It was good for me before, and it'll make a difference now, too. I can't think straight with life happening all around me, Francis...'

I sighed. A week. As she did last year, and the year before that. A week, to replenish her energy.

'Is it a good idea for you to be alone when you're not well? I know you've been before, but you weren't...like this...'

I remembered her mother's body in the water, the weight of her in my arms. There was all that sea in Pwllheli...

'I have to try, Francis,' Peggy pleaded. 'If I'm not better after a holiday, I'll go and see Dr Thomas. I promise.'

A few days later, unbeknownst to anyone except Peggy and I, I drove from Llanegryn to Tywyn station, and held her bony body close to mine before she climbed aboard the train to Pwllheli once more. She did not react to my arms, and I lost a few fat tears in the car on the way home. She was never safely mine. I didn't know whether she would return to me.

That afternoon, after preparing a corned beef sandwich for myself for lunch, the shop door opened and Annie bustled in. A quake of nervousness shook my stomach. I was a bad liar.

'Good afternoon!' Her painted lips widened into a smile, her blue eyes shining. 'How are things today?'

'Fine, thank you,' I answered, the falseness of my grin hurting my cheekbones. 'Yourself?'

'Yes, fine as always.'

She moved to come behind the counter, through to the kitchen in the back, as she always did.

'Annie.' She stopped before reaching the counter, her brows arching in a question. 'Peggy isn't here, I'm afraid. She'll be away until next week.'

Annie stared at me for a long time, the question itching to trip off those rose-tinted lips. She waited for more details, but I remained silent, as I had to.

'Pwllheli, again?'

I nodded. 'That's right. She's gone to see her friend, as she did before.'

Annie stared at me without a smile. I could see her choosing her words carefully.

'Isn't it funny, Francis, how she never mentions it to me before she goes off to see her friend.'

I felt the sweat heating my face. 'Yes.'

'And she never tells me what she's been doing when she comes home.'

I looked down at the counter. We both knew that there was a secret.

'Is she all right, Francis?' She fixed me with sapphire eyes.

'Of course,' I mumbled, turning away from her.

Annie turned on her heel, and left without saying a word, leaving nothing but questions in the empty space where she had stood.

'Where's Mam?' asked Huw, loading his fork with Smash, some sausage, and a smear of ketchup. I took a mouthful of food, and tried to sound normal.

'She's gone to Pwllheli to stay with a friend,' I answered. 'She'll be back next week.'

Huw set his fork down on his plate, and glared at me across the table. 'This is disrespectful to me, you know. The lies. I'm almost eighteen, and I'm a part of this family, too.'

I carried on eating. My face felt hot.

There was something unjust in the way that I had to face the questions when Peggy went away. I was the one subjected to the suspicion in people's faces.

'Do you think I don't notice when she's unwell? Her illness is a part of my life – I know it as I know Mam herself.'

My knife and fork fell to the plate, and I covered my face with my hands. I had failed to protect Huw from the darkness. Whatever made me imagine I could?

'Where is she, Dad? At the hospital?'

'In a guest house in Pwllhelli,' I sighed. 'Alone. She says it helps. Clears her mind.'

'Was she always like this?' I looked at my son. 'Always this... unsettled?'

I shook my head. 'No... Well. I don't know. It started when she realised we weren't able to have another child...' I sighed again, feeling an odd relief in sharing the information. 'I think she had a definite plan for her life, and a house full of children was part of that plan.'

'Maybe she needs something more. Something else to fill her mind.'

'I think you're right. Something outside Llan... In Bryncrug or Tywyn. Llan is full of ghosts for her.'

'I can remember when the doctor came here, and he told us what had happened to Mam when she was a child.' Huw rubbed his head, as if it worried him. 'Do you think that the fact that she was starved is why she's funny about food?'

'What do you mean?'

'The stuffing herself.'

I stared at my son, perplexed.

'Don't tell me you haven't noticed. Oh God, Dad. Look.'

He crossed the kitchen to the dresser, and opened the door on the lower left. He pulled out a stack of neatly folded tea towels, and from between them fell a rainbow of wrappers – tens and tens of them, chocolate and sweet papers, scrunched up and concealed.

Huw shut the dresser drawer, leaving the wrappers and tea towels on the floor, and moved to the kitchen cupboards. He kneeled beneath the sink, where the cleaning materials were kept, and emptied a whole box of wrappers and secrets onto the floor.

'In the airing cupboard, in the back of her underwear drawer, in the suitcase on top of the wardrobe in the spare bedroom.'

'How the hell is she so thin?' I recalled the shape of her ribs under her small breasts, spied upon slyly as she dried herself after a bath.

'She eats them all at once – sweets and biscuits and chocolate, whatever she can get her hands on. Then she makes excuses why she isn't eating with us, and she doesn't eat anything for days. As if she's punishing herself for stuffing her face like she does.'

I shook my head, overcome with a terrible sorrow. 'How do you know this?'

Huw shrugged, unable to answer. Perhaps I had known, deep down, but I had been so keen to please Peggy that I had shut my mind to all the secrets of her darkness. Had I not noticed that Mars Bars and Marathons were disappearing from the shop? Had I not spied empty packets in the bin, and silently sworn at Huw's teenage appetite? Had I not accepted all her excuses for not sitting down with us to eat as truth, without thinking to question her?

'She doesn't do it all the time,' explained Huw. 'Only when things are very bad.'

There was a silence. Where was Peggy now?

'I'm sorry, Dad,' Huw smiled. 'But this food is horrible, and Auntie Annie said that I was welcome to eat with them. Would you mind? She always offers, and I want to see Susie, anyway.'

I stared at the powdered potato congealing on our plates.

'Of course.'

After he had left, I sat in the quiet kitchen, listening to the clock dripping away the seconds. I thought of my elegant, graceful wife stuffing fistfuls of chocolate into her mouth until she felt ill. I thought of her hiding the evidence. I did not know that woman. As frightening as that image was to me, it was nothing in comparison to the thought of Huw, my tall, handsome son, a master of his own emotions, searching the corners of his home for evidence of his mother's madness, and finding it in the form of empty wrappers and the lingering smell of cocoa and sugar.

I could tell from her gait as she stepped off the train that Peggy was better than she had been. She smiled, and wrapped her arms around me lovingly.

'A sea breeze,' she said as we walked to the car. 'It blows all the bad things away.'

'There's a better colour in your cheeks,' I answered, as if she had been suffering from flu and not teetering on the edge of insanity.

I regained some hope on the journey home. Peggy gazed through the window at her homeland, the hills which had always cradled her, and she looked happy. I placed my hand over hers. She smiled and squeezed my fingers.

It was tea time when we arrived, and Llan was silent and still. I carried her suitcase through the shop, and watched her face as she came into the kitchen and saw Huw standing over the Rayburn, a plate in his hands.

'Biscuits, Mam! I made them for you.' He wore an embarrassed smile. 'With Susie's help. Welcome home.'

'Goodness... Thank you,' said Peggy, unused to the attention. 'You didn't have to. It was only a week's holiday...' She bit a corner off one of the biscuits. 'Good God! These are lovely. I'll have to go away more often!'

'Sit down, Mam,' ordered Huw, full of an uncharacteristic enthusiasm. 'Take off your coat.'

Peggy did as she was told. Huw made a pot of tea, and we sat around the table. 'Dad and I have had an idea.'

Peggy raised her eyebrows.

'A café, in Tywyn! We can sell Dad's ice cream, and you can bake cakes, and...'

'What?' Peggy asked, confused.

'It might get rid of your sadness. It's a great idea, because you're organised and you can run a business. Dad says he couldn't do the books without you...'

Peggy turned her big empty eyes to me. 'You told him?'

The words hit me like a fist. She did not have to voice the word that was on her tongue: I heard it in the silence. *Traitor.*

'I knew before my father,' said Huw, quietly. 'And I want to do something to help. The sea breeze, Mam. It's good for you.'

Peggy's smile returned as we discussed plans, and an enthusiasm came to her as we chatted about the possibility of opening a café. But when I stood up to clear away the dishes, Huw lost in his plans for the new café, Peggy turned to stare at me over her shoulder, and I saw the disappointment in her wide grey eyes.

Merfyn Thomas
Estate Agent
1970

Peanut Butter and Honey Milkshake

2 tbsp smooth peanut butter

2 tbsp honey

a cup of milk

a cup of vanilla ice cream

Whisk until smooth.

I wandered around the café for a while before they arrived, trying to find something positive to say that might sell the place, a convenient lie so that I could return to the office bearing the victorious flush of someone who'd closed a deal.

Pulling my finger along the dusty shelves behind the counter, I knew that this would be a hard sell. An ugly red-brick building that had been squashed between the elegant Edwardian houses on the promenade in Tywyn. The building should not have been there. They should not have allowed the existence of such a blot on the dignified beachfront. I was not the one to sell such a place. Not I, with my old-fashioned tastes, my hatred for all the modern buildings which looked so squat and square and functional amidst this old town.

I stood behind the counter of this building which I despised, staring at the rain picking at the windows.

She appeared behind the glass like a ghost, her face clouded by the streaks of rain, as if I was watching her through a dream. She looked black and white, colourless, like a statue.

Her hand rose to wipe the rain from the pane of glass, and I watched her huge dark eyes as her gaze wandered over the tired cafe. My stomach churned as I realised that those stone-grey eyes would find me in the next few seconds.

The breeze blew a wisp of hair over her face. She looked so still, so beautiful.

She pushed the door, and the sea breathed a spray of rain into the café.

'Mr Thomas?' she asked, her voice deep and soft. I moved from behind the counter, rushed to offer her my hand.

'Yes. Mrs Phyllip?'

She nodded, and smiled awkwardly as she shook my hand.

'Call me Peggy, please.'

Her hand was cool in mine, the skin like silk in my palms.

'Will your husband be joining us?' I asked to fill the silence.

Peggy smiled again, as though she sensed my uneasiness. Her lips were thin and reddened by the cold, her mouth slightly open, showing straight, white teeth. She pushed the unruly wisp of hair behind her ear – a childlike movement in the body of a woman.

'He's parking the car.'

I nodded. I had a script, as if I was an actor, but this was the first time I had felt ridiculous reciting it.

'I'm sure I don't have to tell you that this is a prime location for a café. On the beachfront, like this, it will be full to the brim over the summer months...'

Peggy stared into my eyes for a few seconds, and then, unexpectedly, a laugh escaped from her wide mouth. I raised my eyebrows, but she gave no explanation.

'The price is very reasonable, given the condition. You could almost open for business immediately...'

She was not listening to me. She wandered slowly around the café, gently touching the white plastic tables, the metallic counter top, gazing into the corners and shadows. I had never seen anyone view a property in this way before, examining the details and not the whole. I watched her silently until the door opened once more.

'Goodness, what terrible weather!'

Francis shut the door behind him. He removed his hat, and offered his hand to me. He smiled warmly as we shook hands, and suddenly, my mind threw up an image of him caressing his wife, pushing her nightdress from her shoulder... I swallowed, and looked away from him, afraid that he would see her bare shoulders in my eyes.

'I was just telling Mrs Phyllip how busy this place is during the summer...'

'We're local. We know how busy it gets. It's a good location.' He placed his hat on one of the tables. Francis was a handsome man, his dark hair combed back with a sheen of Brylcreem, and he had a square, masculine jawline and thick dark eyebrows. But he was short, shorter than his wife, and they seemed to me an odd couple – mismatched.

'I was the one who wanted to see the building, to see if the kitchen was big enough. And to make sure that it didn't need too much money spent on it,' said Peggy without looking at me.

'Well, as you can see, it's in near-perfect condition...'

'I would want a long counter, from one end to the other,' she interrupted, looking around the cafe as if she could see her plans materialising before her eyes. 'With red and white stools along it, instead of these little tables.'

Peggy looked up and caught her husband's eye, and they both laughed. I felt as though I was intruding on a private moment.

'She has vision,' said Francis by way of an explanation. He fetched his hat, before asking his wife, 'Have you seen enough?'

She nodded, her eyes still fixed on her husband.

'How soon can we get the keys?' asked Francis.

'A few weeks,' I answered, waiting for the rush of adrenaline that came with an easy sale. It did not come. Peggy's presence clouded everything.

After discussing contracts, bank details and timetables, Peggy and Francis left and I watched them walking towards the car, arm in arm, leaning into the wind. Francis opened the car door for his wife, admiring her lean body as she folded herself into her seat.

I switched off the light, and fetched the keys from the counter. As I turned, I noticed that Peggy had left a lone fingerprint on the glass display counter, and for a while I stared at it, round and grey as her eyes.

In the months that followed, every passion and vivid enjoyment bled from my life. I would pass the little café on the beach sometimes, when we had a house for sale on the promenade, looking for her tall figure, her dark hair.

The builders arrived as soon as the deal was done, though I never saw either of the owners there whilst the work was being completed. I became uncomfortable, aware that I was always looking for her. At last, a new sign appeared above the door in swirly red script, *Phyllip's Ices*, and a picture of an ice cream cone beside it. Then, a few weeks' pause. Nothing opened on the promenade over the cold months – not the amusements, the shops, or the café. And then, one afternoon on the edge of spring, the lights were on in the squat red-brick building, and the door was open. I drove my small car past it and parked at the far end of the promenade, but my heart was pounding. I sat alone in the stillness, imagining what it would be like to walk into her new business venture.

The cafe was transformed, just as Peggy had promised – a long counter of red vinyl, and high stools lined up beside it. I was surprised to see that it was almost full. A gang of youngsters in uniform had come here after school, and a middle-aged man read a newspaper through the steam of his coffee. Peggy stood behind the counter in a plain blue dress, her hair tied tightly into a bun at the nape of her neck, her fingers tight around a tall glass.

'You've caught me.' She smiled at me, and nodded to the glass in her hand. 'This is the first time today I've had five minutes to myself.'

I sat on one of the stools, and grinned at her. 'It is whisky you have in there?'

She laughed. 'Banana milkshake is better than whisky.' She took a long gulp through a straw. 'Do you know, I hadn't even tasted milkshake before we bought this place. It's a revelation.' She rolled her eyes with pleasure, as if she was looking heavenward in appreciation of her drink.

'Are things going well?'

'The young people have discovered the place.' Peggy nodded in the direction of the schoolchildren, laughing in the corner. 'They like the milkshakes even more than I do! And the ice creams are selling well, too. Francis makes it himself, you know.'

'Do you have many customers during school hours?'

She grinned. 'The pupils who are meant to be running cross country tend to come here to hide. They pretend to be running, but they're actually in here, stuffing themselves with cake.'

'Goodness. You'll be responsible for a generation of fat people in Tywyn, then.'

Peggy laughed, and finished her milkshake. She turned her back to wipe her mouth with the back of her hand, and the gesture made me swallow, hard.

'Are you going to try one?' she asked.

I raised my eyebrows.

'A milkshake. We have banana, chocolate or strawberry. I'm working on different flavours.'

'A coffee for me, please,' I said, feeling too self-conscious to order a tall glass of sweetened milk, though that is exactly what I wanted.

Peggy placed a cup of coffee on the counter, before turning to the schoolchildren to take more orders. She took the dirty dishes to the kitchen, before returning to the cafe with a mixing bowl in her hand, full of flour and sugar and soft, yielding butter. She had no spoon. She used her hands to mix the ingredients, and her concentration was centred on her task, her lips slightly parted. Without warning, she looked up and caught me staring at her, and she smiled, showing her teeth.

'Scones,' she explained. 'My grandmother's recipe.'

She reached into the carton on the counter behind her, and fetched a smooth egg. She broke it into another bowl, making sharp shards of the once-perfect shell.

'You do it all? Bake all the cakes, and everything?' I asked, and tried to tear my eyes away from those hypnotic hands in the bowl. 'You have no help?'

'I have someone who comes in part-time to help. I'll have to find more if it gets busier during the summer.

She moved rhythmically as her hands kneaded the dough.

'But not Mr Phyllip?'

The question felt like an imposition, and Peggy paused for a few seconds.

'No,' she answered simply.

'The shop in Llanegryn is very busy, I'm sure,' I said to ease the awkwardness.

She smiled, and brushed her forehead with the back of her hand, leaving a line of flour on her pale skin.

'Yes,' she agreed.

By the time I had finished my coffee, a dozen scones were baking in the oven, and the school children were yelling their farewells before escaping, bubbling with energy and laughter. The sincerity of their goodbyes to her: ''Bye, Peggy, see you tomorrow'; 'Thanks for the milkshake, Peggy!' made me envious. A middle-aged woman, so popular with youngsters? Did she not have a son that was older than them? I had spent my school years battling for easy greetings like those.

'I'd better go,' I said, leaving my money on the counter.

'Come again,' Peggy grinned, and the smile reached her eyes. 'I'm determined to get you to try a milkshake before summer is out.'

Though I tried to fight it, it became a habit of mine to call into the café after work each day. During my working day, my mind wandered to those busy hands, pouring water or slicing a cake, her dark hair slowly escaping its knot on the back of her head.

We could not chat every day: sometimes, she was too busy serving drinks or baking, and a friend came every Monday afternoon, and they chatted without pause, occasionally laughing. Annie, the friend, would stay from lunchtime until the café closed, and the two of them never ran out of things to say. Only women, I decided, and children, perhaps, could form a bond so tight. Even marriage had no hope of replicating anything like it.

Sometimes, though, the place was quiet, and those were the days I longed for. I would pray for wind and rain, because that would mean that others would shy away from the promenade, and that Peggy could give me the attention I craved.

She chatted easily, though she barely mentioned Llanegryn and her family, which pleased me. I could pretend that they did not exist, that there was no world outside this warm, sweet-scented café. I rarely had to contribute to the conversation, and Peggy, of course, would work as she talked. I became familiar with the way she took the hot cake tins from the oven using the skirt of her apron, the way she milked her thumbs when she washed her hands. Once, when she was in the kitchen in the back of the café, I caught a glimpse of her through the small circular window, eating a large piece of sponge cake. She was not smiling, not savouring, but pushed the cake into her mouth forcefully.

After a few weeks, as I stood above the grill in my home, waiting for my morning toast to colour, I realised that I loved her. A weight of crippling sadness pressed down upon me for reasons I could not explain, and I switched off the grill and returned to bed. I did not go to work that day: I stayed at home, alone, in stillness and silence, waiting for my affections to drain away. I wondered if she missed me.

The following day, after being reprimanded by my boss for not coming to work and for not telephoning, and after selling a cottage riddled with damp to hopeful newlyweds, I made my way to the café, as usual. It was a grey, humid day, and though it was almost summer, the beachfront was quiet. I walked along the promenade towards the cafe, and watched the waves licking at the damp sand. The colour of a storm was on the horizon, and the bay was empty of boats.

150

Crossing the road, my throat tightened as I saw her there, sitting outside the café on one of the wooden benches, her thin legs crossed neatly. She did not see me, and I became still, for a while, watching her. She faced the sea, her mind elsewhere, and the expression on her face was peaceful, child-like. I had not seen that look before. I felt dirty for watching her when she presumed herself to be alone.

'Enjoying the sea breeze?' I asked, and there was something in the slow, easy way her face transformed into a smile that made me wonder if she knew I had been watching her.

'There's hardly a breeze at all,' she answered. 'I thought I'd take advantage of this five minutes of quiet. It's been busy here all day.'

'And now here I am, intruding on your peace.'

She widened her smile. 'That depends on whether you're happy for me to sit outside while you have you coffee. It's like an oven in there.'

I looked at my shoes, and pressed my lips together. She did not wait for an answer, but disappeared inside to make some coffee. At that moment in time, nothing felt more intimate than the promise of sitting side by side on a bench, looking out onto a grey sea.

I sat, and she came out holding my coffee cup, and a tall glass for herself: another milkshake, the colour of sea foam.

'It's hot – be careful you don't burn your mouth,' she said as she sat beside me. I tried to guess whether there was any significance in the way she spoke to me so easily, as if we had always known one another. She pressed her lips around the straw, and sighed contentedly after taking a long sip.

'A new flavour?' I asked, pointing to the glass.

'It's wonderful,' she groaned. 'I wasn't sure whether it would work, but even Francis agrees with me on this one. Peanut butter and honey. Heaven.' She turned her eyes to me. 'I'll make one for you, if you like.'

I shook my head. 'Coffee will do for me.'

Peggy tutted playfully, shaking her head. 'How can you bear a hot drink in this heat? It's so humid...'

'It's just a habit, I suppose.'

I took another mouthful of coffee – it was strong and bitter, just how I liked it.

'You might like milkshake, too. You'll never know until you try.'

I didn't know how to reply, and so I didn't. We sat, drinking quietly whilst the nearby waves breathed a rhythm. Occasionally, one of us would say something, would start a conversation that didn't lead anywhere, but mostly, we were comfortably silent.

'It must be nice, working by the beach.'

'I wouldn't say I'm a sea kind of person. I don't romanticise the ocean like people tend to.'

I turned to look at her.

'I don't dislike it, and it doesn't frighten me. I'd just prefer to be in the mountains.' She glanced over her shoulder, looking at the mountains that cradled Llanegryn.

'You'll make a fortune here, come the summer holidays,' I comforted, before realising that it was probably vulgar to discuss money.

'Perhaps, yes.' She smiled, with a faraway look in her eyes. 'But we were doing well in the shop.'

'May I ask... Why open the café, then? If you would prefer to be in the mountains, and money isn't the objective...'

'I wasn't... It was Francis and Huw...'

Her voice tailed off. She turned her face away from mine, and the silence became long and awkward.

She stood, at long last, and smoothed her skirt with her palms.

'I have a coffee cake and a tray of Chelsea buns to make before tomorrow morning. And the after-school crowd will be in before long.'

I smiled at her, and our eyes met. Was it my imagination, that look? The look that meant something?

'I'll see you tomorrow.'

She smiled, but it was a tight little smile that did not reach her eyes. She disappeared into the café, and I remained on the bench, alone, uncomfortable in the heat.

Was this not the proof I had been waiting for – that Peggy was unhappy with her husband? A glimpse of disenchantment, a chance for me to...

I stood up, a new energy powering my stride, and for the first time since childhood, my legs felt the urge to run.

Francis Phyllip had obviously sent his wife to manage his new project in town, and now she was consumed with longing for her home. How could he bear her heartbreak? She was so...

I strode down the steps to the beach, paraded to the water's edge, as if I was going somewhere. As if I had a destination.

If only she could see that I was not really an estate agent, not inside, not a man who wore chapel shoes to walk on the beach... No, that man was a disguise for who I was. The real me would not turn down milkshake for a bitter coffee.

Things became busy in the café, and though I still made my daily pilgrimage for coffee, it was always throbbing with tourists. By the time the schools had shut for the long holidays, Peggy had employed two other to work in the café full-time, and she never had the time or energy to offer anything more than a smile or a perfunctory greeting.

I often thought about that afternoon on the bench, the closeness of her body like a long-lost dream. As if it had never happened at all. Peggy wore a disguise of contentedness like a well-worn mask-No one would have guessed from her smiles and girlish giggles that she would have preferred to be elsewhere.

But occasionally, I would see something in her... A tiredness in her eyes, a slackness on the edges of her mouth. My mind created reason upon reason for this unhappiness, and each and every one of them led me to the conclusion that she would be happier with me.

'Where have you been?' asked Peggy, rushing over to me as soon as I sat down. It had been a week since I last saw her, and I realised, for the first time, how painfully thin she was. I could make out the shape of her bones under the collar of her blouse. The cafe was busy, filled with chatter and the sound of tinkling cutlery on crockery. She filled a cup of coffee and passed it over the counter to me, and I nodded my thanks with a small smile. Peggy stared into my eyes, with concern darkening their colour. Had she missed me this last week?

It would have been so easy, so very natural, to obey my instincts and reach over to tuck that wisp of hair behind her ear, and feel her cool skin under my palms. My fingers itched for her.

'With my mother. Being spoiled, enjoying her home cooking. It was nice.'

'Does her coffee taste as good as mine?'

She stared at me, challenging my absence. I felt guilty for abandoning her.

'My mother only drinks tea,' I answered, weakly. 'She says that coffee is too bitter.'

'She's right. There's something foul about it. I don't know why we enjoy it so much.'

One of the customers asked for another cup of tea, and I lost Peggy. Her coffee grew cold as she fulfilled the needs of everyone else – pouring tea, mixing milkshake, fetching biscuits and slices of cake to set on round white plates, clearing dirty dishes.

After an hour, when my second cup of coffee had been emptied, I stood up and hung my jacket over my arm. Peggy looked up from the coffee machine, and caught my eye for a few long seconds. I offered a shy smile, and the one I received in return was enough to maintain the fantasy that she returned my affections on the long evenings of the warmest months.

That summer belonged to her. Had I fallen asleep and awoken by her side every day, I could not have thought about her any more than I did. It was a baking hot season, crawling with moneyed tourists looking for a second home. I sold more houses than anyone else in the office. Peggy had ignited a fire in me that raged its heat into every part of my life.

The café became the hub of the town.

What was better on a hot day than a milkshake, sipped from a tall glass whilst sitting on one of the long benches outside the cafe? Peggy teased me for drinking only coffee. She could not have known how I ached to try one of her sweet milky concoctions, pastel-coloured and sweet, but I was afraid of her eyes watching me as I savoured a brand new taste.

My eyes would trace every pearl of sweat that trickled down her blouse as she worked. I watched her lips widening in a smile as she greeted her customers. Once, I stared at her long, bony bare feet on the white floor tiles as she removed her shoes for a few seconds during a quiet spell. Beautiful feet, and the suggestion of nakedness enough to drive my mind into a ridiculous frenzy. Is that how she looked beneath her clothes? Were her ribs as clearly defined as the bones in her feet, the bow of her hips as rounded as the ball of her heel?

Come the first weeks of September, summer cooled. The tourists returned to their homes in the Midlands, leaving empty shops and abandoned pavements where they had stood. Peggy's café had attracted the locals, too, and it remained busy whilst the other cafés stood empty, but gradually, people's appetite for ice cream and milkshake faded, and the café became quiet after its successful summer.

On a Friday afternoon in mid-September, a cold wind blew in

from the Irish sea, and ushered the last remaining stragglers from the tables. Two girls dressed in their gym kits, full of laughter and joy, were the last to leave, and finally Peggy and I were alone.

Was it my imagination that thickened the air with tension?

I forced myself to look up from the stains of coffee at the bottom of my empty cup. Peggy was still on the other side of the counter, and she was staring at me.

I was so sure that she wanted to touch me.

'Another coffee?' she asked, hoarse and awkward.

'A milkshake, please.'

She stared at me, and then her face broke into a wide, beautiful smile.

For once, I did not attempt to hide the fact that I was watching her every move. She loaded the mixer with milk, ice cream, honey, peanut butter. I grinned as she licked the remainder of the honey from the spoon. She smiled, too. By the time she set the tall glass on the counter in front of me, I felt as if we had made love.

'I hope you like it. Not everyone does.'

A tear of condensation slid down the glass, exactly like the beads of sweat on Peggy's skin that I had studied over the summer.

'Taste it,' she demanded, and a shiver of desire came like an early winter over my skin.

I lifted the glass to my lips, and swallowed a mouthful of the milkshake I had so longed for over the hot months. It was even better than I had expected. A comforting, familiar taste, and yet cold and sweet enough to stun my tongue. The taste of summer. The taste of succumbing.

The taste of Peggy.

'What do you think?' she asked, hoarsely.

I reached across the counter, and held her hand. She was cold and soft as a breeze. I looked up at her face, and she did not express any surprise that I was touching her. She did not pull away.

'I love my husband,' she said gently.

I didn't know if she was telling me, or telling herself.

Voices approached. We snatched back our guilty hands, and the café door opened. A young couple wandered in hand-in-hand, and asked for a pot of tea. I looked up and tried to catch her eye, but she didn't look at me all afternoon.

I spent my weekend in a daze. My tongue ached for the taste of peanut butter and honey, my fingers twitched with desire for hers. She had not pulled away from my touch, whatever her words had been. She had not pulled away from me.

I sat by my desk at the estate agent's on Monday morning, counting the hours until I could go and see her. I was glad when the telephone rang: anything to take my mind off her.

'Evans Estate Agents?'

'Merfyn?'

My back straightened. She was telephoning me. At work. She, too, must have been thinking, thinking about me... Dreaming, perhaps...

'Peggy.'

'Are you free to come to the café in about an hour? Before it gets busy at lunchtime?'

'Of course.'

I wasn't, really, but anything in the diary could be postponed for her. She wanted me there when it was quiet. When there was no one else around.

The sight of her bare feet flashed into my memory, and I sat still at my desk for a few minutes, listening to the dead tone of the telephone, imagining her waiting for me in the deserted café.

He was there.

Francis Phyllip stood behind the counter in a white apron,

pouring hot water into a teapot, laughing with the only customer in the café. I could not see Peggy, and I almost turned and ran. What if he wanted to hurt me? What if Peggy had confessed her love for me? He was shorter than me, but he looked strong. He could have set it all up. He could have forced Peggy to telephone me, creating this trap...

Francis glanced up, and gave me a cheerful smile.

He was handsome, damn him. I had convinced myself in his absence that he was too short for her, his features too nondescript to be interesting. But no – he was film star perfect.

I ventured into the warmth of the café.

'Mr Thomas! Thank you for coming at such short notice.' He nodded to a stool on the other side of the room to where I usually sat. I felt wrong-footed, viewing the place from this angle.

'You're welcome. It's no trouble.'

'Tea? Coffee? Or one of these milkshakes?'

'Black coffee, please.'

'I don't know...' Francis shook his head as the poured the coffee. 'Peggy told me that these milkshakes would sell. I must admit, I had no faith at all. But goodness! People can't seem to get enough of them! I'm a cup-of-tea man myself, you see. Every time.'

'Me, too,' I answered, hoarsely. I still had no inkling whether he knew about what had happened on Friday. The milkshake, the meeting of fingers. Was he playing with me?

'Is Mrs Phyllip here?'

'She's in the back, sorting. She doesn't feel well, so she asked me to come in and give her a hand.'

'Oh.'

She was there, then, behind that door. I could not see or hear her, but she was close. Was she listening to us?

'She wouldn't ask for help unless she really needs it. She knows how much I hate shutting up the shop.'

The Brylcreem in his hair shone under the café lights.

'Why...' I started, and Francis shook his head, as if stirring himself from a dream.

'I'm sorry. I should have explained straightaway. We'd like to put the café on the market.'

I squeezed the handle on my cup between thumb and forefinger. 'Oh! Well... Of course...'

'We'll be shutting today, at the end of the day. Peggy is loading the boxes.'

'Today?' I spat, hearing the panic in my own voice. 'But you're doing so well!'

Francis smiled, showing a set of perfect teeth. 'The café has been a success. But I miss my wife, and she wants to come home...'

'Are you sure?'

Francis paused, and looked at me, puzzled at the edge in my voice, and his answer was calm and quiet. 'She hasn't been happy here since the very beginning. We had decided back in spring that we would sell up after a summer season. The café is making a far better profit than it used to, and I expect that to be reflected in its price.'

'Of course.'

She had been unhappy. She had longed for her husband and home. I had not been enough to make her want to stay.

'It was a test, I suppose, and a successful one. Yes, we want to sell the café, but I can hardly complain that my wife wants to be with me, can I?'

He laughed lightly. I wanted to punch him.

The kitchen door opened, and there she stood. My Peggy. She wore her hair in a long plait down her back, so different to what I had seen before. She paused for a second, then smiled weakly and hurried to fetch a bowl from the shelf.

But she had not managed to disguise her first reaction to seeing me. Disappointment. Distaste.

The café sold almost immediately, for a sum considerably higher than had been paid for it the year before. Peggy returned to her comfortable, safe life in the shop in Llanegryn. I left Tywyn a few months later, looking for a new life, a new feeling. Slowly, the redness of the scars she had left upon me faded, and gradually, whole days passed without me thinking of her.

And yet, in the darkest parts of my heart, the memory of the pain I had felt upon seeing a sweet smile exchanged between husband and wife remained. Sometimes, between sleep and wakefulness, the taste of peanut butter and honey would return to my tongue, and I would recall her long fingers.

I would remember.

Susan Vaughan
The Reverend's daughter
1970

Llanegryn Curry

8oz diced chicken breast
sliced mushrooms
sliced red pepper
2 chopped onions
thumb-sized piece of ginger peeled and grated
lime juice
12 fl oz single cream
1 tsp brown sugar
fresh coriander
1 tsp dried coriander
1 tsp dried cumin
1 tsp dried turmeric
chilli, to taste

fry the chicken with the onion for a few
minutes until the meat is browned and the
onion softened. Add the mushrooms and red
pepper, and cook for a further few minutes. Add
the ginger, the lime juice, the sugar and spices,
and stir well. Add the cream, and simmer →

for a few minutes. Stir in the chopped coriander before serving.

After Huw Shop left, I would pick at the scars he had made by walking the same paths that we had wandered together, re-living old conversations, poring over memories of past touches that had turned into ghosts when he left Llan. If I sat by the river on the small bridge in the common, I could see his bedroom window, the sky reflected upon it. I knew he was no longer there, but a part of me still clung to the hope that I would see him.

It was a moping kind of afternoon in an Indian summer, the threat of autumn abated for a week or so, warming the village as if it was July. Huw had been gone for a month, but I could not forget him. The memory of him seemed to get more powerful with every promise I made to myself that I would remove him from my mind.

'It wouldn't be fair on you to carry on,' he had said as we walked up the Black Road six weeks before. A cruel, feeble excuse. 'Manchester is another world, Susie, and I don't know how often I'll be able to come home to see you.'

'But it's always been you and me!' I turned to look at him, his pale face and dark hair separating me from my favourite view, down to the seaside in Tywyn. My favourite place, ruined by the words of my lover. I would never again be able to struggle up the steep incline of the road and enjoy the bleakness of the high ground without seeing his mouth twisting around cruel, severe words. I wouldn't be able to stand at the highest spot and look down at Llan, Bryncrug, Tywyn, the river snaking its way into the sea without feeling a twist of pain that he had brought me here, to this most sacred of places, to leave me.

'And you know how much I adore you,' Huw said, running his fingers through his hair. 'But I'm moving away...'

'You don't have to!' I pleaded, hating the desperate tone of my voice. 'You belong here!'

'But... I don't think I want to be here anymore. I've been bored here since leaving school, with nothing to do...'

'You work in the shop! A good, reliable business...'

'I don't want to be a shopkeeper like my dad and grandfather. I want to break the pattern.'

'You could have helped your mother with the café! It was too much for her to handle on her own.'

Huw looked away. He was already wearing his city clothes, though he was not there yet – a colourful striped shirt and velveteen flares. He didn't look like my Huw at all.

'Go, then!' I spat, venomously, losing all dignity as I hurried down the hill. 'Go to the girls in mini-skirts, go to a place where nobody knows you, nobody cares about you. Bloody fool!' And though he shouted my name, I didn't turn back, running away from him as fast as I could until the air hurt my lungs. I went straight to the chapel, where my father was tidying the hymn books after the service. He was still wearing his collar.

'What is it, Susie?' he asked.

'He's finished with me.'

The river of tears came as soon as I sank into his comforting arms. I planted my face in my father's shoulder, and regretted that Huw Shop had ever been born.

It would have been easier if I had more reason to hate him. But I didn't. Apart from the abandonment, he was a wonderful man. I had loved him always, and reaching back into my store of memories, he always featured in the sweetest ones. From that first kiss behind the wall of the chapel to the tender touches on my soft flesh, he had been gentle with me since he'd been old enough to share his toys.

He wasn't like other people: Not over-emotional or easily riled like other boys his age. My school friends came to the conclusion that he was either odd or weak, but I saw the strength of a rock in his choice words and straight face. He lived his life to a familiar pattern, and became uneasy when anything changed. One kind word from Huw equalled a novel of clichés from any other boy.

I watched him once, at the football ground in a neighbouring village, as we sat at opposite sides of the pitch to one another. As the players argued and scored, sprinted and fought, the spectators reacted instinctively – on their feet, gesturing, screaming at the referee, their loyalty to their team boiling the blood in their veins. Huw was different. He stood amidst his friends, his hands deep in his pockets, his eyes fixed on the game. No arguing, no exclamations, not a smile or a grimace. Their boyish, immature behaviour was beneath him. Only I could touch him.

A few hours after the football game, as we lay on a bed of moss in a copse on the bank of the Dysynni, Huw traced his finger gently down the flesh of my bare arm, and said simply, 'I love you, Susie.' And though I had said the same to him a hundred times before, and though such words should never count after making love, I believed him.

This sort of love was unfamiliar to me. My parents were friends, and I doubted if they had ever felt the fire that existed between Huw and I. I was born to be beside him.

My mind insisted on wandering back to the Black Road as I sat by the river in the common, the only pale, weak thing in that tangle of moss and grass and leaves. The kitchen window of Huw's home was wide open , and I could hear his mother singing 'The Shepherd of Aberdovey' as she went about her work. The melancholy melody suited my mood perfectly.

I rose, and wandered slowly along the path. My mother had insisted that I help her with the groceries, though I hated going anywhere near the shop now that the memory of Huw tarnished the place. Damn him. Though he was far away in a bustling city, he still managed to ruin things for me.

Mam was filling her basket by the time I reached Phyllip's shop, and she looked up as I moped in. Francis smiled, too, a sweet, hopeful smile. I had never seen him in a bad temper.

'How are you, Susan?'

'Very well, thank you, Mr Phyllip.'

'Been for another walk?' asked my mother as she put a tin of salmon into her basket. 'The soles of your feet will wear thin if you carry on walking so much.'

'Well, it's perfect weather for a stroll, isn't it?' interjected Francis. 'Winter will be here soon, and we'll all want to be indoors.'

'That's true enough,' Mam agreed. 'Jack will be in to settle the bill tomorrow.'

'There we are. Now, you both go through to the kitchen. Peggy will tell me off if I don't insist. I'll come to fetch my tea in a minute. She's been baking biscuits, and she said I wasn't allowed one until you came...'

I didn't want to go. I would have to see the table at which we used to sit, the plates we ate from, the cups in which Huw took his tea. Milk and two sugars. But I did not dare refuse. I didn't want to make a fuss, didn't want them to know how much it hurt.

Peggy sat by the kitchen table, completely engrossed in a magazine. Her hair was tied messily on the back of her head, and I thought, for the hundredth time, how odd it was that she and my mother came to be best friends. Mam was always so well groomed, and Peggy didn't care at all about her hair, and she never wore make-up.

'Isn't it an easy life for some, flicking through magazines all day,' Mam said with a grin. Peggy leapt to her feet, and switched on the kettle.

'I can't tell you how wonderful it is to be home after slaving in that café for so long. I don't think I so much as glanced in a magazine for a whole year. Sit. I'll make tea. There are biscuits, too, if you like. A cinnamon recipe, from the newspaper, but I think they'd be nicer with a few nuts thrown in.'

Mam and I sat by the table, watching Peggy prepare the tea. I gazed at her face as she poured the boiling water into the teapot. She had the same lips as Huw – Thin and raspberry-coloured.

'How are you, Susie?' she asked. I didn't know how to answer.

'Longing for him, as am I, I'm sure. He was told off for upsetting you, you know,' she added, gently, her sympathetic grey eyes on mine.

'I'm all right,' I said, hoarsely.

'No, you're not,' Mam said with a sigh. 'You're not all right. You need something to do, Susie, to take your mind off everything. You could go to college...'

'I don't want to.'

Marrying Huw and bearing his children had been my lifelong plan. I had no other ambition but to be beside him. I had never considered an alternative.

'I don't blame you,' said Peggy, setting the cups of tea on the table before us. 'I'd be no better off having read more books, to be honest. And tell me the truth, Annie, do you think you would have learned more by going to college? I'm talking about the important things, now, the things that are of use to us, day to day.'

Though I was heartbroken, Peggy managed to raise a smile in me. She was never afraid to disagree.

'But you and I had other things to do, didn't we Peg? You worked in the shop, and I had to keep the vestry and chapel clean and tidy.'

'Susie will find her own way, as we all do.' Peggy smiled at me. 'And we mustn't talk about her as if she isn't here.'

I forgot my grief, for a while, in the easy, amusing chatter between Mam and Peggy. My childhood had been narrated by these voices. As I had played with Huw and his Matchbox cars in that corner of the kitchen, our mothers had chatted and laughed.

'Look at what I've been reading,' said Peggy, passing her magazine across the table to Mam and I. I looked at the large black and white picture of a dark-skinned boy, a hopeless look on his beautiful face, and the headline written in bold print: 'Who Will Love This Child?'

'I didn't bring my glasses,' Mam murmured, hating to be reminded that her sight was deteriorating. 'What's it about?'

'It's all about the children in the cities,' explained Peggy. 'The black children in the orphanages. Most of them stay there until they're grown... People who are looking to adopt are usually white, and they want children who look like themselves.' Peggy shook her head. 'So these are the children who are left behind, who live their whole life without parents. It's terrible.'

'I'm sure the chapel committee made a donation to that kind of charity last year...' said Mam.

'Well, that's great, but money isn't going to sing lullabies to them, or wrap them up safe in their beds at night, is it?'

Mum sniffed, offended. 'I worked very hard to raise that money, what with the coffee mornings and the whist drives...'

'Oh, don't take it to heart, Annie,' Peggy said, quickly. 'Of course, you did your best, as you always do. And I'm sure that money made a difference. What I meant was...well...I'm not too sure myself, to be honest.' She wrapped her thin fingers around her cup, and said slowly, 'I'm just thinking that I could perhaps help in a more practical sense...'

Mam set her cup back onto the table, indicating the seriousness of the subject. 'Peggy, you're not thinking of taking in one of these children?'

'Keep your voice down!' Peggy hissed. 'I haven't mentioned it to Francis yet. He has a lot more common sense than I do...'

'But...' Mam touched her hair, as she always did when she was lost for words. 'You can't bring a black child to a village in the middle of the Welsh countryside!'

'Why not?'

'Well, he'll get teased...'

Peggy shook her head and waved away the objection, as if it was nothing more than a house fly in her face. 'People pick on children for all sorts of reasons.'

Mam sighed, but she didn't say another word. She knew, as I did, how determined Peggy could be, and that she wouldn't change her mind.

'Francis won't let me, anyway,' said Peggy, tracing her index finger along the lip of her cup thoughtfully. Though I was only eighteen, I knew better. It was clear from the smile that shadowed his lips when his wife was around that Francis adored her. He would do anything to please her. When she had gone to Tywyn to run the café on the seafront, leaving him every morning, the whole village became concerned that the sparkle in his eyes and the lightness in his voice had gone with her. Selling the café and returning her to him became a matter of urgency. Francis would share his home with all the orphans in the world if it pleased her.

'Peggy...' Mam began again, but she was muted by the look on her friend's face. Peggy gripped the handle of her cup tightly, and her eyes became serious.

'I need something good,' she said in a low voice, and a new idea came to my mind that perhaps I did not know Peggy at all.

In my memory, it feels as if Jonathan arrived the very next day, though, of course, it wasn't that simple. Peggy and Francis travelled to Liverpool twice (Huw had travelled there from Manchester and had met them for lunch. I pictured the scene, imagined the cafe, what clothes Huw had hung upon his muscled frame, what he had eaten...) Half the village were on their doorsteps when Francis' blue van arrived back, the words 'F. Phyllip, Grocer' in italic writing on the paintwork. I had been walking, again, on the common and up the narrow lane to the church before turning back to the village, my ankles dotted by stinging nettles.

I was walking down the road which snaked through the village when the van passed, and spied the three faces inside: Peggy, thin and pale, and Francis, square and masculine, and between them the round, brown face of a five-year-old boy. Peggy waved at me enthusiastically as they passed, flashing her teeth in a grin.

She looked happy.

Mam and I were invited to the shop for a cup of tea the following day.

'Invited!' exclaimed my mother with a cackle. 'Peg never did anything but order me over there before now!'

Still, Mam wore one of her Sunday dresses for the visit, as if a small boy would care about her clothes.

The smell came like a ribbon down the street to meet us. Something new, something different. Until that second, everything in my life had been safe and familiar, but I could never overestimate the feeling of a brand new smell, the boundaries of my experiences demolished.

It was like finding a new colour.

'What's that stink?' Mam asked as the smell became more pungent, but I didn't answer her. It was enchanting and wonderful to me, making me ravenous though I had not long eaten. How could something smell sweet and sour at the same time?

The shop was thick with the new smell, like an invisible fog blanketing the place. I could have stayed there all day.

'...And the cat has thrown up *three times* since this stench came...' Mrs Llewelyn stood by the till, pointing an accusatory finger at Francis, though she was almost half his size. Her cheeks were rouged by bad temper. 'And the whole street is complaining, I'll have you know. I'm surprised nobody has called the police about it!'

Francis smiled serenely at us.

'Go through to the kitchen. They're waiting for you.' He turned back to Mrs Llewelyn. 'I'm afraid there's nothing I can do about the smell. Peggy has to cook, doesn't she..?'

'Foreign muck!' spat the old woman, as she crossed her arms under her hanging breasts. 'I knew it'd be like this! You start taking people from their natural habitat, and standards begin to slip...'

At the utterance of those words, I felt something stirring in the ashes where my heart had been. Something was returning, a flash of the soul that I had presumed stolen by Huw.

'Mr Phyllip?' I said before disappearing through to the kitchen. Francis looked up, surprised that I was interrupting the argument. 'I was just thinking how lovely the scent is in the shop today. I hope you'll be stocking whatever ingredients Mrs Phyllip is using. I'm sure that many people in Llan will want to make use of them.'

Mrs Llewellyn stared at me, her mouth like a cat's behind.

'And also, somebody's letting their cat vomit all over the pavement. It really isn't hygienic. If you find out who it is, please let me know so that I can mention it to that nice young policeman.'

Francis bit his lip to supress a smile. Huw used to do exactly the same.

'Thank you, Susie. I'll see what I can do.'

Peggy was pouring the tea when I walked through to the kitchen, and Mam was sitting by the table, watching the little boy pulling a wooden train along the windowsill. He was breathtakingly pretty, eyes the colour of the dresser in the kitchen, and skin like milk chocolate. His lips were thick and full, and his hair like a sponge on his head.

He looked up when I walked in.

I fell in love with him immediately.

'Hello,' I said, before Peggy had the chance to introduce us. 'I'm Susan. But you can call me Susie, if you like.' It felt odd to speak English, here in this kitchen, where Welsh had always reigned so naturally.

He didn't look too sure of me, but he still answered. 'I'm Jonathan. I live here now.'

I padded across the room, and sat cross-legged on the floor beside him.

'I like your train.'

'Peggy got it for me,' he answered, his Liverpool accent thick on his tongue. 'She and Francis got me lots of clothes, and some toy cars, too. I got the Shell Oil lorry, a massive big one. The doors open and everything!'

'Goodness,' I exclaimed, mimicking his enthusiasm. 'I've never seen one with real doors on it before.'

The smile I was awarded by Peggy as she brought me my tea made her look like a stranger – a smile that reached her whole body, somehow.

'Good girl, Susie,' she said quietly, before returning to the table where Mam sat eyeing me thoughtfully.

I became a child again that afternoon. Jonathan and I left Peggy and Mam to chatter over endless cups of tea as we played with the lorry and the train, created imaginary battles between the tin soldiers that had been found, dusty and forgotten, under Huw's bed. Jonathan could become lost in his imagination, and sometimes I would watch his face as he pretended to be a soldier, stabbing the bayonet into the Shell lorry... He forgot himself, forgot his new home and the insecurities of a new family. It was a wonderful sight.

'As much as you seem to be enjoying yourself, Susie, we'll have to go home,' said Mam after a few hours. 'Your father will be wanting his tea, and I haven't even thought what to make yet.'

I rose to my feet, and Jonathan watched me. I smiled at him, and he returned the gesture shyly.

'This smell is wonderful, Auntie Peggy,' I said, watching the steam rising from the pots and clouding the window. 'What is it?'

'I was just telling your mother,' she answered, looking doubtfully into the largest saucepan. 'I want Jonathan to feel right at home, so I bought plenty of ingredients, enough to feed the masses, whilst we were in the city. If the masses are happy to eat curry, that is. I want him to eat the things he had at home, the things that are a part of his culture. Food can be such a comfort, can't it? And although he's as polite as can be, he hasn't tasted a single thing since he arrived.' Peggy shook her head, her forehead creased with worry. 'I must have got the recipe wrong.'

'How does it taste?' I asked, gazing into the pot. It looked like some kind of soup, the sauce a watery custard consistency, with meat and vegetables floating in it.

'We're not terribly keen,' Peggy confessed. 'Taste it, Susie, and see what you think.' She fetched a spoon from the drawer and offered it to me. 'You're a good cook, maybe you'll have an idea as to what I can do to improve it.'

I dipped the spoon into the scented sauce, and lifted it to my face. The smell was unfamiliar, odd here in Peggy's messy kitchen in Llan.

I tasted the curry, chewed the chicken, and swallowed.

It was divine. Salty and sweet, creamy and fresh and completely different to anything I'd ever tasted before.

I immediately reached for another spoonful.

Peggy laughed behind me. 'I think she likes it.'

'It's lovely, Auntie Peggy,' I sighed with pleasure. 'I've never tasted anything like it before.'

'You might as well take it with you,' she answered hopelessly. 'We've hardly touched it.'

'Do you have the recipe? May I have it?'

'Yes, yes, of course. All sorts of spices, and ginger, and onions.' She filled a huge bowl of the concoction for me to take home with me. 'The recipe in the magazine asked for coconut milk, but I couldn't find any, so I've used cream and a bit of sugar. And a bit of the coconut block we have in the shop. The same one I use to make macaroons.'

'Will you write the recipe out for me sometime?' I pleaded. 'I might be able to order the spices through the post...'

'I bought a box full of them, my love. And it doesn't look as if they'll get used up. You're welcome to them.'

As we said goodbye, Jonathan left his toys on the window sill, and pulled on my sleeve as if he had an important secret to impart.

I kneeled beside him, and he cupped my ear with his small hands, and whispered, 'Will you come and play with me again, please, Susie?'

'Of course!' I answered, delighted to have pleased the child. 'Maybe, if Peggy says it's all right, I can take you for a walk. There's a common, and a river, and lots of fields, and other children I can introduce you to.'

He smiled, showing his dainty white teeth shining in the middle of his beautiful brown face.

I don't know what was responsible. Was it the curry, a new smell and taste, that soothed my wounded soul, or Jonathan, the little boy who became as besotted with me as I was with him, and his wide-eyed wonder at the things I had taken for granted, the details of my humdrum life. He was fascinated by the fish in the river, the voles in the garden, the slow worms lounging under the sun in the fields. I became someone new in his company, developing a core that was solid as Bird Rock.

Amid discussion and plotting between Mam and Peggy, I was asked to mind Jonathan for three days a week, to try and teach him some Welsh – a plan that pleased Peggy, as she wanted him to be able to converse, at least, by the time he started school. It suited my mother, too. It gave me a purpose, a job, and put a certain responsibility on me that she thought would be beneficial.

Almost a fortnight after Jonathan had arrived, we set out from the shop, a picnic wrapped safely in my backpack. It was one of those kind days between summer and autumn, before the leaves had blushed but after they had started to dry, and the sharp breeze had begun to blow away their vivid green.

Jonathan and I walked the lane towards Bird Rock. He picked the wildflowers from the verges and stuffed them into his pockets, whilst I offered a narrative of Welsh words for him: 'Look, Jonathan

– It's a *deryn* – a bird!' or 'Look at that *mynydd* – that mountain!' He accepted the new words without question, taking an interest in everything. Some of the words he didn't even know in English, because he'd never come across an *aradr* – a plough, or *eithin* – gorse. He looked so small in the flat-bottomed bowl of the valley, gazing up at the farmhouses as though they were mansions. I don't know whether this quiet place had ever seen a boy like him before, and yet he looked so right, the lovely earthy colour of his face and hands against the green of fields and forests.

'It's such a big place!' he said, looking down the valley towards Cadair Idris, looming like a knife point in the distance. He meant, I suppose, that it was a big place to be so empty – only a few farms dotted the fields and they crouched, nestling in the corners of fields and the shades of hills and crags. To me, the city from which Jonathan had come was far bigger, a never-ending expanse of claustrophobic criss-crossed streets.

After climbing the gate to Big Rock Field, Jonathan and I settled on a large, flat stone, and I reached for the picnic that Peggy had prepared for us. I opened the greaseproof paper carefully. Beef in curry powder, flat bread, raw onion, sliced thinly. It didn't look appetising, even with my increasingly adventurous palate. Peggy had taken to smothering everything in curry powder, thinking that it was what Jonathan was used to, though I had always thought that curry was Indian, and Jonathan's heritage was African.

Jonathan picked at the bread, but he didn't touch anything else.

'You haven't eaten much since you got here, Jonathan. Do you not like the food?'

He turned his eyes away, but nodded. 'Yes, thank you,' he answered in his thick accent. 'It's very nice.'

'You know, you can ask Peggy for anything, and she'll cook it for you. They do have a shop, after all.'

I chewed on a piece of beef, and tried not to grimace as I tasted the powder, thick like flour on it.

'Can we go fishing one day?' asked Jonathan.

'Of course! I like fish – it's *pysgod*, in Welsh. I'm sure my father has a rod and a net somewhere that we could *menthyg* – that means borrow.'

At the end of the afternoon, I was tired but triumphant after witnessing Jonathan's first Welsh word ('Look, Susie! It's a *deryn*!' as he spied a heron rising, as if heaven-bound, from the river). I took the boy to my home for the first time. My brother, who had long flown the nest, had left a box of toys under his bed. There was a bag of marbles that I was sure Jonathan would find enchanting.

The house was quiet. Dad was in his study, and Mam was weeding in the back garden. I fetched the marbles.

Jonathan wandered from room to room, staring at the pictures on the walls and the ornaments on the shelves.

'Your house is dead posh,' he said, quietly respectful.

'My mother loves cleaning,' I explained with a grin. I much preferred the homely chaos of Jonathan's home than the impersonal clean lines of Rose Cottage.

'Look, Jonathan, *bwyd*. Food. Two minutes, then I'll take you home.'

He followed me into the kitchen, watched as I lifted the lid of the pan.

'Did you cook it?' he asked, and I nodded.

'I put the meat and vegetables in this morning with a splash of water, and it's been simmering all day. It's just about ready now. It's a kind of stew... We call it *lobsgows*.'

'Lobscouse?' asked Jonathan, with a hint of something I had not heard before in his gentle voice. 'We had that in Liverpool.' He swallowed, and gazed up at me with those wood-coloured eyes. 'It was my favourite.'

'*Lobsgows* is your favourite?' I repeated in disbelief. Jonathan nodded.

'Sit by the table, *cariad*, my love,' I commanded, reaching for a bowl. I half-filled it with the stew. The beef had melted into soft pieces, and I reached for a spoon. The food disappeared within a few minutes. I refilled the bowl.

I watched the small boy devouring, grasping the spoon tightly in his mouth lest he lost a drop. I sliced two thick pieces of bread, freshly baked that morning, and spread butter thickly upon them. He ate it all. I had made a fruit cake the previous day. He ate two slices of that, too.

I smiled triumphantly. He had eaten!

I settled in the chair beside him. 'What other foods do you like, Jonathan?'

'Chips! And suet pie, especially with chicken. Toad-in-the-hole. Sunday roast. And once, in the home, we had pork with crackling. It was brilliant.'

His eyes widened with the memory.

I laughed gently. 'Why didn't you tell Peggy, *cariad*, my love? She's been making all this curry thinking it's what you're used to...'

Jonathan stared at me in confusion. 'Why would she think that? I'm from Liverpool!'

Peggy and Francis were stacking tins onto the shelves when I walked into the shop behind Jonathan, and they both greeted him warmly.

'Did you have a nice day?' asked Peggy in heavily accented English. Jonathan nodded, opening his fist.

'Susie gave me these marbles!'

'Well, that's very kind.'

Francis smiles at me appreciatively. 'Thank you, Susie.'

'May I play with them in the kitchen, please?'

'Of course, but don't put them in your mouth!'

After he had disappeared into the kitchen, I stood, silent and still, and Francis and Peggy stared at my victorious grin, expecting me to explain myself.

'Well?' Peggy asked finally.

'He ate a great deal today, Auntie Peggy.'

She stared at me, agog. 'Of that picnic I made?'

'No. The lobsgows I had at home.' Peggy shook her head in disbelief. 'Honestly! And some fruit cake. And when I asked him what he liked to eat, do you know what he said? Roast dinner, and toad-in-the-hole, and that sort of thing!'

'But why didn't he just tell us?' asked Francis.

'He was probably trying to please you. But honestly, he has a good appetite for nice, home-cooked food. Exactly what you'd usually make.'

Peggy's face broke into a smile, and she sighed with relief. 'Susie, you're worth your weight in gold, you really are. Jonathan! Come in here for a minute!'

Within seconds, Jonathan was back in the shop, a blue marble playing between his thumb and forefinger.

'Jonathan, is there anything in the shop you fancy to eat?' asked Francis kindly.

'No, thank you,' answered Jonathan, with an edge of nervousness to his voice.

'Don't worry, *cariad*, my love. I've told them about the food you like, and, to tell you the truth, I think that Francis is relieved that he won't have to eat any more curry.' I smiled at his anxious little face. 'They just want to know what you like, so that they can fill up your belly.'

Jonathan walked around the shop slowly, gazing at the shelves around him, as if he was facing an army. 'I like corned beef. And peas. And anything with Heinz Tomato Ketchup. I like baked beans... I think I like most things in here, you know.'

Peggy laughed with relief.

'And I like Mars Bars,' he added abashedly.

Francis bellowed a belly laugh, and passed a chocolate bar to his new son. He smiled a contented, easy grin.

'Did you like the lobscouse that Susie made?' asked Peggy as Jonathan tore the wrapper from the chocolate.

'It was lovely, *cariad*, my love,' he answered, before taking a generous bite.

Huw Phyllip
Peggy's Son
1976

Plum Tart

8 plums   2 egg yolks
8oz plain flour   4oz cold butter
4oz dark muscovado sugar

Beat the eggs [yolks] with four tablespoonfuls
of cold water. Rub the butter into the
flour. Slowly mix in the egg. You may
not need it all. Roll out the pastry and
cut it into a disc.

Halve the plums and remove the stones.
Fry them with the sugar and about 2oz
water in an ovenproof dish. When the
water has begun to thicken, place the pastry
over the fruit, and bake for about 25
minutes. When removed from the oven,
turn the tart out onto a plate so that
the pastry is at the bottom.

Serve warm, with cream.

Once, when I was eight or nine years old, my mother took me to the hairdresser in Tywyn. Before then, she had cut her own hair and mine with the aid of nail scissors and a black plastic comb. Dad would cut his own hair over the sink with a razor blade, leaving tails of black hair in the white porcelain.

It was Annie that convinced her, I think, when she pointed out the crooked parting where Mam's hair met her scalp in zig-zags, and the way my hair was starting to curl over my collar. Annie went for a shampoo and set every week, and kept her hair in a tidy little perm like the Queen, and somehow she convinced my careless, chaotic mother to pay someone to do our hair.

I didn't much care one way or the other, and my hair was buzzed short, like a soldier's, in a few minutes. I moved to one of the other chairs by the door as Mam took her turn.

My attention was stolen by a comic for a while, but when I glimpsed up, I pushed Roy of the Rovers aside and concentrated on my mother, face to face with herself in the looking glass. There was a stillness about her that I hadn't seen before, an emptiness in those familiar grey eyes.

The hairdresser busied herself around Mam, combing her long, dark hair until it fell like silk over her shoulders. I rarely saw her hair loose like that. It made her look like a wild woman, raised in the hills by wolves.

A kernel of fear hardened in my belly. She wasn't my mother, this effigy of a woman. A ghost had possessed her, had taken her place.

Patsy, the hairdresser, chatted incessantly as she straightened my mother's parting and reached for the glinting scissors, but Mam didn't react. She stared into her own eyes, her face as empty and emotionless as a corpse.

Patsy cut the first wisp of hair, and it sounded like something being torn. I watched the unwanted hair flutter to the ground, leaving a question mark on the white tiled floor.

My mother was still. The world spun around her.

Her eyes are the colour of stone, I realised suddenly, without having considered it before – the stone walls around Hare House, or the big rocks that jutted out from the water in the river. Perhaps that's what happened to her, I imagined – perhaps the stones in her eyes had throbbed and grown inside her, freezing her face and body, cold and devoid of feeling in the hairdresser's chair in Tywyn.

Her hair fell about her feet like feathers. I would have liked her to wear her hair loose, sometimes, instead of in the plait down her back or the bun at her nape. She looked younger, softer.

'Would you like me to tie it back for you?' asked Patsy, and Mam nodded gently. Without enquiring further, Patsy reached for the brush and for a long time, the pulled it rhythmically through my mother's hair. It looked out of place, to me, like something girls would do on the school yard at playtime, pathetic and child-like.

Patsy twisted my mother's hair, and pinned it high and tight, like a film star. She fixed it with a sweet spray of Elnett.

'There you are!' Patsy declared proudly. 'Do you like it?'

Mam nodded, looking dangerously like a stranger with her hair so grand. She stood up, and removed the black cloak from her shoulders.

'Are you sure?' Patsy bit her lip, made uncertain by my mother's lack of enthusiasm. 'I could do something different with it, if you like...'

'No,' Mam smiled tightly. 'It's perfect. How much do I owe you?'

In the car on the way home, I watched my mother eyeing herself in the rearview mirror, looking at the way a small change to her hair seemed to transform her into someone else.

She was the most beautiful woman I ever saw.

Between Tywyn and Llanegryn, she stopped the car by the old bridge and switched off the engine. I could hear the whisper of the river, the wail of the gulls.

She lifted her arms and removed each and every one of the pins that held her hair in place, and it fell, flowing like a flood around her shoulders. She combed through her hair with her fingers, before pulling an elastic band from her wrist and using it to tie her hair back, untidily, in a knot. She looked exactly as she had when we had left the shop that morning.

She started the engine, and started towards home.

'But it was so pretty!' I exclaimed from the back seat.

She glanced at me in the mirror, and smiled softly.

'It was, wasn't it? But I didn't feel like me, Huw. I looked too much like someone else.'

Some memories remain, always, at the surface of the mind, a comfort or a sharp blade of guilt to pore over at quiet moments. Others seem to hide in the shadows of the brain, before rising unexpectedly and stunning the imagination with their unexpected detail.

The memory of my mother at the hairdresser's was like that.

I didn't know that it was in my head until I left home and moved to Manchester, having decided that home was a fluid, foggy ideal. I had settled into city life with ease, and the years begun to separate Llanegryn and me. I became sure that Manchester was where I was meant to be, on the cold pavements, in the shadows of grey buildings.

In a crowded pub in the city centre one Saturday night, a young woman brushed passed me on her way to the bar, the smell of Elnett sweet in her hair. I was back at the hairdresser's shop in Tywyn, Mam gazing at herself in the looking glass. Question marks of hair on the floor, and my mother, still as a stone in the chair, looking and feeling like someone else.

'Can I buy you a drink?' I asked suddenly, my voice hoarse, as if letting the Elnett-scented girl escape would be letting the newfound memory go, too. I had never offered to buy a stranger a drink before. I had barely spoken to any women since arriving in the city, and I was certainly not looking for a girlfriend. I was happy in my own company.

'I'm doing rounds with my friends,' smiled the girl, her blue eyes shining under mascara lashes.

'That's a shame.'

'Are you from Wales?' she ventured in Welsh.

'Bloody hell... Yes! And you?' I answered in my mother tongue.

'Of course I bloody am!'

She flashed her teeth in a smile.

'Oh yes... Of course. How did you guess..?'

'You have a strong accent.'

The pub barked with sharp English consonants. I had not noticed then how soft the vowels of my language sounded.

'Where are you from?'

'Bethesda. But I've lived in Hulme for two years.'

'What brought you here?'

'Nursing. And... Well. City life.'

Weeks later, as she hid her nakedness under a thin cotton sheet on my bed, Maria confessed the truth as to why she had left her village. 'I thought I could leave myself there. Escape from every stain on my history, every memory.'

I stared at the shape of her body in the twilight of the room, inhaled the Elnett which arose from my pillow.

'I didn't think I had any roots at all. But it's not like that. I can't seem to escape from myself.'

I could not bear to confess that I understood her perfectly.

I could not say that I heard the Llan river whispering through my sleep, my mother's sweet voice singing softly in the confusion between sleep and wakefulness. Perhaps it was acceptable for man to long for his land, his country, his people, but it was somehow shameful for me to pine for my mother as I did.

Maria rose from the bed, and dressed herself. I swallowed my shock at seeing her naked body for the first time. The protruding bones of her shoulders. Small slack breasts above the lines of her ribs. A skeleton of a girl, her skin tight about her bones. I turned away, stunned by the lack of flesh on her body.

I shut my eyes as Maria washed and applied her make up, and I thought of Susie's naked body, of Susie washing herself in the river on a hot day, the trees above throwing lace patterns across her skin. The curve of the mountains echoed in her nudity, as if she was crafted as a tribute to the land: breasts and buttocks and pale, thick legs. A fullness to her stomach, comforting and yielding, and the triangle of hair between her legs soft as moss. Cheeks blushed by the sun, and the smile. Oh! That smile! The gap between her front teeth dizzyingly sexy.

Maria appeared in the doorway, her clothes loose on her frame, her hair perfectly pinned and Elnetted.

'What are you thinking?' Her painted lips widened into a smile. 'You looked like you were in another world.'

'I was remembering Llanegryn in summer,' I answered, aware that it was a white lie. Even without Maria to complicate my thoughts, I felt guilty for recalling Susie's soft skin after all these years. She was married now, and had two young children. I had forfeited my right to the gap between her teeth.

'Do you miss it?' Maria asked, and the question plunged like a blade into my gut. I could only nod my answer, and stun myself with the severity of my longing.

I waited almost a year before taking Maria to Llanegryn. Though I hadn't asked her yet, I knew that we would be married. She was like me... Full of faults, escaping from a nameless horror that she could not quite place. I saw such sorrow in her big, blue eyes, and though we had been together a year, there was a sense of mystery to her, as if she hid herself from me, as if there were parts of her that I was not allowed to know.

'I didn't think it would be like this,' said Maria, almost accusatory, from the passenger seat as we drove to Llanegryn. She was twitching with nerves as we left Tywyn and moved up the valley, the leaves blushing on the trees around us.

'Why? What did you expect?'

'I didn't think it would be so beautiful.'

I turned the car down the lane towards Llanegryn. Everything was the same.

There it was: the shop. 'F. Phyllip, Grocer' above the door, and the windows a kaleidescope of colour – boxes, packets and jars.

I switched off the engine and sighed. Why had I been so keen to escape from this place? What had made me think that city life could improve upon the comfort of my village?

The shop door opened, and two figures hurried out, stood smiling on the step. My parents. I glanced at Maria, who was smiling nervously, clutching at the hem of her skirt.

What would her first impressions be of them?

Dad, handsome and swarthy, with his constant unyielding smile. Mam, by his side, her hair greying to the same shade as her eyes, long thin arms and slim wrists, bony, pale fingers. I opened the door, and was greeted by a homely autumn breeze.

'Mam, Dad, this is Maria.'

Maria joined us, and I could not help but notice the quarter second of shock in my mother's eyes as she saw my girlfriend for the first time. It was rare for Mam, she was adept at hiding her feelings. She reached for Maria's hand, and smiled warmly. A soft wind danced though her hair, and I shivered.

'Maria and I are going for a walk,' I announced over the breakfast table. 'Does anyone want to come? Jonathan?'

My brother shook his head, his mouth full of toast. He swallowed, and took a swig of milk from his glass. 'I'm making the pudding today, and I'm going to do something special because you and Maria are here.'

He grinned, showing his teeth, before standing up and taking his dishes to the sink. He reached over Mam's shoulder to steal one of the carrots she was peeling, and smiled sweetly as she raised an eyebrow at him. At twelve years old, he was already taller than her, and loyal as a sheepdog. He would sit by the kitchen table each afternoon, pretending to do his homework as they chatted and laughed.

Perhaps it would have been natural for me to feel envy towards their closeness, but, in truth, my brother's arrival was a relief to me. I was relieved of my responsibilities as an only child. What did it matter that I had run away to the city? Jonathan was so sweet-natured, so gentle, and he seemed perfectly suited to a small village community. Better suited than I had ever been, perhaps. I did not return home often enough to know whether he had suffered our mother in one of her dark periods. I didn't even know if she still suffered from those bouts of melancholy.

Maria and I pulled on our coats, and left the shop. Dad was whisking ice cream in a big blue bowl, with cherries like balls of flesh within it. He waved at us as we went.

We walked through the village in silence, arm in arm in the cold wind. Maria did not say a word until we left the village on the lane, Bird Rock jutting proudly in the distance.

'How could you ever leave such a place?' she asked quietly.

'I wanted to belong to somewhere new.'

'And do you?'

I stopped suddenly, floored by the question. Did I belong to anywhere but here?

'You. I belong to you.'

She smiled. She looked out of place here. Two worlds meeting

186

gently. She was meant to be in the city, as I was, lit orange by streetlights, her hair the only sunshine in a grey place.

We resumed walking. Since I had made the city my home, my visits to Llanegryn would stun me with the vividness of their colour: the fields of green, the bright blue sky, the pure white of the feathers which had escaped the backs of the seagulls. It was autumn, and the valley bled its colours, red and orange and bright yellow, onto the lanes.

'I like your mother,' said Maria. 'She's not as I expected her to be.'

'In what way?'

'I don't know, exactly. I had an image in my head of a short, round, red-cheeked woman. She's more...mysterious than I expected.'

'Isn't everyone?'

Maria cocked her head in thought, before answering. 'No, not everyone. Sometimes, I see something in your mother's eyes. It makes me wonder whether she likes me.'

'Of course she likes you.'

But I knew what she meant.

I would catch my mother glimpsing Maria, and see something close to fear in her eyes. At meal times, certainly, she watched Maria pushing a single potato around her plate, before setting her knife and fork down tidily and claiming to be full. When Maria wasn't looking, Mam would stare at her face, her bony arms and wrists.

'Have you argued with you mother, Huw?'

I swallowed. 'What makes you ask that?'

Maria chose her words carefully. 'Something between you. I can't put my finger on it.'

'No, there's never been an argument. But...'

'You don't have to tell me,' Maria comforted after I paused.

'She wasn't very well as I was growing up.'

'What was the matter with her?'

'I'm not sure. A darkness would come to her every now and again. I think she feels guilty for it now.'

Maria nodded, as if she understood. I felt a breeze of relief at unloading a small, significant secret that had been like a thorn in me.

'You didn't make this!' I exclaimed as Jonathan carried the plate proudly to the table. 'Don't lie!'

'I did,' he answered, setting the plate in the centre of the table ceremoniously, pleased at the fuss. 'It's easy.'

'He's very good in the kitchen, you know,' Dad interjected proudly. 'He helps me with the ice cream, and he does seem to have a talent for it. What was that flavour you came up with?'

'Lemon and ginger,' he answered proudly, slicing large pieces of the plum tart and placing them tidily on plates. He added a spoonful of thick cream to each one, a cloud at their edges.

'Well, thank you very much!' I said, picking up my fork and eating.

The tart was delicious: golden brown, soft pastry, fruit that tasted of summer, a caramel that was sweet enough to set my teeth on edge. A perfect balance between fruit and sugar.

'Good God,' I said, utterly sincere, now. 'This really is lovely, Jonathan.'

He grinned through a mouthful of pudding. I looked at Mam to see her reaction, but she wasn't looking at me. No, she stared at Maria, a nightmare unfolding on her face.

I turned to look at my girlfriend. She looked as if her heart was breaking, as if the piece of tart on her fork was poisoned. I tried to swallow my concerns, pretending the fear wasn't there.

Damn my mother for showing me Maria's weaknesses. Damn her for staring at her so sympathetically over the table. Damn her for making me think, for making me tot up the clues that had been there since the very beginning.

Maria was *very* thin.

I remembered the first time I had seen her naked body, the edges of her frame like cliffs upon her. I had grown used to her shape, now, and her excuses: 'I've already eaten'; 'I had a huge breakfast'; 'I don't feel very well.'

I watched as she ate every morsel of that plum tart, finishing ten minutes after everyone else. She looked as if part of her had died.

'It was great, Jonathan,' she said in a half-whisper. 'Thank you. And thank you, Mrs Phyllip. Excuse me, please.' She stood up, and disappeared upstairs.

'I'd better go to the shop,' said Dad, rubbing his stomach with satisfaction. 'Though I really could sleep after that feast. Thanks, Peg. Thanks, Jonathan.'

'You go and watch telly for a while,' Mam told Jonathan after Dad had gone, and he left Mam and I facing each other over the table. The remains of the plum tart was between us, red and glistening like a battleground lost.

'Maria is a sweet girl,' said Mam, sadly. 'My heart bleeds for her.'

I stared at my mother and felt the urge, for the first time, to really hurt her. Punch and kick, scratch and spit. I would not have realised that Maria was unwell had I not brought her home. Had I not seen my mother looking at her in that way.

Yes, I recognised all the excuses she had for not eating. I had heard them all when I was a boy.

'Can you see yourself reflected in her?' I spat, my voice venomous.

Mam looked down at the table, and nodded slowly. 'Yes. I can.'

'Mam... I don't want this. Not again.'

The edge had left my voice, and I felt defeated. As if I had already lost Maria.

'I'm sorry, Huw.' Mam raised her grey eyes to mine, and the

memory of those eyes in a rearview mirror, years ago, flashed into my mind. 'I'm sorry that you recognise that darkness in her.'

'Will it go? Can I get rid of it?'

She swallowed, unable to give an answer that would satisfy me. 'You can try.'

I stood up, and ran upstairs. Maria was not in her bedroom, and I tried the bathroom door. It was unlocked, and she stood before the looking glass, leaning over the sink. She stared at my reflection.

In the toilet bowl, the plum tart was like a bruise against the white porcelain where she had thrown up.

'I'm sorry. I had to get rid of it.'

I held her tightly in my arms. Now that I knew, it was painfully clear. Her jutting bones stabbed into my flesh, as if her body was battling my touch. But Maria wrapped her arms around me, and wept.

I could only hold her, and whisper that everything would be all right, and plant my face in her sweet Elnett-scented hair.

Annie Vaughan
Peggy's Best Friend
1987

Christmas Toast

4oz unsalted butter   2oz icing sugar

1oz honey   1½ tsp cinnamon

Pass the sugar through a sieve, then mix all the ingredients well.

Serve on toast, pancakes or crumpets.

I had never been brave. When I was a child, I had been afraid of everything – dogs, cats, darkness, the landing in our home.

Though I would never admit it, I was not much better as an adult. I eyed the shadows in Rose Cottage with trepidation, and lay awake in bed when I knew there was a corpse awaiting burial in the vestry across the road. I remained a child inside. My shell was ageing, wrinkling with the years, but my fear remained intact.

I never confessed it to Jack, knowing how pointless and baseless it was. Not until a Thursday afternoon in mid-October, when we had returned from the hospital. Our coats still on our backs, sitting by the kitchen table, Jack and I shared our first awkward silence.

'They were very positive,' Jack began, staring at my face. 'A very hopeful outlook. That's what you must remember, Annie. That's the part you must concentrate on.'

'Yes,' I agreed, wanly.

'And some people don't experience any side effects at all with the treatment! Well, you remember old Lewis, on a hell of a dose of chemotherapy and still out lambing!'

'Yes.'

'Courage, Annie, that's the thing. Being positive. If you believe everything will be all right, it *will* be all right...'

'But I'm not courageous, Jack,' I admitted, suddenly, my voice like a child's. 'I'm afraid of everything.'

'No!' Jack insisted, panic blushing his pale skin. He was frightened of my tears. 'I've never met such an able woman...'

'That's what you think,' I said, hearing the quake in my own voice, in my breast, in my stomach. 'You have no idea how afraid I am...'

I had known for years that Jack and I were friends, not lovers. The sweet and loving looks that were exchanged between Peggy and Francis did not exist between us, nor the long, languishing evening conversations. I loved him, yes, in a way. He was a good father, and a good husband. But sometimes I wondered how it

192

would feel to be worshipped, to be desired by the very instinct of a man. I had read the forbidden novels, had watched the late night films. I knew what love could be, and I knew that I had never been truly lost in anyone else.

It wasn't until that second, seeing the concern on his face, that I started to believe that perhaps Jack did love me, properly, warmly, devoutly.

I could not explain. Not now, when I knew that his fear was as great as mine. Exposing it would shake the foundations of who we were more than any cancer could.

'We have to be strong... And sensible...'

'Yes,' I agreed, tired, swallowing those words that I wanted to say. 'It's all right, Jack. I'm all right. I'll get through it.'

I stood slowly, and the chair groaned as it scraped the floor. I had always told the children off for doing that when they were younger.

'Are you going to call Susie?'

Of course. Susie. She would be waiting by the phone, waiting to hear what the doctor had said. She had tried to insist on coming with us to the hospital in Aberystwyth, and I'm sure Jack would have appreciated her soothing presence. But I could not allow it. I couldn't make a party out of a diagnosis in a grey, blank room.

'I'll phone Susie later on. When I've decided what to say.' I pulled the zip on my coat. 'I'm going to see Peggy.'

Jack nodded, but he didn't look away, as if he was expecting more.

'Is that all right?' I asked, quietly.

'Of course,' Jack answered, averting his eyes to the crumbs on the kitchen table. I left the kitchen, and left the Reverend's house. As I pulled the heavy oak door behind me, I felt guilty for abandoning Jack to the silence, leaving him alone to relieve the bruises in his mind.

The shop seemed dark after the bright light of day, and I stood inside the door for a few seconds, shivering. Peggy stood behind the counter, putting the orders into cardboard boxes. She froze when she saw me. We stood in silence, eye to eye.

'Come in, properly,' she ordered at last. 'You're shivering.'

I followed her through the shop and the dark stockroom, into the kitchen at the back. The remains of lunch were still on the table: half a loaf, a butter dish, a wedge of cheese, cracked and dry under the light.

'Stand by the Rayburn,' she commanded, switching on the kettle. 'I'll make tea.'

I stood, as I had done countless times before, with my back against the Rayburn, feeling its heat thawing me.

'Will you get better? Can they treat it?' Peggy asked over the wheeze of the kettle. No one but her had the right to ask in that way. From anyone else, the question would have been coarse and disgusting.

'They think so. But I'll have to have chemotherapy, and radiotherapy, and God knows what else...' I covered my eyes with my hands. 'I don't want to, Peggy.'

She was silent. I heard the click of the kettle, and the sound of water being poured into the teapot, the ugly, brown one she had inherited from her mother. I listened to the cups being placed on the table, the sugar bowl, the milk bottle.

'Sit down with me,' she insisted, gently, and I pulled my hands from my face and obeyed. She poured the tea, and opened the biscuit tin. She stirred a spoonful of sugar into my tea.

'What do you mean when you say you don't want to?' she asked, quietly.

I sighed, and felt the fear bubbling inside me, quaking the core of my body.

'I'm going to be so very ill, Peggy... Throwing up, and sweating, and losing sleep... For months and months... And I know it's a terrible thing to say, because at least they can treat it, but Peggy...'

I glanced up, and half expected to see disappointment or shock in those stony eyes, or tears, perhaps. But after staring at me for a while, Peggy moved her chair close to mine. She placed her thin hand over my swollen fingers, and silently, a relief rushed like adrenaline through my sickly body. I could tell her the truth, always, without chastisement or rebuke. I didn't have to be brave with her.

'It's all right,' she comforted.

'I'm scared, Peggy,' I admitted, in a half-whisper. 'Scared of the sickness, the injections, the poison, the hospital and the machines...'

'I'd feel exactly the same as you.'

'And I don't think that I want to suffer it all, Peggy. I could refuse the treatment, and let nature take its course... It isn't as though I'm a young girl with everything ahead of me... The children are all grown up...

Peggy thought about it for a while. Her eyes fixed through the wide window, watching the dark treetops swaying away their sunset-coloured leaves.

'I can understand why you think like that,' she answered, finally. 'But I think you should accept the treatment. Yes, you'll be ill, and yes, it is frightening. But I know you well enough to know how aware you are of your responsibilities. And taking the treatment is another one of those.'

'How?'

'Your responsibility to Jack, and the children. Susie especially. You have a responsibility to battle for this life you have with them, and face your fears, because they're worth it.' She rested her cup on the table, and turned to me. 'Imagine how angry you would be if Jack was in your situation, refusing treatment because of fear. If he was willing to leave you, the life you have, because he didn't want to throw up or have night sweats?'

'But Peggy, Jack and I aren't the same as you and Francis. We're not lovers. There's no big romance.' I sighed, the words finally given light after decades locked away inside me. 'I should be telling him, not you.'

Peggy nodded, sadly. 'I know. But it doesn't change anything. He's your husband, and you love one another, whatever shade of love it may be.'

She was right, of course. I never managed to work out whether I was seriously considering letting the cancer devour me, unchallenged, or if the shock of the diagnosis had thrown up the idea. I wondered whether, if it wasn't for Peggy's quiet reasoning, her ability to accept everything I said without judgement or scorn, I may have allowed myself to refuse treatment and die without a fight.

I nodded quietly, whilst thinking that my first battle was already lost. The battle to be allowed to make the wrong decision for cowardly reasons. It would have been easier to concoct weak arguments than to face the mountain of suffering that was about to strike my loyal old body.

'I'm so selfish, Peggy,' I said suddenly, wiping the hot tears that escaped from my eyes. 'I should be thinking of the family, comforting them, but I can't.'

Peggy reached out and held me, and I allowed myself, for the first time since I could remember, to weep in somebody's arms.

I rested my head on her bony shoulder, and, for ten minutes or more, I voiced all the selfish, horrific fears that had been swelling within me. She accepted it all. Every ugly, sharp syllable. And then, we sat back in our chairs, and Peggy ate with an almost feral appetite – biscuit after biscuit, shoved whole into her wide mouth, a dusting of crumbs on her thin lips.

Over the following months, Peggy crossed the threshold from being a friend to being a sister. I hadn't realised before then that there was any real difference, but there is. She came to know me better than anyone, better than Jack, better than my children, perhaps better than I knew myself.

Sometimes, not as often as I should have, I would remember to thank her for her care. Her answer was always the same: 'You'd do the same for me,' and I would nod. But I didn't know if it was true. I didn't know whether I would know how to be like her.

She sat with me in the hospital ward, my veins attached to poisoned pipes. Sometimes, Susie would find someone to care for her children, and she would come. Sometimes, Jack came. But I was happier when it was just Peggy and me. Susie and Jack worried incessantly, eyed the bald patients, trying to hide their fear. Not so Peggy. She always brought with her a bag full of magazines, and a box of sweets or biscuits that would be passed around the ward. We never endured an awkward silence.

The fear never ever abated, of course, and a new tension grew between Jack and I, threatening the quiet contentedness that had been there before. I felt that he was holding back, looking for a path into a long and difficult conversation. I could not abide his silent company, and for the first time in our marriage, I avoided the rooms in our home in which he sat.

At lunchtime on one windy Sunday, Jack carefully set down his cutlery on his half-cleared plate. 'Annie – do you listen to my sermons?'

'Of course!' Sometimes. The cadence of his voice was a part of the comfort of chapel, along with the cold, hard seats, the tired hymns, the dusty, damp smell of the prayer books. The words themselves didn't seem important.

'So you know about the existence of heaven, and you know what a joyful, peaceful place it is. You know that you needn't be afraid..?'

I stared at Jack across the table. At that very second, I truly hated him.

'I wanted to remind you, that's all.'

I, too, set down my cutlery as he had done, and stared at him coldly across the remains of the roast. 'My heaven is my children, my grandchildren, Peggy. You.' I rose from my chair. 'There will be no joy for me without you.'

I left the room, and felt insulted and patronised by the chapel, by God, and most importantly, by the man I had married.

One evening, in the middle of a week made tired by chemotherapy, I lay in the bath, massaging shampoo into my scalp. As I pulled my fingers away, the hair came away too. I lay in the water for a long time, staring at the dark hair in the white foam, before washing my hair and standing up, drying myself as the plughole gulped the dirty water. Then, knowing that Jack was safely napping in his study downstairs, I wrapped myself in a towel and tiptoed to our bedroom.

I stood before the looking glass.

The lamp light was dim, and I could only see a ghost of myself in the reflection. I didn't look ill. Over the years, I had battled to keep my narrow waist, keeping myself slim and neat, and I regularly had my hair dyed and set in a little salon by the station in Tywyn. Would the months of treatment I had remaining steal my curves? Would my body become bony and jagged where it was meant to be soft? Would my face crease under the influence of all the poison?

I could stride down the street in Tywyn, and no one would realise that I was ill. Make-up could disguise the paleness of my skin. But as I ran my fingers through my hair and felt more strands coming away at their roots, I knew that the cancer was about to leave a most obvious mark on my appearance.

It was irrational. But that night, nothing felt worse than the prospect of losing my hair. Losing my cared-for, tended pride and joy; losing the essence of my soft femininity. One of the things that had attracted Jack all those years ago, and my lifelong crowning glory. My hand become a fist, and I wanted to punch that looking glass until it was nothing but shards and blood. How could this be? It was the treatment that was doing this to me, not the cancer. What use was such cruel medicine? What use was a solution that stole the meat from a woman's bones, its poison eating her from the inside until she wanted to die?

'I'm losing my hair,' I told Peggy in the car the next morning, trying to sound nonchalant. Peggy was driving. Peggy always drove. She lifted her eyes from the road for a second, and looked at my head.

'I know that you can't tell yet, but it is happening. I noticed last night, in the bath.'

'It will grow back afterwards, you know. Don't worry. And until then, we can do as you like. We can use scarves, or turbans, or a wig...?'

I touched my head self-consciously. 'Yes, a wig, I think. But I don't want to look like one of those awful men that wear toupees.'

Peggy giggled. 'I promise, I won't let you go out if you look as if you were wearing a rug on your head. No, they make very good ones now, you know. You'd never tell that they were wigs at all.'

'Really?' I asked, suspiciously. 'Do you know anyone who wears one?'

'Goodness, yes, lots of people,' She smiled. 'As do you. But we'd never know about it, because the wigs are so convincing.'

Five minutes later, I had to ask Peggy to stop the car in a lay-by outside the village of Pennal, and I stood in the cold, vomiting my breakfast into the verge. I had not felt any illness before that, but it wasn't the last time that we had to stop on our way to the hospital. I can only clearly recall that first time, the violence of my weakened body heaving, sitting in the car seat afterwards, exhausted. And I shall remember forever the silence between us for the rest of that journey, lost in these new, tangible symptoms of mine. This was it.

The cancer had arrived.

Though I had read every pamphlet and book that I could stomach, not one of them managed to describe that drugged, uneasy feeling that I suffered each morning – as if my mind refused to awaken, a fog of sleep gathered thickly around me. They called it tiredness, but I had been tired before, when the children were young. This seemed utterly different. I had determined to survive, to exorcise this cancer and live to an old age in the comfort of my village. But this exhaustion, and the pressure to keep fighting – I wanted it to end. I wanted to sleep, longer and deeper than I had ever done before.

For the first time, Peggy and I found a comfortable silence between us. I was too tired to chat. If she ever felt an awkwardness, Peggy never let on. She still accompanied me for the chemotherapy, though the journey became longer and our friendship changed. I leaned on her as we walked into the hospital, and she became my carer, bringing me tea and food and magazines.

'Peggy,' I said weakly one morning, my forehead pressing against the window of the car. It was cold, and the windows were steamed up. I could see Peggy's breath like smoke from between her thin lips. 'I'm so tired, Peggy.'

'I know. I know.'

'I can't admit it to anyone but you.'

'You'll get better. Think of spring.'

I gazed at her. Her eyes were on the road, her hair soft as a ball of ribbon on the nape of her neck. Small creases spread from the corners of her eyes. She was nothing like me. I was neat and fashionable. I didn't leave the house without powder and rouge on my face. I never saw her wearing make-up, and she was too bony and angular to be pretty. And yet, my best friend, whose mind plaited with mine in an endless knot, was the most beautiful person I'd ever seen.

She caught me looking at her, and smiled. 'What is it?'

'Are you being positive for my benefit? Or do you really believe I'm going to get better?'

She turned her eyes back to the road, and thought for a while. I think she was deciding whether to give an easy answer, or an honest one.

'I am being positive, but for *my* benefit. I can't contemplate walking the lane without you, come spring time.'

Honesty, of course. That's what made her easier company than the others. That's what made her a true friend.

'I'm worried about Christmas,' I said, voicing the concern for the first time. The car passed under a curtain of trees, and the shadows darted across our faces. 'I want everything to be perfect. I want to be at home, with my family, in case this is my last Christmas.'

'Of course.'

'Susie has offered to make the Christmas dinner. But all the other meals, and all that energy the grandchildren have... I'm so tired, Peggy.'

Peggy moved one hand from the cold steering wheel, and touched my cheek with the gentleness of a mother. 'Don't worry, Annie. You'll have the best Christmas ever. And when you're tired, you must sleep. I'll be there, I promise.'

There can be no peace of mind in the midst of illness. Happiness is impossible when sickness is at the foundations of existence. That was how I felt at Christmas dinner that year. My husband, my children, my children's children feasting joyously, wearing jaunty paper hats, and laughing at bad jokes. I looked around me, and felt nothing but sorrow that I was so very happy.

If the cancer won, if I died... I would be so, so sad to leave these dear people, this huge family tree that had pushed its roots under mine and Jack's feet and grown to be a comforting shade above our heads.

'Are you all right?' Jack asked quietly, placing his hand over mine. 'You're a little pale.'

'Tired,' I replied, as if the word could begin to do justice to the complete lack of energy that stilled the marrow of my bones.

'Go to bed. Everyone has eaten. You've done well.'

I didn't want to go, regardless of the heaviness of my eyelids. I would miss them, up in my bed: I would miss the laughter, the easy chatter.

The doorbell rang. Susie rose from her chair, and disappeared into the hall.

In a few seconds, Jonathan appeared in the doorway, his usual wide smile plastered on his lovely face. A chorus of 'Merry Christmas!' arose from my family.

'Merry Christmas.' Jonathan moved around the table towards me, and kissed my cheek softly. I could smell his aftershave, spicy and sweet like Christmas. 'Especially to you, Auntie Annie.'

'Are your parents having a nice day? And Huw and Maria?'

'They've all eaten until they feel ill. I think I cooked too much, again. Huw looks as if he's been in the ring with Ali!'

'Susie made us a lovely dinner, fair play to her.'

'We thought she might. That's why... Well, Mam wants to invite you all over to the common to play games. A treasure hunt, for the adults and children. An opportunity for you to get rid of those pudding bellies! And she thought that you, Auntie Annie, might like to rest a bit whilst everyone is out, so that you can feel lovely and rested by this evening. What do you say?'

Peggy even knew the timetable of my body clock. She knew that the hours between lunch and dinner were the most difficult, the most sleepy.

As I climbed the stairs to the bedroom, I heard them wrapping up in coats, hats and scarves. Parents fussing, children brimming with energy, desperate to run. How I would have liked to be with them, and seen Peggy's treasure hunt. But I slept within seconds of lying down, the Christmas dinner warming me from the inside.

'Mam?' Susie whispered. 'Mam?'

I opened my eyes. The room was dark, but the landing light was enough to show me my daughter's shape, sitting on my bed. Voices wandered up from downstairs as stories were regaled, and somebody laughed.

'What time is it?' I asked, groggily.

'Seven. You've slept for hours.'

'Oh!' I gasped. 'You'll be wanting a bite to eat, and...'

Susie placed a comforting hand on my shoulder. 'We've had a little supper in the shop, Mam. We've only just come back. Don't worry.'

'Only just come back?'

'Yes. Look, I brought you some toast. It's been too long since you ate.'

I sat up in bed, and Susie switched on the lamp. Soft light, yellow as butter, flooded the bedclothes.

'Take your medicine first.'

I grimaced as I took the cupful of thick liquid from Susie's hands. The foul, bitter taste stung the back of my throat, and I looked over to the plate on Susie's knee, hoping for something that would get rid of the taste.

'It's Christmas toast, Mam – it's special. Peggy made the butter. It's delicious.'

She put the plate on my knee, and I stared at the thin slices.

'My dear Peggy.'

'She's been wonderful, Mam. She must think the world of you.'

'She'd done a treasure hunt for the children, had put clues in little golden envelopes and had hid gifts all over the village. And then, when it started to get dark, Francis came out and ordered us all into the shop. The children were allowed to choose something from the sweetie counter, and then toast for everyone by the Rayburn. Special toast, Mam – Christmas toast. Taste it!'

I looked at the toast. I had no appetite, but its smell was wonderful, spicy and sweet...

'You'll like it, I promise,' said Susie, and I chewed a corner of the toast.

Yes: Christmas. Cinnamon and honey and butter, and crunchy toast between my teeth.

'And then, Francis let the children play shop in the shop, filling the baskets and playing with the till and everything! They loved it. Little Mali told me on the way back that this was the best Christmas ever!' Susie laughed. 'Then, parlour games in the kitchen, and some tea and Christmas cake before we came home. Peggy missed you, Mam. She gave me a plateful of food and a jar of this special Christmas butter for you.'

It was lovely. Better for my weak stomach than the heavy Christmas roast, and tasted, somehow, of the magic that I used to believe in as a child. I ate it all.

'Don't cry, Mam. You'll get through it.'

Susie wrapped her arms tightly around me, and I could feel the comforting folds of fat around her pressing against my blighted, skinny body.

I admit it. I was jealous of Peggy, at the Christmas afternoon she had spent with my children. I envied the way she had seen little Mali playing shop amidst the packets and tins.

That's not why I cried.

No, those tears came from somewhere else, from somewhere primal, from the depths of some unnamed, buried emotion: the taste of Christmas on a piece of toast; handwritten clues to a treasure hunt in the coldness of a December day; a small car negotiating frozen roads to the hospital; long, thin feet walking alongside mine along the lane. Appreciation, as strong as love, its honey and cinnamon and butter flavour hiding the bitterness of the medicine on my tongue.

Sion Phyllip
Peggy's Grandson
1990

Chocolate Popcorn

1 tbsp cocoa powder	2 tbsp brown sugar
2 tbsp butter	1 tsp cinnamon
1 tsp ginger	160g popping corn
2 tbsp oil	

Warm the oil in a saucepan with two or three of the popcorn kernals, and wait until they pop before adding the rest.

Pop it all, remembering to place a lid on the saucepan, and then place to one side in order to cool.

Melt all the other ingredients in a saucepan.

Mix the popcorn and sauce in a paper bag, and shake well.

'Hey, Sion,' Nain whispered. 'Are you going to get up?'

I opened my eyes and sat up. Nain Peggy had opened the curtains to another grey day.

'I've got some honey porridge on the stove for you.' She smiled, happily. 'Taid is asking if you could give him a hand in the shop. I've told him that seven is a bit young to start working, but he thinks you're grown-up enough.'

'Of course I am!' I answered, hoarsely. 'Taid swears that he's never had such a good helper!'

'Well, you'd better get on with it, then. There's a delivery of sweets coming in an hour, and he'll need a hand with those.'

She smiled at me one last time, and walked towards the door. 'Your clothes are warming on the Rayburn. Come down when you're ready.'

The bedrooms above the shop were cold, different in every way to the rooms in our modern house in Bethesda. It was always warm at home. Still, there was something comforting about the weight of all those blankets on my skinny frame as I slept in the small bed. The chill of the house made the warmth of the kitchen even more inviting.

I hurried downstairs in my pyjamas. I popped my head through the door of the storeroom, and called 'I'll be with you in a minute, Taid!' He would have been there for hours, sorting the papers and taking the fresh bread delivery from Tywyn.

'Good boy,' Taid answered as I darted into the kitchen.

'There you go,' Nain said, her hands lost in suds in the sink. 'That's your porridge on the table. Eat it before it gets cold.'

I sat in my chair, and planted my spoon in the midst of that thick breakfast. I always had Coco Pops or Sugar Puffs at home, with a purple vitamin pill on the side that tasted like a sweet. I had refused Mam's porridge time after time, but Nain's tasted different – sweet and creamy, like heavy warm blankets inside me. I ate it all, and enjoyed it.

After washing my face and brushing my teeth, and swapping my flannel pyjamas for jeans and a thick jumper, I hurried to the shop, feeling important. Taid never spoke down to me, and always gave me proper jobs to do to make me feel like a man. I knew he was proud of me. He'd introduce me to everyone that came into the shop, a satisfied smile on his thick lips.

'I have an assistant today, Mrs Roberts.'

'Ooooh, so you have!' Mrs Roberts stared at me through her thick glasses. 'Who is he?'

'This is Sion. Huw's boy. And goodness me, he's a good worker! I'll be out of a job if he carries on like this!'

Mrs Roberts laughed, and reached into her old-lady-bag for her purse. 'Does he pay you, sweetheart? Here you go.' And she pressed a cold pound coin into my hand.

'Thank you!' I said, appreciatively, as I had done to all the old ladies that had lined my pockets that week. 'You're very kind.' I enjoyed my job.

After a bellyfull of warm lobscouse for lunch, Nain and I pulled on our coats and started out for a walk in the village. Auntie Annie had gone shopping to Aberystwyth that day, so it was just me and Nain walking though the grey afternoon.

'Do you see that house? With that odd-looking bent tree in the garden?' Nain pointed with a long, bony finger. 'Mrs Davies lived there. A kind woman, and she looked after me when I was about your age.'

I looked at the house, and tried to imagine Nain there when she was a little girl. I couldn't imagine how she had been. She was so old, and so tall. 'Dad says I'm like you, Nain.'

She stopped, and turned her eyes to me. 'Does he?'

'Yes. Do you think I am?'

Nain started walking again, and thought for a while before

answering. 'Well, you're tall, like me, and thin. And your eyes are grey.' She smiled. 'I do hope that I'm like you.'

Further down the road, Nain paused by a big, wide gate, leaning her weight on the railings. She nodded towards a small house in the fields. 'Hare House. That's where I went to live when I was your age. The most wonderful place on earth.'

It was far from everywhere, and Bird Rock jutted out, almost threateningly, behind it. But yes, I could see what it was like. It would be a wonderful place to play.

'Were you lonely?'

I thought of all the friends that I had on my street at home.

'No. I was with my family.'

'Did your parents like it there, too?'

'I lived with my grandparents, sweetheart.'

'Really? Why?'

Nain ran her tongue over her thin lips. 'My father died, and my mother was too ill to look after me. But I was lucky. My grandparents were so kind.'

As we walked back towards the village, I listened to Nain telling me about her childhood in Hare House, but my mind was whirring. I loved coming on holiday without Mam and Dad, but yet, I wouldn't want to live without my parents, never mind how kind Nain and Taid were to me. It wouldn't be natural, would it?

Back in the shop, Taid grinned upon seeing us return. 'Are you ready to start working again, Sion? I have something to show you...'

'Yes, yes, I'm ready. I hope it hasn't been too busy for you...'

'I managed. Did you have a nice walk, love?' He asked Nain as she moved though into the kitchen.

'Oh, yes! The fog almost completely lifted. Tea?'

'Please. Right, Sion, the time has come. As you're old enough and sensible enough, would you like me to show you how to work the till?'

The till! I had been allowed to do everything in the shop except touching the machine on the counter and dealing with money. And now Taid was teaching me how to do that, too!

It became one of the most enjoyable afternoons of my childhood. I stood on a bottle crate in order to reach the till, read the price stickers on the stocks, and fed the numbers into the machine. Took the money and gave change. Taid never lost his cool, even when I made mistakes and took my time. Even the customers smiled. By the time I spun the sign on the door from 'Open' to 'Closed', I felt like a man.

'Would you like to go to the pictures tonight, sweetheart?' asked Nain over tea. 'They say that there's a very good film on at the moment.'

'Yes please!' I answered brightly though a mouthful of bara brith. 'Can I use my money to buy popcorn?'

'No, no. I'll buy the popcorn. I may even get some for your grandfather, if he behaves.' She smiled, teasingly.

There was nowhere in the world like Tywyn Cinema – a cold cave of a place, old-fashioned and charming. Huge portraits of the Marx Brothers, Laurel and Hardy and Charlie Chaplin stared down from the wall. I didn't like the look of Harpo. He grinned madly at the audience, flashing his teeth like a growling dog, his empty eyes following me.

I remember nothing of the film, only that safe feeling of sitting between my grandparents, my hand planted deeply in the box of sugary popcorn. Complete contentment. I looked up at Nain and Taid's faces either side of me, lit up by the moving images on the screen. They were perfect.

The next evening, between tea time and *Pobol y Cwm*, I sat by the table reading a comic. Nain was drying the dishes, and she turned to me.

'You like popcorn, don't you?'

'Mmm, yes.'

'Did you know, people can make popcorn at home.'

'Yes, I knew that. Mam does it sometimes.' I liked hearing the little red bag popping in the microwave, but the popcorn itself was tasteless. Nothing like what was sold in the pictures. 'It's not as good as cinema popcorn.'

Nain opened drawers and cupboards, fetched a saucepan and a few ingredients. 'Well, let me change your mind.'

I was doubtful, but I smiled at Nain, not wanting to seem unappreciative.

'Come and give me a hand, would you?'

Nain had no microwave, so she warmed the kernels of corn in a saucepan on the Rayburn, a dinner plate in place of a lid on top of it. At the same time, she gave me instructions on what to place into a second saucepan: butter, honey, spices and chocolate, and a little sugar. The scent that arose from it was wonderful.

After the sauce had cooled, and the kernels had bloomed into popcorn, Nain fetched a large paper bag from the shop, the kind of bag Taid would use to wrap a large loaf for a customer.

She poured the popcorn into the bag, and turned to me.

'Careful now – no burning! Pour the mixture on the popcorn.'

'Into the bag?'

'That's right.'

I lifted the saucepan slowly. Mam would never let me do anything so dangerous. I poured the hot brown syrup over the popcorn until there was not a drop left.

'Now, put the saucepan down. Take the paper bag, and make sure you close it tight with your fingers. That's it. Now, shake it?'

'Shake it?'

'We want the syrup to cover all of the popcorn, so you'd better do it properly.'

I shook the bag as Nain washed the saucepans, and then, when she told me to, I emptied the bag into a large bowl on the table.

Every piece was glistening, and I licked my lips.

'This is better than cinema popcorn, Nain.'

I pushed another piece into my mouth. Nain shoved a fistful between her lips, and smiled with a bulging mouth.

'I'm so full,' she said. 'But they're too nice not to eat!'

'Do you know what's brilliant about you, Nain? You like sweets and biscuits and cake just as much as I do.'

'You're right, I do.'

'You're like a child, but you're old.'

She swallowed her mouthful, and stared at me. 'I still feel the same as I did when I was a girl, you know,' she said, softly.

'I'm glad,' I answered, before taking another mouthful of popcorn. When I looked up, Nain was smiling at me, the tiniest smear of chocolate at the corner of her mouth.

Jack Vaughan
Annie's Husband
1997

Affogato

Vanilla ice cream
Espresso

Pour coffee over the ice cream.
Eat immediately.

I did not realise that Annie and I were old until I happened upon our reflection in a shop window in Tywyn one cold afternoon in autumn.

My shoulders were slumped and all the hairs on my head, once a vivid red, were now silver. Annie had become heavy and swollen after that unnatural thinness of chemotherapy. She remained the most beautiful creature that I had ever seen. I could see nothing but her glittering eyes, and that wonderful gap between her front teeth. She had no idea how much I loved her.

Once I had noticed our oldness, I saw signs of it everywhere... The familiar pattern of our weeks, the heavy flowery print on our wallpaper, the food we ate, versions of what we used to eat half a century ago.

My hands. They were the biggest shock. The hands of an old man. I examined them daily, turned them over to see the pink palms. How had this happened to me? How had my body become so creased? Surely, this was not life: A fleeting series of events, decisions, births and seasons?

I had expected it to be easier.

Yet, I was one of the lucky ones! I hadn't been ill, or lost a child or a lover, I hadn't battled for my freedom or for a good cause. Is this what caused this recent restlessness? The fact that it had all come so easily to me?

Annie and Peggy still walked every day. I would watch them, sometimes, from the bedroom window, their strides becoming slower with the passing years, Annie becoming plump and Peggy's back curving slightly under her coat.

Llanegryn evolved with each year that passed – more cars, less conversation, the children becoming adults and having children of their own. A new reverend came to take my place, but he had five other chapels, as well as Llan, and Annie and I were allowed to remain in the house. It was far too big for us by that time, and only the grandchildren's visits to remind us of the cruelty of empty rooms, to show us the loneliness of a home that was still.

As autumn brought sunset's colours to the village, Francis Phyllip shut his shop for the final time, scarred by the arthritis brought on by years of lifting heavy boxes. Jonathan returned, a gentle, sweet-natured giant, his smile unchanged from all those years ago. He had been a chef in a hotel in Llandudno, and had given up on the bitter managers and moaning customers. The shop windows were covered in newspaper, and no one except for his parents was allowed to know his plan for the old shop.

There was something odd about seeing Francis wandering the village.

He hadn't been truly free since he had taken his father's apron and had taken over the running of the shop. There was something child-like in his movements as he leaned over Llan bridge to look for fish in the water, or reached his work-worn hand to pluck some honeysuckle to his lips, sucking gently to taste that shot of sugar. He lifted his eyes to the pattern of the slates on the roofs, or the uppermost branches of the trees in the common and watched as they waved gracefully. He had always been a sweet-natured man, but it wasn't until he was old that I realised that there was truly no bitterness or hatred inside him at all. I never heard him speak an uncomplimentary word about his wife. I remembered the vicious tongue of his father, but when Isaac Phyllip was mentioned, Francis only said, 'He must have had a difficult time of it, losing my mother when I was a newborn.'

A part of me thought Francis a coward, weak and devoid of passion. I knew that Peggy had suffered cruelly at the sharp words of her father-in-law, and I had never heard of Francis stepping in to protect his fragile wife. Perhaps I was old-fashioned, but it seemed to me that Peggy had been given too much freedom to do as her whims pleased, in the vain hope that she might forget the darkness of her childhood.

'What do you mean?' Annie snapped at me one day when I

mentioned it to her. 'What are you talking about?'

'The holidays on her own by the sea, the café in Tywyn. Not to mention Jonathan!'

'Jonathan is a godsend!'

'Yes, he is. But it was a ridiculous idea to adopt a black Scouser and bring him here...'

'It's not that ridiculous, or it wouldn't have been so successful.'

I sighed. Annie's loyalties lay with Peggy, not me.

'Peggy was starting to come undone, then. She was unhappy in the cafe, and she lived in fear that she was becoming her mother. She needed something to give her stability. She needed to save someone, as someone had saved her. And that's what kept her from falling apart, I think... She followed the example of everyone who had ever been kind to her.'

I couldn't be sure that that was true. Her mother's legacy was difficult and complex. But after the shop had closed, my opinion of Francis changed, and I followed that old cliché about old age: everything that had once been black and white became a misty grey.

Both finding ourselves with an excess of time, Francis and I became friends. We would walk, as our wives did, and swap books. I hadn't realised until then that Francis was a voracious reader. I don't know if he himself had realised until he had the time and peace to sit down and enjoy a novel.

Then, as Jonathan started work on the shop, a new sign was erected on the dark lane beside Llan bridge – *For Sale*.

Riverside.

A couple from Birmingham had been using it as a holiday home for decades, but they had been complaining that the stairs were too much for her varicose veins. The house would not be for sale for long, I told Annie one day over breakfast. It was perfect for use as a holiday home, small and neat and close to the river. I hated that house. I could remember Jennie's empty face as she sat in her chair in the kitchen, the proof of the neglect of her daughter poisoning the place with its scent.

'Peggy and I went to Riverside yesterday,' said Francis, much to my surprise, as we both walked up the Black Road one morning. 'We're thinking of buying it.'

I stopped in my tracks. 'Are you serious?'

He nodded. 'We'd give the shop to Jonathan, and give our savings to Huw. It makes sense.'

'Well, yes, when you say it like that. But why go there? Why would Peggy want to return to such a...' I failed to find the words.

'She wasn't sure herself until she went back there. But she seems very keen now. She says it would create some sort of circle in her life – being born and dying in the same place.'

We walked in silence for a while. Years ago, it had been easy to climb the steep hill of the Black Road, but now my knees creaked like an old machine.

I had tried for years to rid my mind of the image of Peggy as a child – her bony wrists, her dirty clothes, the matted fur of a rat in a casserole dish. It all came back vividly as I climbed the hill, along with another flash of memory, white as an angel: Jennie's corpse in a shroud of a nightdress, in the river.

After crossing the cattle grid, Francis and I rested for a while, enjoyed the view. The Dysynni river shining in the weak autumn sun, Bryncrug nestling at the foot of Moel Gocyn, and Tywyn, a sliver of buildings on the coast.

'Don't think I'm overstepping the mark,' I said, quietly. 'But are you sure that this is best for Peggy's health?'

'Her mental health, you mean?'

A dozen lines furrowed Francis' forehead. The scars of years of concern.

'I know that she's been better in recent years,' I added, slowly.

'I'm just worried that being in Riverside might lead her back to a place of darkness.'

'Do you know, it's almost thirty years since Peggy suffered a bad patch.'

I stared at him. 'No!'

'Yes. She went away to the seaside for convalescence for her mind when Huw was a young man, and within six months we had Jonathan.'

'The darkness never returned to her after Jonathan came?'

'I think it threatened her a few times. When Jonathan went to college... I was worried then. They're so close. But when I think she's about to go down again, she'll go for a long walk, all day, sometimes, and she seems better, then.'

'Do you know where she goes?'

Francis shook his head. 'I never ask.' He smiled at me. 'Women are so full of secrets, aren't they... Perhaps it's better not to know what's in their minds.'

As we walked back down to the village, Francis said, 'You should have seen her in Riverside, Jack. Wandering from room to room, telling me what used to be there when she was a girl. She seemed to change, in that cottage, her back seemed to straighten a bit. She looked younger.'

That seemed frightful to me, a slow anti-ageing which could only end in Peggy once again becoming that little girl.

Francis added gently, 'Peggy never told me about her life with her mother. I remember her, then... She worked in the shop, and would stay later and later, as if she didn't want to go home. But she never told me why her mother went to the asylum, what happened to her there.'

I don't know whether he was questioning me, probing for information. I didn't say a word.

'She stood for a long time in the doorway to one of the bedrooms. It was a pretty little room, painted a lovely spring green and with thick carpet on the floor. But she didn't go in, just stood in the door, looking. 'This was my room,' she said. 'The walls were white then. No carpet. Just white walls and a cold bed."

I remembered the dirty worn sheets on her bed, and though it was a lifetime ago, I could still recall the details. One of the floorboards creaked, and the windows were darkened with dirt. In the attic above, rats shuffled and squeaked.

'I saw her, then,' I said, hoarsely, because I felt that I had to. 'I arranged for her to go to her grandparents.'

'I know,' Francis replied, head lowered.

'She knew nothing about them,' I added, conjuring the memory of Mr Pugh Hare House walking up the road to fetch Peggy to her new home. 'That was the first time they met. She had a vile childhood in that house. Are you sure she's all right to go back there?'

'How can I be sure?' He answered with a question. 'And yet, Peggy seems determined that it's what she wants to do, and I have to trust her judgement.' Francis' eyes met mine. Two old men, still asking questions. 'You know Peggy, Jack. Well enough to know that nobody really knows her at all.'

Visiting Peggy and Francis in their new home, a few months later, was a surreal experience. Walking over Llan Bridge, exactly as I had done over half a century before. Up the lane towards the church, the dark cottage stood on the bank of the river, which sighed its water to the sea, barely a mile away. Annie held onto my arm as we walked, unusually contemplative, as if she, too, could feel the past's presence around us.

'They've done well with the garden, haven't they?' she said as I paused to let her be first through the gate. It was Jonathan's doing, and he had worked hard though he had plenty to do in the shop. In the fortnight that had passed since Peggy and Francis had become the owners of Riverside, Jonathan had painted the walls, fitted a new kitchen, and had planted herbs and lavender along the garden borders. When their roots took hold, the path would be thick with their scent. I could imagine Annie and Peggy there in the spring, sitting on the bench underneath the kitchen window, steam rising from their mugs of tea and the sweet, musky smell of lavender pervading their clothes and hair.

Peggy opened the door before we knocked, her face illuminated by a girlish smile.

'Come in!' she said, before stepping aside for us. I had never seen her more different to her mother, though she, too, had stood on that very threshold. Jennie had never smiled like this, and she had not lived to wear furrowed skin and silver hair.

I could not deny that Riverside had been transformed into a pretty and cosy home. It was perfect for Peggy and Francis. But old shadows lurked behind the smell of paint, under the thick carpet, unforgotten memories, dark and cold. I silently berated myself. Peggy and Francis were clearly happy here.

My eyes wandered to the corner of the kitchen where Jennie's rocking chair used to be. I seemed to feel the empty dead stare of her grey eyes in the warm kitchen.

I turned away, and caught Peggy's stone-coloured eyes. She had been staring at me. We were the only ones who remembered what it had really been like, and it was unspoken between us, like a heavy secret. I did not want to share her history.

Each room reflected some long-ago horror. I smiled and muttered positive comments about the heavy curtains, the patterned wallpaper and the thickness of the windows. I despised that place. Was it my imagination, or was Peggy watching me closely from the corner of her eye, looking for a flicker of something in my reaction?

'We'd better go,' said Francis, straightening the blue tie he wore with his only smart suit. 'Jonathan will be waiting for us.'

We chose the uneven path through the common instead of the flat smooth surface of the road. Peggy and Annie led the way, arm in arm, their summer dresses clashing prettily in the breeze, their bodies slightly leaning into one another. Francis and I followed, our best shoes shining with the remains of a late afternoon shower which lingered in the grass. We were old people walking the paths of our youth. A lump formed in my throat as I thought how we would look to any outsiders looking in, each of us carrying the years we had lived in our walks. I had read, once, that the human body renews itself entirely several times during a lifetime as old cells made way for new ones. Was there anything left of the two young newlyweds who walked the common arm in arm in Annie and I? Were there still traces of the fragile young children in Francis and Peggy?

The whole village had crammed into Jonathan's new café for the launch of his new venture. Though it had become autumn and the breeze was cold, there were people standing on the pavement outside the café, sipping wine, faces shining with laughter. It seemed that the occasion itself offered its own kind of warmth. Everyone smiled as we arrived in a silent tribute to the fact that this new café used to be Peggy and Francis' old shop.

The place was transformed. The dark old counters that had held rows and towers of boxes and coloured tins had gone. In their place there were light-coloured wooden tables, with a posy of white flowers in the centre of each. The walls were painted a soft light blue, dotted with dozens of picture frames. The cafe was lined with black and white and sepia photographs of the village as it once was. On the back wall, behind the counter, a photograph of a young Peggy and Francis standing outside the shop, stared out at the party. They must have been newlyweds when the photographs were taken, and a knot formed in my stomach as I looked at it. How kind and thoughtful of Jonathan to choose this image to preside over his new venture, and how sad the stillness of the photograph of a young couple, yet to live their best days.

The guests all turned their attention to us as we arrived, and applauded Peggy and Francis warmly. Jonathan came to take our coats, and Susie disappeared to the kitchen at the back to hang them up. She had cared for him ever since he had arrived in Llan when he was five, and she still treated him as if he were one of her children. Jonathan found seats so that his mother and Annie could sit by the big window, as if this party was for them. Someone summoned him, and he disappeared into the shiny metal kitchen which had once been the shop's storeroom.

I watched Francis' as he gazed at the new details of the decor which covered his old shop, looking for signs of longing, of a pining for the days when he had been young here. But no – he seemed only to be admiring the clean walls, the light-coloured wood and the comfortable chairs. He noticed that I was watching him, and a smile brightened his face, a real smile, from the heart.

'My father would have hated it,' he said, smiling mischievously. 'I think it's wonderful.'

'Even the smell has gone,' I remarked, trying to recall that comforting scent: the salt, the paper, the ham and spices and brown sugar...

Francis nodded. That old aroma had been masked by the smell of paint and coffee and newness.

The evening was a resounding success, and the wine and coffee and Jonathan's delicious little cakes were all devoured by hungry, eager, smiling mouths. The young and the old folk of Llan laughing and chatting, and pretty grey ribbons of cigarette smoke wandered in from outside through the open door. The old photographs on the walls and the young eyes that examined them, looking at the way the streets used to look when there were no cars lining them. Jonathan and his friends giggling at old hairstyles and fashions that I had barely noticed in passing.

'I found a suitcase full of these old photos in the attic,' Jonathan smiled. 'It seemed a shame for them to be unseen.' Before that moment, I had doubted Jonathan's business plan, had thought it foolish to imagine that a café might thrive in a small country village like Llan. But I had been wrong. It was a haven of Jonathan's laughter and warmth. It was certain to succeed.

Jonathan must have been baking all day long. He spent the evening carrying loaded plates from the kitchen, small bites of food he would be serving in the café – loaded sandwiches, small quiches, cakes and pastries shining with sugar and caramel. Peggy and Annie were the first to be offered everything that came out of the kitchen, and Jonathan's inquisitive face searched theirs for a reaction.

'Try this!' he said, bringing Annie a long plate on which he balanced a small cup and a dish. He placed the dish on the table in front of her, and offered her a long silver spoon. 'I'm not sure that Llan is ready for a dessert like this, Auntie Annie... It's quite different.'

Annie peered into the bowl and cup. 'Ice cream, and... What's this? It smells like coffee.'

'That's right, it's a small black coffee. Pour it onto the ice cream, and eat it straight away.'

He offered her the spoon again.

'I never really drink coffee, only tea,' Annie hesitated, but she took the spoon. She wrapped her fingers around the cup, and slowly poured the coffee over the ball of creamy yellow ice cream, as if she was afraid of what might happen.

She loaded her spoon with the ice cream and coffee, and tasted it.

My wife shut her eyes. I could see her Adam's apple slipping towards her chest as she swallowed slowly, lazily. Brief seconds of abandoning herself to the pleasure of a new taste, a wonderful taste, and I saw Annie making the gestures of a young girl in her old woman's body. I had never been able to make her feel like that.

She smiled at Jonathan in admiration, and took another spoonful.

'You like it, Auntie Annie?' She nodded her answer, raising a smile to Jonathan's thick lips. 'I'll put it on the menu, then. They call it *affogato*.'

'It's wonderful. So, so wonderful,' said Annie after she had finished it all, leaning back on the sofa with a peaceful, satisfied smile on her round face. She turned her eyes and found me staring at her. Our eyes locked for a few seconds, and we shared a conpanionable smile.

She looked happy.

It was nearly midnight when we finally left the café, and Jonathan looked exhausted. The empty plates and cups threw tens of reflections in the warm light… The leftovers of a celebration. Peggy and Annie offered to wash the dishes, but Jonathan refused.

'I have a machine to do all that, and anyway, I'm not touching it until the morning.'

The village slept as we walked home, the darkness of night and the orange glow of the streetlamps meeting at the edges of shadows. It felt like it was only the four of us – Annie and I, Peggy and Francis – left in the whole of Llan.

Peggy and Annie walked in front, as before, arm in arm, their steps made smoother by the wine. I couldn't hear what they were talking about, but every now and then a peal of laughter escaped from their bellies and their mouths, the laughter of girls. Francis and I walked in a companionable silence. A smile played on Francis' lips, a comfortable contentment on his face. It had been a good evening. One of the best.

'Good night,' Peggy whispered as we came to the bridge.

'Good night,' Annie whispered back, flashing a wide smile at her best friend. 'Shall we go to the café tomorrow for a pot of tea?'

Peggy nodded. 'Half past ten?'

'Tea and affi… affa… That coffee and ice cream thing!'

Peggy giggled at my wife's thick tongue, before taking Francis' arm and heading home. The lane to Riverside seemed darker than the rest of the village.

'Did you enjoy it?' I asked Annie later as I lay in bed. She was taking the pearls from her ears as she stood in front of the mirror, her body comfortingly round beneath her flowered nightdress. I knew the answer, of course, but I wanted to hear the comfort of her voice before I slept.

'Very much. It was a lovely evening.'

She turned her eyes to the reflection of my own in the mirror.

She sighed at my gentle teasing, and looked at herself once again. I fell asleep as I watched her rhythmically combing her hair, the bristles of the brush whispering through her white curls like a soft breeze.

Annie died that night.

I awoke at eight, and listened to the wind angrily rattling the windows. She had her back to me, and I could feel her weight by my side, but it took a few minutes for me to pinpoint what it was that made the bedroom feel odd that morning. The silence. I had awoken to the sound of her breath every day for fifty years, and sometime during the night, she had become silent.

I lay there for a while, delaying the moment when I would have to look at her lying dead beside me. I felt the coldness of her flesh creeping across the sheets towards me. My Annie had never had any trace of winter within her.

I turned to face her. She was pale and half smiling, as if she was recalling lovely things.

I watched her, examining the stillness and searching for my wife in her face, in the form of her body beneath the sheets, but she wasn't there. Only her shell remained, and the details and detritus of who she had been.

I got up, dressed myself slowly. Grey trousers, green shirt, a tie, socks from the drawer. I combed what was left of my hair. I washed my face and brushed my teeth, before returning to the bedroom and pulling the duvet right up to her chin, to keep her warm.

I don't know why I didn't phone Susie to tell her. I made myself breakfast instead, surprising myself with a voracious appetite as if I hadn't eaten for days, and I made a mound of toast, ate it with home-made jam. I wasn't used to slicing the bread, and so the slices were ragged and crooked. After washing the dishes and having a cup of tea, I sat in my easy chair in the study, watching the grey skies, the wind blowing the clouds across the sky. I didn't pick up the paper when it landed with a soft sigh on the mat, but listened instead to the wind trying to break into the house, the morose ticking of the clock. These would be my last moments with Annie before the busyness of death descended. Had I not been a part of that busyness myself many, many times for the families of Llan? And so, for an hour, I sat in my chair, knowing that Annie was lying in our bed upstairs. I wanted to keep her to myself for just a while longer.

At half past ten, I pulled on my heavy coat, and left the silent house. The wind whipped the legs of my trousers as I walked up the road towards the café. The autumn leaves danced joyfully on the grey road, and I paused for a while to watch them spinning, the wind whipping them up in a pirouette before letting them fall like feathers to the road.

Peggy and Francis were sitting in the same chairs as they had done last night. In the warmth of the café, coffee scented steam clouding from the cup on the table in front of her, Peggy turned as I reached the door. I caught her eye through the window, and her smile faded.

I shouldn't be the one on the doorstep. It should have been Annie.

The heat of the café comforted my wind-bitten face as I stepped over the threshold. The smell of coffee warmed the air. Jonathan stood behind the counter, slicing a Victoria sponge into fat triangles. He gazed at me, perplexed.

'Jack?'

'Annie died,' I answered, turning to Peggy.

She opened her mouth to say something, and then failed to find the words. Her grey eyes searched the lines in my face, searching for an answer to a question that she did not know.

'I woke up this morning, and she had gone in her sleep.'

With a heavy sigh, Jonathan set down his knife, and came over to me.

'Uncle Jack. I am so sorry.'

Francis arose from his chair, and placed a firm hand on my shoulder. Tears greased his eyes.

'Jack. Jack. Oh, poor Annie.'

I nodded, feeling the heat of emotion pricking the back of my eyes. I allowed Francis to lead me to the chair beside Peggy, and I sat. Peggy stared at me, the weight of a whole life in her eyes.

'I'm sorry,' she whispered.

'So am I. Your loss is as great as mine, Peggy.'

And as we sat, the bitter raw pain of what had happened permeated the four of us – Jonathan, Peggy, Francis and I – And we stared at the empty space on the sofa where Annie had sat the previous night, her sickle-shaped smile and tinking laughter in perfect harmony with the villagers' chat.

Jonathan disappeared into the kitchen, and returned with small round bowls for us, spoons curving out of them. '*Affogato*,' he explained as I gazed at the bowls. 'Annie enjoyed it last night. I'll phone Susie.'

And so, the three of us ate ice cream and drank hot coffee in the small café, listening to the wind, and the sound of spoons scraping porcelain. Appreciating the new, unfamiliar taste. The bitter coffee and the sweet ice cream, the coldness and the warmth.

'This was the last thing she ate,' Peggy said after her bowl had been emptied. I turned my eyes to her, but she focused on the leaves dancing outside on the empty street. 'It's a wonderful taste to have in your mouth as you go to heaven, isn't it?'

And she was right. She was right.

Huw Phyllip
Peggy's son
2008

Easy Mince Pies

Puff pastry

milk

Buttercream

mincemeat

Sugar

Cut the pastry into discs. Place a spoonful of mincemeat in the centre of a disc, and some buttercream. Grease the edges of the pastry with milk, and place another disc of pastry on the top.
Brush the top of the mince pie with milk, and sprinkle with sugar.
Bake on greased baking paper for approximately 20 minutes.

Driving from Bethesda to Ceredigion on cold, grey roads that were heavy with lorries, I came to the conclusion that the only thing that had the ability to shock me was myself.

Fifty-four. I sounded old, though I still felt like a youth travelling on this old road, these hazardous corners and narrow miles a familiar journey. The road home. It was rife with danger.

I had shocked myself that day by jumping into the car, barely five minutes after I had taken the phone call at work. Jonathan, his voice soft and apologetic. I imagined him, standing outside the hospital, his mobile phone clasped tightly to his ear and the Thursday morning traffic sighing on the roads.

'Can I go?' I asked the manager after speaking to my brother. 'Something has happened.'

He raised his eyebrows questioningly.

'My mother's had a stroke.'

I remembered his face as I slowed down through Ganllwyd, the speed limit signs flashing like an ambulance. The silent 'O' that came to his lips, the mask of sympathy. 'Of course,' he said after a pause. 'I hope... Well. I hope she's comfortable.'

The car radio lost its signal. I listened to the hazy whispers that came from the speakers in its place, a few words discernible in the hiss.

The turning towards home came and went, and I passed it by on my way to the hospital in Aberystwyth. When was the last time I'd driven this way? I could not remember. Was it when Maria and I were new to one another, and had taken a dirty, damp tent to the Royal Welsh Show, had camped in a field with people like us, drinking and dancing and laughing until we became exhausted? Years had passed since then, yet I could still remember her face as she slept in that tent, a scar of dried mud slashed across her face. My memory was dominated by such small, inconsequential details, losing whole years to the dark fog of my my mind, leaving only snapshots of what had been.

'Shit, Huw,' I had heard Maria's voice tightening when I had phoned her earlier. 'Is she going to be okay?'

'I don't know,' I answered, knowing that I didn't have to tell Maria. She would already know how I was feeling. There was something terrifying and comforting in it – she knew me so well. Lying to her would be impossible.

'Are you going to see her?'

'I'm on my way to Aberystwyth, now.'

There was a pause.

'I'm glad that you're going to her. I know it won't be easy.'

Damn her, my wonderful wife, for reminding me of things I didn't want to think about. Damn her, for knowing how my mind worked.

'Phone me tonight, will you? And send my love to your mother, and your dad. And Jonathan.'

The radio signal returned in Corris, and I turned up the sound until it blared, until it drowned out my mind. Chippy English voices discussing politics and news and other important things. None of it seemed significant with the knowledge that my mother may die soon. What if she died whilst I was driving? What if she was already dead?

Aberystwyth was quiet, the students having returned home to celebrate Christmas. I parked outside the hospital, and watched a green star flashing in the window of one of the houses, winking provocatively at me. Did they imagine, whilst decorating their home for Christmas, that people visiting the hospital would have to accept its unashamed joy, would have to face the grin of its flashing bulbs?

Sion would have adored it. It was exactly the kind of tasteless, tacky decoration which filled him with glee. I promised myself that I would buy one on the way home.

The hospital was confusing, as if the same corridor was recreated over and over again, the heavy metal lift opening and shutting its

233

doors repeatedly with a wheeze. I did not get lost. The name of the ward had been seared in my mind since Jonathan spoke it on the phone.

I was taken to a cubicle by a tired-looking nurse.

My father sat in a high-backed chair, his hands over my mother's, his lips whispering soft, kind words. He looked up as I came in, and gave me a small smile, but he didn't get up.

'Look who's here! It's Huw. Come all this way to see you.'

My father suddenly seemed old to me, his hair unkempt and his collar untidy under his jumper.

'He's been incredible,' the nurse said, quietly. 'Both him and your brother. They haven't left her for a single second since she arrived. Most people run out of things to say in a one-sided conversation, but your father hasn't stopped. He says he's reminding her of the olden days.'

'Mam?' I said, and the limp figure in the bed turned to look at me.

She opened her mouth to speak, but she could only grunt. I swallowed hard, and stared at her.

'The stroke has affected her speech,' the nurse explained. 'It's a common side-effect. Patients usually regain speech after a while... You'll be chatting in no time, won't you, Mrs Phyllip?'

The nurse gently pushed me towards the bed, before leaving the room.

I approached my mother, entranced by her face. She stared back at me, child's eyes in an old face. For the first time, she looked fragile and vulnerable.

She tried once again, and I saw the way one side of her face was pulled down. One eye half-asleep, cheek frozen, one corner of her mouth resolutely dragged down. Half Mam, and half stranger. A voice in my mind questioned cruelly. *Which half is the real her, the dead half or the one still clinging to life?*

'Oh, Mam.'

I held her hand, trying to compensate for the vicious voices in my head. She wrapped her long fingers around my hand, soft as a lover's touch. I couldn't remember the last time we had held hands. It must have been when I was a young child, walking side by side on the road.

'Are you all right?'

She tried to answer, but the sound was gutteral, feral, and her tongue failed to form the words. A stream of spittle escaped from the corner of her mouth, and wound a tinsel-silver path down her chin. I reached for a tissue from the box by the bed to wipe it away, swallowing, swallowing, swallowing my tears.

'It's difficult to see her like this,' my father comforted, stroking her hair with the tips of his fingers. 'But she's still Peggy, inside.'

The door opened.

'Huw!'

Jonathan rushed towards me, and embraced me tightly, warmly in his thick arms. I was tall, but Jonathan was gargantuan, and had gained a comfortable pot belly since he had opened the café: a satisfied stomach of cupcakes and hot chocolate. There was a tenderness, a softness to his movements and a gait that was at odds with his size.

'Is he gay?' Maria had asked me once, and I hadn't known the answer. I had never thought of him as someone who would bestow his love onto anyone except for our parents.

'I went for a cup of tea. Are you all right? How was the journey?'

I nodded. 'Fine. Have the doctors..?'

Jonathan moved over to Dad, and stood behind him, placing his firm hand on our father's shoulder. I noticed my mother's eyes following him, their greyness fixed on his face.

'We can only wait. Once Mam can speak again, they'll be able to assess how she's been affected.'

Jonathan smiled. 'But we can see in your eyes that you can understand everything, eh Mam?'

Mam gurgled a foul sound from the depths of her throat.

Her eyes filled up with frustration, and the grey, tearful sheen reminded me of things I had tried, for years, to forget. I shut my eyes, tried to blacken the image.

The café was empty without her. Her easy chair in the corner was cold, the table bare without her empty mugs. I inhaled deeply, trying to find an old, familiar smell... Ham and sugar, spices and ice cream... But the shop was all gone, only the photographs on the wall to testify that it had ever been here.

'Glass of wine?' Jonathan asked from the kitchen, and I followed him before setting down my bag on the floor. Before I could answer, Jonathan had fetched two fat goblets and was pouring generously. We stood by the kitchen table, sipping the cold dry white wine without even removing our coats. Everything was as it had been left that morning, when Mam had a stroke over her cup of tea. Cake mix had been left in a bowl on the side, a cube of butter sweating on the table, and a half-drunk cup of coffee, stone cold on the windowsill.

'Fair play to them, letting Dad stay in the hospital overnight.'

Jonathan nodded. 'The nurses all adore him. I caught two of them crying, touched by how tender he was being with Mam.'

I thought of my father's gentle eyes, his easy smile.

'Don't worry about Mam,' said Jonathan, eyeing me closely. 'She'll be fine.'

I nodded, embarrassment stirring within me that my little brother was comforting me. I should be the one who was comforting him... It was he, after all, that would bear the brunt of having to face the empty space in the café if our mother died.

Though it was almost eleven, Jonathan made us sandwiches whilst I had a shower. I turned the dial until the water was as hot as I could stand it, until my skin almost hissed with the heat. The steam rose in ribbons around me, and I watched my reflection in the mirror as it slowly swallowed me, and made me invisible.

Jonathan had poured each of us a second glass of wine. After he had eaten his sandwiches, he pulled a rhubarb tart from the oven and a tub of home-made ice cream from the freezer.

'Eat your sandwiches,' he demanded, and I sat by the table. He had remembered my favourite sandwich filling. Cheese, pickled onion and peanuts. I raised my wine glass as I chewed my first mouthful.

'Do you remember everyone's favourite foods?' I asked. 'Is that why the café is such a success?'

Jonathan grinned, his straight white teeth pearly under the kitchen lights. 'No. Only the family.'

We ate in silence, and I considered his words. He didn't know how that small word, 'family', warmed me. He uttered the word without thinking, not realising how precious it was.

'The café is a success because it's become an unofficial meeting place for the W.I.' Jonathan cut a piece of his rhubarb tart with the corner of his fork and soaked it in soft ice cream. 'And the agricultural society, the mother and baby club... People come here in big crowds, to chat.'

'You've done so well. I had misgivings, I must admit... Llanegryn is so far from everywhere...'

Jonathan shook his head thoughtfully. 'You probably feel that way because you've found a home somewhere else. But when I was away from here... Everywhere else seemed far from everywhere, because they were so far from my home.'

I finished my sandwich in silence, and refused dessert. The second glass of wine loosened the knots in my shoulders, and as I poured another, Jonathan and I settled into easy chat. I couldn't remember being alone with him before, not even when he was a boy. The house was so busy then. And now, of course, I never visited without bringing Maria and Sion, and Sion insisted upon his beloved uncle's constant company.

I had certainly never shared three bottles of wine with my brother before.

'Do you ever regret leaving?' Jonathan asked, his tongue thickened by the alcohol. For a second, I was reminded of the feral, grunting sounds of my mother in her hospital bed, and I thought of her thin, bony body under the sheets, her grey eyes watching the dark cubicle at night.

'No. Well. I do think about it, sometimes...' My own voice sounded unfamiliar, the vowels dragging lazily.

'Think about what? Coming home?'

I shook my head. 'If things had been different... If I hadn't gone to Manchester, if I'd come back here afterwards instead of going to Bethesda.'

'But you're happy there...'

'Yes. Very happy. And Maria and Sion are wonderful.'

My description of those closest to me sounded clichéd and insufficient. I thought of Maria, right now, asleep in our bed at home, so very different to that Elnett-scented blonde in the pub in Manchester a lifetime ago. She had held the upper hand over her demons for years now, but occasionally my imagination liked to remind me of how damaged she had been, once.

'I love them more than I thought was possible.'

Jonathan raised one eyebrow, as if he could hear the 'but' in my voice.

'But everyone imagines a different life, don't they? What if I had taken Dad's place, had taken over the shop. What if I'd gone to university. What if I'd have stayed with Susie, settled here with her...'

Her even white teeth flashed into my mind, and the sexy gap between them.

'That would have been wonderful,' Jonathan sighed, before adding hurriedly, 'Not that I don't adore Maria. But, you know...

My brother and my best friend... You would have been well suited.'

'No, we wouldn't,' I answered with a small smile. 'I wouldn't have been happy, thinking what would have happened had I gone to the city. I would have been resentful.'

There was a pause before I dared ask, 'Is Susie happy?'

Jonathan nodded enthusiastically. 'Yes. You know that her father has gone to live with her and Owen? She loves having him there. They're very close.'

I was glad. I remembered her, an integral part of my childhood. Here, in this kitchen, a dirty-faced doll in the crook of her arm, her tiny fingers pushing a Matchbox car, curls tucked behind her ears, and the smell of tea and clean laundry rising from the stove. Mam and Annie chatting and giggling by the table, the sound of the shop doorbell ringing every now and again.

'We'd better go to bed,' I said then, trying to avoid a discussion about the old days. 'We'll have to be up early to go to the hospital.'

Jonathan nodded, but he didn't move. I knew he had something to say, and so I waited.

'I'm glad you came, Huw,' he said slowly. 'I know it means the world to Mam. And Dad, too.'

I nodded silently. I knew what he meant.

'She talks about you every day, you know,' he added, quietly. 'Loves you very much. The same as you love Sion now.'

'No.' I stood, heavy-headed with wine. 'Don't... It's complicated.'

Jonathan held up his hand, a gesture of surrender. 'I'm not pretending that I understand. I just wanted you to know that I'm glad you came.'

I nodded, the secrets filling my mouth, threatening to choke me. I could not release them. Not now, not to Jonathan. I didn't want to pass the burden of knowledge on to him. I smiled, wanly, before saying good night and climbing the stairs. I slept in my clothes, soundly, dreamlessly, and awoke to see the frost patterns, pretty as Christmas decorations, on my window.

A fortnight later, the whole family congregated in the Old Shop Café to feast and pull crackers, the Christmas tree winking through the window at the grey pavements outside. Jonathan had worked hard, obviously anxious to ensure that his first Christmas with Maria and Sion would be perfect.

Dad stayed by my mother's side, holding her hand and making her endless cups of tea. Slow as silence, the smell of the turkey wafted through the house that morning, sharpening our hunger and causing our stomachs to grumble impatiently.

My mother sat at the head of the table, her plate piled with wonderful tastes. She ate slowly, using only her right hand, her face lopsided as she tried to avoid making a mess. Her left eye was half-shut, the right darting from face to face, trying not to miss anything. It made her look untamed, like a wild animal, and I looked away, trying to banish a memory that was trying to force its way into my mind.

For the first time, my mother was eating without enthusiasm, and I hadn't realised until then how the food she had eaten had made her who she was. Before the stroke, she'd enjoyed each mouthful with a feral joy, ripping it with her teeth, like a child who hadn't eaten for a long time. Now, she didn't seem to taste at all.

Later, as everyone else watched a children's film, I succumbed to my tiredness, and lay on my bed – the bed I had slept in for the first eighteen years of my life. Jonathan had transformed the room, along with the rest of the house. Soft cream carpets to swallow the sound of footsteps, elegant blue walls and thick plastic windows. But he had kept a few things, too, as a tribute to the little boy who'd lived here. Old fashioned Matchbox cars in the corner and a Roy of The Rovers poster framed on the wall. The bed was in the same place, and the little wooden chair in the corner.

If I shut my eyes, if I reached that blissful moment between being asleep and awake, the years would clear away like fog, and I would be a child again.

I dreamt. Awake, I could control my memories, but sleep was a cruel kind of relief, resurrecting old horrors, refusing to be tamed.

A cold night in the depths of winter, the wind moaning through the windows. I don't know what woke me. The wind, perhaps, or the owl that ruled the common by night. I lay in bed for a while, watching the shadows of the trees dancing menacingly behind the curtains.

I was a greedy ten-year-old, and was willing to take full advantage of living in a shop. Without a sound, I threw back the bedclothes and slid my warm feet into slippers. It was freezing, but it would be worth enduring the cold to get my hands on the Aztec Bar that was waiting for me in the shop.

I crept downstairs. The old clock measured its loneliness in hollow ticks.

I turned the doorknob to the shop slowly, and the smell greeted me like an old friend.

There was a sound.

I looked into the shop, my heart punching my ribs rhythmically, loud enough to hear.

Mam, in her white nightdress in the centre of the shop, a bowl of honey ice cream in her pale hands, melted until it was nothing but custard. Dried ice cream clung to her lips and the tail of her plait, crusty like a scab.

She was horrific.

'Mam?'

She turned to look at me quickly, her grey eyes flashing. 'What are you doing here?'

'I'm hungry. Mam, are you all right?'

She rose quickly, her feet moving as swift as rats. Her fingers still clung to the bowl.

'Don't tell anyone, will you, Huw?'

·I swallowed. Why was I suddenly afraid of the woman who had protected me throughout my childhood?

Because she didn't look like my mother.

'What about? The ice cream?'

She shook her head. 'Oh Huw,' she sighed. 'I did a terrible thing. But you mustn't tell anyone. Not even your father.'

'What did you do?' I asked in a whisper.

'Never trust me. I am my mother's daughter. Dangerous.'

She turned her eyes to me, slowly, and they had the coldness of stone within them.

'Are you listening? Don't come close, or I might hurt you.'

'Huw?'

I awoke. The day was fading into twilight through my bedroom window, and Jonathan stood above the bed, a steaming mug in one hand and a plate in the other.

'Here you are. You've been asleep for two hours... I thought I'd better wake you, in case you don't sleep tonight.'

He set the mug and plate down on the bedside table, and studied my face. 'Are you all right?'

'Yes. I was dreaming about things that happened, long ago.' I sat up and rubbed my eyes. 'You woke me before the worst part. Thank you.'

Jonathan stared for a while, and decided not to ask any more. He gave me a small smile, and disappeared.

Hot chocolate, thick as melted chocolate, and a mince pie with an unexpected layer of soft icing in it. I lay on my bed, waiting and drinking and listening to the television mumbling downstairs.

Sometimes, I imagined that the whole thing had been a dream. The ignoring, the benign neglect, the lack of interest. My mother seemed so different now, and, as I always did when these thoughts came to me, I muttered a prayer of thanks that my father had been so patient and careful of me. He was the one that cut my nails, read to me in bed at night. Did he realise how bad she had been? Did she ever look at him through empty eyes, as if he wasn't there at all? Did she whisper those same barbed, wounding words to him across the dark shop floor?

I rose from the bed and went downstairs, the empty dishes in my hands. I could hear my father telling a tall tale in the lounge, and the gleeful chuckles of Maria, Jonathan and Sion.

Mam was sitting by the kitchen table. She looked up at me as I put the dishes in the sink.

'I slept for a long time, Mam.'

She nodded, and lifted a piece of mince pie to her mouth. She failed to open her mouth wide enough, and the pastry crumbs snowed down to her jumper. She set the mince pie down on the plate, defeated.

I sat in the chair beside her, and gingerly picked the piece of pie with my thumb and forefinger. She opened her crooked mouth, and I pushed the sweet mince pie into it gently.

She stared at me as she chewed, before swallowing and opening her mouth for more. Piece by piece, I fed my mother the entire mince pie, her grey eyes staring at me throughout, as if searching for something. I could not remember a more tender moment between us, and that made me feel like a failure, cold and hard as stone.

'Sorry,' said my mother, her words still slurred and thick after the stroke.

'It's all right,' I answered, though I did not know what she was apologising for. I placed my large hand over her slim fingers, and thought how sad it was that things had come to this.

Peggy
2010

One night, when the wind's teeth were at their sharpest, I dreamt that another spring had come, all the wild flowers in bloom. I dreamt that I was reborn, just like last year's Welsh poppies, the gnawing in my joints gone, my back straightened, my hands, once more, smooth and young.

In my dream, I walked through the common, and noticed the details that had long ceased to amaze me: the branches hanging lazily, gently waving their leaves; birdsong in the hedges; the glassy sheen of the stones at the bottom of the river, worn smooth by the water. I was barefoot, and wearing a white summer dress that I hadn't seen the like of since I was a young woman.

I raised my eyes to the far end of the common, and smiled. People, tens of them sitting on the grass, a few wandering around, many of them laughing. Someone was spreading thick blankets over the grass, and laying heavy wicker baskets on them. The promise of a picnic, the promise of a feast.

I awoke in Riverside in my old tired body, with the promise of another futile day. Francis snored softly by my side.

I stayed in bed for a while, not quite ready to face the coldness. I hadn't had a dream like that for years, with every detail vivid and colourful. I had smelled the spring flowers and had felt the dandelion clocks tickling my ankles. I hungered for the food that waited for me in those wicker baskets, longed for the company of those people... Did I know them?

At last, I got up from my bed, silently thankful for the central heating that Jonathan had insisted upon installing in Riverside after I had the stroke. At the time, I had complained about the cost, but the radiators had brought a new warmth to the old cottage, filling the cold, dark places that had been here when I was a child.

'Good morning.'

Francis stretched his arms, and lay still for a while, breathing away the sleep from his mind.

'Good morning. Did you sleep?'

'I was reading until the early hours. What time is it?'

I looked over at the digital clock blinking the time on the bedside table.

'Half past eight. Go back to sleep.'

'Are you sure?'

'I'm going for a walk, and then to the café. Come over when you get up.'

'All right. Will you open the curtains? And the window?'

'It's cold.'

'It's warm in bed.'

It was the effect of a lifetime of shopkeeping, I think. The conclusion of having to get up before dawn and working until the sun had set. Since retiring, Francis had fallen into the comforting habit of returning to bed in the afternoon, or sleeping in late in the morning. He liked to have the window open, even when there was ice on the panes, as if he was challenging daylight and showing off to the sun that he was, at last, allowed to keep to whatever hours took his fancy.

I pushed open the plastic-framed windows, and a fresh breeze cut into the room. The cold reached through my thick nightdress, and steam curled like cigarette smoke from my mouth. This was the kind of morning I had loved when I was younger, the sky a cloudless blue and the cold sharp enough to hurt the soft skin of my cheeks. Weather for walking, weather that highlighted the mountains and hills at their most magnificent. The view from the highest point of the Black Road would be wonderful today, surrounded by the jagged mountaintops and the sea sparkling on the horizon like a bracelet. I had seen that view a thousand times, in all weathers and seasons, and yet I yearned to see it again, to tire myself by climbing that hill and then to fill my lungs with the cold air that blew in from the sea. I would never see that view again, and the tragedy of that loss struck me in the stomach. That road had become too steep for me.

I was dying.

I didn't know how I knew. A change, I think, in the world that surrounded me, a softness on the edges of my life that was like energy spent. Even the colours had become less vivid, as if grey was bleeding into everything.

The change in me had started after the stroke, when I was struck dumb, watching everything from the outside. I saw how the world would be when I had died, and found that the flowers would go on growing, the spring would return once more and Llanegryn would survive, mercilessly.

At that time, when I had been close enough to death to inhale its metallic, rotting scent, I wished that the stroke had killed me. I was saved by doctors and drugs, and for what? A few extra years of burdening my husband and sons; more time to recall with longing the touch of Francis' skin when we were young enough to excite one another; time to remember the sound of Annie's laughter. Remembering, always, everything. To live can be cruel.

My body took time to warm up in the morning, and today was no different. To the sound of Francis' snoring, I put on layers of cotton and wool, covering my soft wrinkled flesh. I never looked at myself in the mirror any more, but sometimes, as I tugged on a pair of socks or as I soaked in the bath, I looked down at myself and loathed what the years had done to my body. I wasn't fat, but that didn't matter anymore. Aprons of flesh hung from my stomach and breasts, as if my skin was too loose for my body. I may have felt better had I filled my skin with a little fat.

I stepped down the stairs, one at a time, my hands bent and bony on the bannister. The living room was a den of shadows until I opened the curtains and let the beautiful morning into my home.

In the kitchen, the smell of last night's supper lingered: cauliflower cheese and bacon, a feast of sharp saltiness. Jonathan had left some cake on the side, but I would not eat it. I had lost my appetite, and the only foods I wanted were creamy and tasteless – rice pudding, bread-and-milk and porridge, barley pudding. Baby food, I realised as I flicked the switch on the kettle. I had always lived for food, and there was a great sadness in my lack of interest now. A quiet surrender to the slow death that was creeping upon me.

I felt better after a sip of tea. A milky coffee in the café would awaken me properly, and after pulling on a thick coat and a woollen hat, I ventured out into the cold, as I did every day. Even the emptiness of my days had their rhythm. To the café until lunchtime, chatting with Jonathan or Francis or the customers, or reading a book. Home after lunch and counting the hours with television schedules, throwing myself into the lives of soap opera characters. Then, after the café closed, Jonathan would bring us our tea, and we would sit by the kitchen table, our knives scratching the plates and our voices soft in light conversations. After Jonathan returned to his home above the café, Francis and I would lay out a deck of cards and would play blackjack until late. Sometimes we would talk about Huw, but it was mainly about Jonathan.

His life was his café and his parents. It wasn't fair or natural, but Jonathan insisted that he was happy. As there was no evidence to suggest otherwise, I accepted that a quiet life in Llan with Francis and I for company was enough for Jonathan.

I walked slowly though the garden and noticed that a crust of frost had appeared on the edges of the path, the edges of the leaves twinkling prettily. The gate groaned as I pushed it open. I took care as I walked down the lane. It was slippy. I held onto the wall, my fingers as rough as the grey stones.

I paused for a moment on Llan Bridge, as I did every morning. The same ghosts always lingered in the water, and for a second I believed that the sun's reflection was a scrap of white cotton in the water. The jagged, angelic memory of my mother, dead in the water, was a daily spectre, and I had grown not to fear it.

Two young mothers with babies on their knees sat on a sofa in the café. They looked up and smiled as they saw me coming in from the cold. I smiled as I looked at the fat red cheeks of their children, their mouths wet and their eyes wide. A stab of something painful came to me as I remembered Huw as a baby, when everything was different. I swallowed back the urge for a little baby to hold, a wonderful warm bundle of something to love. In a whole lifetime, I had not found anything sadder than the longing for another time.

'Good morning!'

Jonathan came from the back of the café as I hung my coat on the peg and pulled off my hat before tidying my hair with my finger.

'Did you sleep? Where's Dad?'

'He was awake until late, reading that book you bought him for Christmas. He's still in bed.'

'The window wide open so that everyone can admire his pyjamas, I bet.'

I nodded, smiling, and sat on the sofa by the window. Orchestral music was drifting in from the radio in the kitchen, and the smell of coffee warmed the place. Though everything had changed, I felt that sometimes, if I breathed deep enough into the chambers of my lungs, I could smell the shop – sugar and spices, ham and pickle and seasoning...

'Here you are.' Jonathan placed a mug of coffee on the table in front of me, the froth like sea foam. 'I have a bit of baking to do... Shall I fetch a book for you?'

'Please.'

Jonathan fetched the novel I had been attempting to read. It had become harder to immerse myself in books, the words refusing to penetrate my mind. I found myself re-reading the same pages over and over again, until the words finally meant something. Jonathan left the book on the table before disappearing into the kitchen. I could hear him singing along softly with the music on the radio as he worked.

I didn't attempt to read the book – my mind was busy enough without the mess of its characters.

I didn't regret what I had done.

Perhaps I should have done. Perhaps that was the problem. But after years of considering it, I could not imagine how I could have lived a happy life had I not done something. No, I did not regret the deed itself, only the fact that I had shared it.

I shut my eyes, tried to stop the memory from returning once more. I tried to fill my mind with the sound of Jonathan's voice singing in the kitchen, the chatter of the young mothers in the café. But it was futile, and I was magicked back to another time.

'Mam?'

Huw, just a boy, standing in the back door of the shop, the features of his face lost in the twilight. My stomach, aching after too much ice cream, the flow of sugar diluting my bloodstream. I could imagine it in my veins, a thick, golden syrup. It had inebriated me.

'Don't come too close, or I might hurt you.'

I disgusted myself for losing control in front of my little boy. I failed to stop the words from building on my tongue, failed to restrain my need to utter them all.

Was it true? Could I hurt my own son? I was so afraid of my inheritance, frightened that I had the cruel tendencies of my mother.

'What did you do, Mam?'

Huw would never tell! He was a good boy. Mam's boy. He would understand and would keep my secret. He would know why I had to—

The relief of telling someone!

So I told him.

That I had killed my mother.

'I don't want to be here any more.' That is what she said, on her last evening, her grey eyes already dead.

I was so tired, and had started, like her, to despise life. Given a few months, I would fear and hate everything. We were so alike, I felt as though the boundaries between mother and daughter had become blurred, as if people would soon mistake us for one another, or even believe me to be her mother. I was not allowed to visit Hare House, and there was no possibility of succumbing to my instincts with Francis when she was to be cared for. She was corrupting my life.

It was a matter of choosing. Mother or me.

When she uttered that sentence, surrendering all our battles, I decided to help her, for both our sakes. I didn't have to think about it. It was the only way.

That night, I stayed awake in bed until after midnight, and crept down to the kitchen with a pillow in my hands. She was asleep in her chair, the darkness creating shadows under her eyes.

It was so easy.

I pressed the white cotton lovingly over her face.

She waved her arms, scratching my flesh, quaking like a rat in a trap. She didn't have the energy to overpower me, or maybe she didn't want to. After a while, her arms stopped flailing and she became still.

I removed the pillow from her face, nervous that she may have been faking. But even in the darkness of the kitchen, she was clearly dead. She looked somehow empty, as if all the poison and sadness has suffocated her.

I stood in the kitchen, staring at her. I waited for the panic and the guilt. It didn't come. I only felt a calm peacefulness in my mind, and the freedom of being without her.

After pulling on my boots, I took my mother in my arms. I had expected her to be heavy – I had become weak and weedy – but I lifted her as if she was a child. Her hair fell like rats' tails over my arm.

Llanegryn was asleep.

I walked silently towards Llan Bridge, looking up at the blind windows. If anyone was awake now, they could look through their window and see me. But only the whispering of the river broke the silence.

Above the bridge, I stared down at the river. It was low. It hadn't rained for a long time. The water looked black. I held my mother's body close, hugging her now as she had never allowed me to before, and then I turned her over into the river and let go of her forever.

She fell quietly, her nightdress puffing around her like the wings of an angel. Her body hit the water, and I looked at the houses to see if the light thud and splash had awoken anyone.

The village slept.

I turned on my heel. It was an odd feeling, leaving Mam there, as if I was leaving a helpless child. And yet, there was no guilt. I had saved her.

I lit the lamp and sat by the kitchen table, and smiled at the posy of flowers Francis had bought. They were so pretty, even in the wan light of the lamp.

I was a murderer.

My mind explored the word, before trying it on my tongue. There was something lovely about it, like the sound a river makes: murmurer, murderer. Again, I waited for the significance of the word and its meaning to bring a tide of guilt, but it did not come.

I decided to go to Francis in the morning and ask for his help.

In the meantime, I was starving. Not simply an appetite, but truly hungry, and I turned up the oil lamp and searched the cupboards.

By the morning, I had devoured a whole loaf and a pat of salted butter. I felt glorious, reborn, and that morning, the sunrise seemed brighter, the house lighter without my mother's dark, heavy presence.

The guilt came slowly, like a mist creeping into my mind. Perhaps because I was so happy. Francis was so kind, the shop was a success and I was allowed to see Nain and Taid whenever I pleased. This life could never have been had my mother been allowed to live. I would have had to care for her, and sacrificed my life for her.

I had done my best, for her and for me. And yet, as the years went by, after Huw was born, after Mr Phyllip died, when I had found a sister in Annie and when Nain and Taid died, the memory resurfaced. Her white nightgown in the black water, the flow stroking her hair.

Was I becoming like her?

I would awaken at night and sneak down to the shop, eyeing the tins and packets as if I hadn't eaten for days. I would eat until I became drunk on the sugar, the salt and the flavours, until the fire in my mind was dampened.

That is what had happened when Huw had come into the shop that night, finding me bent over a bucket of ice cream.

'No, Mam!' Huw insisted in the half-light. 'Your mother was ill. You didn't kill her!'

I stumbled onto my feet, the remains of the ice cream sticky on my fingers. 'I didn't mean to...'

'Come on, Mam.' Huw put his arm around me. 'Come to bed.'

At the top of the stairs, I turned to my son and saw the worry etched upon his face.

'Don't worry. You only think you killed her, Mam, but it wasn't really you. It wasn't your fault that she killed herself.'

I stared at my child for a while. He was at that stage between boyhood and manhood, an anxious little face that had slipped from my body in a miraculous moment. 'You're right, Huw. I didn't kill her. Not really.'

But as I stared at him, I knew that I had planted a seed of doubt in my son's mind, and that it would grow like a weed in his head.

'I had a dream last night,' I said to Jonathan mid-morning, when he sat by my side to have a coffee. His cakes and biscuits were cooling on the dresser in the kitchen, ribbons of smell warming the cafe.

'What about?' asked Jonathan, blowing the steam off his coffee.

'I was on the common. It was spring, and I was young again. There was a picnic party, and I was on my way to join them when I woke up.'

'Who were they?'

'I was too far away to see. But they seemed familiar.' I sighed as I remembered the feel of the sun on my skin in the dream, the sweet smell of the wild flowers. 'I think Annie was there.'

Jonathan gazed at me as if he was trying to understand what was behind my words.

'The next time I go there, Jonathan, I'm not coming back. It was lovely.'

Jonathan placed his hand over mine. 'Don't say things like that.'

I sighed, and turned away. He was too young to understand that I had to tell him, that I had to be kind. I had planted a seed in Jonathan's mind, and when I was gone he could imagine me feasting on the common on a warm day, surrounded by the people I missed.

That night, I sat on my bed in my nightdress. I was tired, but there was something else, something new, that had disturbed my mind that day. I was unsettled.

The dream. That was it. I was on the verge of dying.

I would be going there again, soon... I would stride from my body to a better, younger shell, and I would leave this cruel winter for an invincible spring. Nain and Taid would be there, Mrs Davies and Annie. And when the time came, Francis would come to join the party on the common, and he would not be a sleepy old man. He would wrap his arms around my young body, and I would smell his salty, sweet scent and put my long fingers through his Brylcreemed hair. Thinking of those two – Peggy, tall and lithe, and Francis dark and muscled – was enough to make my stomach ache with longing. I had never loved with my heart. I always loved with my stomach, the emotion churning like a heavy meal in my belly.

I would have to leave Francis here, though he was as kind and gentle as ever. I would have to bid a farewell to Jonathan and Huw for the final time, and accept that I would never see Sion growing up. The most wonderful people I had ever known. People I had adored throughout their lives, celebrating every smile and laugh. I would never see them again.

And there, sitting on my bed in my home, I cried a river of salt for all the things, all the people, all the seasons and tastes I would not see.

I awoke the next morning to find that everything was pretty, the first buds pushing through the ground. I made two cups of tea and climbed the stairs with the tray in my hands.

'Francis!' I said, climbing back into the warm bed.

He moved slowly, yawned and then blinked at me.

'I've made us breakfast in bed.'

A smile stretched his face. The exact smile that had captured me over the shop counter all those years ago.

'Goodness.' He sat up in bed, and rubbed his eyes.

'Don't get too excited. It's only tea, bananas and digestives.'

'Biscuits? For breakfast?'

'We're too old to worry about what we eat. We might as well enjoy the tastes while we still can.'

I reached for the peanut butter jar on the tray, and spread it thickly on a biscuit, and then sliced a few discs of banana on top of it. It was a perfect breakfast.

'You're very odd sometimes, Peggy.' Francis shook his head with a smile. A loving satisfaction swelled within me as he helped himself to exactly the same breakfast. He groaned over-enthustiastically as he tasted, spraying crumbs over the bed.

I giggled.

'I think I'll go for a walk this morning, all the way to Hare House. Will you come?'

Francis nodded as he chewed.

'Past Beech Grove and Rose Cottage, and the garden where Gwynfor Daniels used to grow tomatoes and herbs.'

'Are you all right, Peg?'

'Of course! And then I think I'll bake something after we come home from the café. A fruit tart, or a savoury pie.'

'What's brought all this on?'

I sighed. 'Thinking about when I was a little girl, alone in that little bedroom. I was so frightened of everything, scared of living my own life.'

'Don't think about that now...'

'If that little girl could see me now, Francis. If she could see all the gentleness and kindness I've seen. You, and Nain and Taid, and Mrs Davies, and Annie. Huw and Jonathan. I'm not like my mother.'

Francis put his arm around me, and I settled into the soft folds of his body. It was my own quiet epiphany. I had become contented, satisfied, well-seasoned, and had lived for the bitter, the sweet, the salty. It was all worth tasting, and it all tasted like home.

Jonathan Phyllip
Peggy's son
2010

Bread

1 lb strong white flour
1 tbsp of yeast powder
2 tsp salt
tsp sugar
½ pint warm water

Mix the yeast and sugar with a splash of water, and wait until it foams. Sieve the flour and salt, and combine them. Add the yeast and the rest of the water. Knead for ten minutes. Mix in more flour or water if the mixture seems too dense or too sticky.
Place the dough in a lined bread tin, and leave in a warm place until risen. Bake in a moderate oven for 40 minutes, or until the crown has browned.

My mother died in the same room as she was born, the room with the little window that looked down over the river. She lay in bed, the blanket covering her up to her neck. She was on her side, her knees pulled to her chest – the foetal position. The curtains danced in the breeze, as if there were invisible fingers tugging at them.

I sat on the bed, and put my hand on her shoulder. I felt the coldness through her nightdress, through the sheet. My father stood by the window in his striped pyjamas, staring at the warming day. His eyes were wide, his hair unkempt.

I had prepared her favourite that morning. A moist ginger loaf, the syrup making it sticky and heavy. I'd waited for her in the café as the customers came and went. I'd waited for her appearance at the door, her coat tightened around her and her hair escaping from her hat. She had never missed her ten o'clock coffee, not since the café first opened.

By half past ten, her absence starting to unsettle me, I looked through the window to the common, and saw a thin stripe of sunshine trying to warm a patch of grass. My throat constricted as the phone rang.

'Jonathan?'

My father's voice, low and gruff, at odds with his usual jollity. I pressed my phone tightly to my ear. 'Can you come over, son? Your mother has gone.'

In Riverside, I kissed her cold cheek. The wrinkles on her face had been smoothed by death. Mam looked young again.

'Oh, Dad.'

'When I woke, I thought she'd got up early. I couldn't feel her here in bed with me.'

'I don't know what to say. It was always obvious how much you adored one another.'

'I still adore her,' my father corrected gently. 'That hasn't gone, wherever Peggy is now. She's left all these feelings behind.'

'I know. I know.' I got up. My body felt heavier than before. 'Get dressed, Dad. I'll make us some sweet tea.'

I padded heavily to the kitchen. In a few hours, the chaos of death would descend. The undertakers, neighbours, people whose arms were full of morbid curiosity and cake. Mam would be lost in the organisation, and the space she left would be hidden for a few weeks.

Her favourite mug was drying by the sink.

In the centre of the table, something was hiding under an ivy-pattened tea towel. I pulled on the cotton.

A loaf. A perfect white loaf, the crown rising in a brown crust. A soft smell clung to the edge of the kitchen.

Mam had not baked anything in years. Why would she, when I did it every day? And yet, something had made her mix the yeast and flour, the water and salt, plunge her old fingers, bent with arthritis, into the dough before kneading it firmly.

I sat in her chair in the corner of the kitchen, and wept.

A few days after the funeral, after Huw returned home, silent and grey, after the visitors stopped calling and the condolence cards stopped coming through the post, I took a walk through the common.

In the ten days since she'd died, winter had faded, and spring had started to show its presence in Llan. New buds, a few swallows and an edge of heat from the sun. In a few weeks, flowers would be blooming everywhere, and the dawn would be arriving before I awoke.

I remembered the dream she had had before she died. A picnic on the common, on a kind summer's day, her youth returned and her friends and her food waiting in the long grass. I paused for a while, searching for her. Though I stood perfectly still, all I saw was a rat creeping through the grass towards the river.

My father had gone for lunch with Jack and Susie and her family in an attempt to bring a new rhythm into his unfamiliar, single existence. He had asked me to sort through some of my mother's things whilst he was out. He had done his best, but had failed to throw anything that had belonged to her. When I agreed to do it, he had sighed with his whole body.

The house was still, odd gaps in the bookcases and kitchen cupboards where Huw had taken a few things. My brother hoped to find our mother between the yellowing pages of her books.

I spent the morning packing books, clothes and shoes into boxes. Every box felt like a betrayal, though I knew that my mother never felt sentimental about her things.

Two bin bags of clothes and half a dozen boxes of ephemera, and the house looked bare and stark, as if someone had stolen its softer half. I hated thinking of my father returning here and finding the chest of drawers empty, nothing but a space where Mam's hairbrush used to be.

The clearing took the entire morning, with tears constantly threatening as I saw her handwriting, the scent of her perfume. Things that had been unimportant until she had died. Everything was a treasure now.

I was nearly finished, only the dresser to sort out.

I recognised the book immediately: hard-backed, brown and yellow marbling on the cover, like cream in chocolate. Her birthday present, together with a heartfelt beseeching that she would write her story. I never spoke of it again, and Mam never mentioned it.

I opened the book: my mother's handwriting filled the page.

It was a recipe: 'Beef Casserole with Mustard Dough Balls', and the name Kenneth Davies written above it. I didn't recognise the name, but that didn't impair my enjoyment as I flicked through the pages. She had noted the things she wished to remember. All kinds of recipes, each one with a person's name attached to it. Some names I knew well, and some were completely new to me. Had these people given her the recipes? No... Huw's name was there, and he had no interest in food. Were they culinary experiments, Mam trying to evoke old flavours as much as she could?

I couldn't wait to take this book back to my kitchen, to cook these flavours bequeathed to me by my mother – an inheritence of sugar and spices and seasoning.

She had left me her story, after all.

I turned to the first page, and smiled as I saw her neat handwriting, blue ink on cream paper.

The Seasoning
by
Peggy

Weights and measures for use in recipes

Weights

imperial	metric	imperial	metric	imperial	metric
½oz	15g	7oz	200g	15oz	425g
⅔oz	20g	8oz (½lb)	230g	16oz (1lb)	450g
1oz	30g	9oz	255g	24oz	680g
2oz	60g	10oz	285g	32oz (2lb)	0.9kg
3oz	85g	11oz	310g	35oz (2.2lbs)	1kg
4oz	115g	12oz	340g	48oz (3lb)	1.4kg
5oz	140g	13oz	370g	64oz (4lb)	1.8kg
6oz	170g	14oz	400g		

Oven Temps

Gas	°F	°C	
½	250	120	very low
1	275	140	
2	300	150	low
3	325	170	
4	350	180	moderate
5	375	190	
6	400	200	moderately.hot
7	425	220	
8	450	230	hot
9	475	240	very hot

Liquids

Pint	Metric	Fl oz
	100ml	3½
	125ml	4½
¼	150ml	5
	200ml	7
	250ml	9
½	275ml	10
	300ml	11
	400ml	14
	500ml	18
1	570ml	20
	750ml	26
1¾	1 L	35

Author biography

Manon Steffan Ros was brought up in Rhiwlas, Bangor, north Wales. She won the Drama Medal twice at the National Eisteddfod (2005 and 2006) and her first novel, *Fel Aderyn* (Like a Bird) was shortlisted for the Wales Book of the Year award, 2010. She won the Tir na n-Og prize for children's literature twice, in 2010 and 2012, with *Trwy'r Tonnau* (Through the Waves) and *Prism* (Prism). Her novel *Blasu* (The Seasoning) was originally published in Welsh to critical acclaim in 2012 and won the 2013 Wales Book of the Year Welsh Fiction category.

More from Honno

Short stories; Classics; Autobiography; Fiction

Founded in 1986 to publish the best of women's writing, Honno publishes a wide range of titles from Welsh women.

We That Are Left *Juliet Greenwood*
August 4th, 1914: It was the day of champagne and raspberries, the day the world changed.
Elin lives a luxurious but lonely life at Hiram Hall. Her husband Hugo loves her but he has never recovered from the Boer War. Now another war threatens to destroy everything she knows.

'Powerful and moving' Trisha Ashley
'It is, quite simply, a riveting read.'
Suzy Ceulan Hughes, www.gwales.com
ISBN: 9781906784997   £8.99

Motherlove *Thorne Moore*
One mother's need is another's nightmare... A gripping psychological thriller from the author of A Time for Silence.
'...a heart-wrenching tale of three mothers and their love for their children... which kept me enthralled until the end.'
Rosie Amber

ISBN: 9781909983205   £8.99

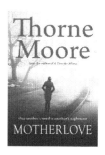

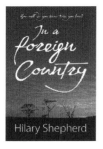

In a Foreign Country *Hilary Shepherd*
Anne is in Ghana for the first time. Her father, Dick, has been working up country for an NGO since his daughter was a small child. They no longer really know each other. Anne is forced to confront her future and her failings in the brutal glare of the African sun.

'Intelligent, subtle and sensitive... a thought-provoking, absorbing and rewarding read' Debbie Young
ISBN: 9781906784621   £8.99

Left and Leaving *Jo Verity*
Gil and Vivien have nothing in common but London and proximity, and responsibilities they don't want, but out of tragedy something unexpected grows.

'Humane and subtle, a keenly observed exploration of the way we live now...I am amazed that Verity's work is still such a secret. A great read'
Stephen May
ISBN: 9781906784980   £8.99

Someone Else's Conflict *Alison Layland*
Jay is haunted by the ghosts of war who threaten his life and his love. A compelling narrative of trust and betrayal, love, duty and honour from a talented debut novelist.

'A real page-turner about the need for love, and the search for redemption... If you like a fast-paced thriller but want more – then buy this book' Martine Bailey, author of An Appetite for Violets

ISBN: 9781909983120   £8.99

My Mother's House, *Lily Tobias*
A poignant story of belonging, nationhood and identity set in Wales, England and Palestine.
The twenty-fourth publication in the Welsh Women's Classics series, an imprint that brings out-of-print books in English by women writers from Wales to a new generation of readers.

ISBN: 9781909983212   £12.99

All Honno titles can be ordered online at
www.honno.co.uk
twitter.com/honno
facebook.com/honnopress

ABOUT HONNO

Honno Welsh Women's Press was set up in 1986 by a group of women who felt strongly that women in Wales needed wider opportunities to see their writing in print and to become involved in the publishing process. Our aim is to develop the writing talents of women in Wales, give them new and exciting opportunities to see their work published and often to give them their first 'break' as a writer. Honno is registered as a community co-operative. Any profit that Honno makes is invested in the publishing programme. Women from Wales and around the world have expressed their support for Honno. Each supporter has a vote at the Annual General Meeting. For more information and to buy our publications, please write to Honno at the address below, or visit our website: www.honno.co.uk

Honno, 14 Creative Units, Aberystwyth Arts Centre Aberystwyth, Ceredigion SY23 3GL

Honno Friends
We are very grateful for the support of the Honno Friends: Jane Aaron, Annette Ecuyere, Audrey Jones, Gwyneth Tyson Roberts, Beryl Roberts, Jenny Sabine.

For more information on how you can become a Honno Friend, see: http://www.honno.co.uk/friends.php